THE UNDERGROUND MOON

MELISSA K. MAGNER

ISBN-13: PB: 978-1-7322506-1-1
EBOOK: 978-1-7322506-3-5

Library of Congress Control Number: 2019913602

Any references to historical events, people, places, or things are used fictitiously. Names, characters, and places are products of the imagination of the author.

Summary: Two sisters find an enchanted forest underneath a hidden well, laden with peculiar trees, a beautiful lake, and an underground moon. The more they return, the more the moon grows, and the older sister begins to realize it isn't as innocent as it seems.

Content Warning: *The Underground Moon* is a dark fantasy horror novel intended for teens and young adults. It contains depictions of the following: suicide, suicide attempt, mental illness, grief, neglect, alcoholism, grooming, gore, blood, gun use, death of a parent, and cursing.

Front cover design by Bespoke Book Covers.

Illustrations by Viktoriia Davydova.

First printing edition 2020, United States of America.

FOR MY SISTER, JACLYN

ACKNOWLEDGMENTS

I would like to begin by thanking my younger sister, Jaclyn, for inspiring me to write this novel and for helping me bring to life the unique bond between two sisters. Few connections are stronger than those between siblings, and for that reason, *The Underground Moon*—specifically the relationship between Rosella and Hettie—will always hold a special place in my heart.

Thank you to my parents, Heidi and John Magner, for their enduring support and their willingness to listen as I developed my plot and characters.

Thank you to my late grandmother, Patricia Kaspar, who inspired me to start my writing journey—and who always encouraged me to stay true to my passion, despite how frustrating the process may sometimes be.

And, of course, a big thank you to my friends and family who continually encourage me to pursue my love of literature and storytelling.

Lastly, a special thank you to Peter and Caroline at Bespoke Book Covers for creating a beautiful book cover, Stephanie Cohen and Ashley Chen for being the best editors I could ask for, and Viktoriia Davydova for bringing my scenes to life with her illustrations.

CHAPTER 1
FIREFLIES

I got my first and only tattoo when I was nine years old, and I cried throughout the entire thing.

Despite how furious my mother was at my father's lack of discretion, I never regretted it. Six years later, I carry that detailed outline of a bird at the corner of my left wrist and forearm, and remember how he always smelled of grass and cigarettes.

Whenever my mother sees it, she rolls her eyes and mutters something about how he had always been a terrible influence. I've never admitted to her that I was the one who begged him to give me the tattoo—that I brought his old machine up to him and refused to leave until he gave me one. I thought a bird would be fitting because my name is Rosella, like the flat-tailed parrots with colorful feathers. I suppose his problem was that he never really knew how to say no.

My mother wishes she had left him sooner, but I don't like to think that way, even though I share her anger. Five years ago, he left us, and we didn't hear of him for another year before we learned he had been beaten to death at some bar in Tampa. Mother says she hates him, but mentioning his name never fails to bring a forlorn look into her eyes. I don't think she's ever truly hated him. I guess some people are like that; they make you love them despite the terrible things they've done to you.

That will never be a problem I'll deal with, though. Falling in love is a waste of time—the way my mother rants about my father even after all these years is proof enough. I always tell my younger sister Hettie that one day, she and I will buy a big house together and live there for the rest of our lives. She usually just laughs and asks if we'll buy a castle. I tell her, "Of course we will."

Hettie is seven. She has eyes like the bluest cornflowers and the most delicate face, surrounded by loose blond curls that reflect the sunlight.

I looked a lot like her when I was her age, but now my hair is more frizzy than curly and pure blond instead of gold.

I don't grow my hair down to my back like Hettie does either; I cut it straight to my shoulders, and even then, it's still a nuisance. In fact, the only interesting thing about me is my eyes. They're a mix of deep emerald and amber, like the forest surrounding my house—the forest I grew up around and loved since I could walk.

I'm not sure I'll ever see that forest again. My heart aches when I think about the things I'm missing: my friends, my home in Oregon, and that very same forest. But after what happened with Mother, it's best for all of us not to go back, at least for now.

It's been less than a month since the three of us moved to Tennessee to stay with my Aunt Vivian. She's younger than my mother by eight years, the same gap as Hettie and me. They were really close growing up, which made what happened even harder.

The adjustment hasn't been easy either. Instead of lush woods and towering redwoods, empty fields surround our home. A few small forests pop up here and there—there's one a few minutes from Aunt Vivian's house—but it's not the same. Summers are even more boring than they are painfully hot, and sometimes the most interesting thing to do is lie outside on the grass and watch the fireflies. I like it better when Hettie joins me.

Tonight, she's more chatty than usual, but I don't mind.

"Do you think the fireflies notice us?" she asks me, keeping her gaze up at the blinking yellow lights.

I shrug. "They probably sense us or something."

"Do they have eyes?"

"I'm not sure."

A few moments of silence pass until she's on to the next topic.

"If you were an animal, what would you be?"

I grin and take a moment to think. "I guess I'd be a bird," I say. "A Rosella."

Hettie laughs. "I'd be a dolphin."

"I think that suits you."

Hettie giggles and makes a dolphin noise as she shifts toward me. She rests her head and her arm on top of my body as though I'm her pillow.

"Can we go downtown tomorrow?" she asks. "We can explore."

I nod. The town is a fifteen-minute bike ride from Aunt Vivian's house if you go fast. Unfortunately, Hettie is the slowest biker I know.

Still, a trip downtown sounds interesting—way more interesting than staying in the house all day and wishing it was September. At least then I'd have something to do, even though school is on my list of things I dislike most. Being a new student at school is something I think I'll dislike even more, and that's precisely what I have to face in a few months. I shake the worrisome thought away.

"As long as we tell Mom before we leave so she doesn't freak out," I say. It's happened once or twice.

Hettie pauses. "She's been sleeping all day."

My stomach sinks in response, but I don't reply. It's a rare day when Mother *doesn't* sleep. The past year has been especially difficult. It seems we see less and less of her as time goes on.

I have to keep reminding myself that it's not Hettie's fault or mine; it's simply unfortunate circumstances. But when I see her sitting very still at the kitchen table, frozen solid like a statue, or when Aunt Vivian tells me not to disturb her because she's been in her dark room for fourteen hours, I can't help but feel like I could be doing more.

And then I feel anger. Anger that my presence or Hettie's does nothing for her. Anger that she no longer seems to want to be a mother. Anger that even her daughters are unable to bring her out of her deep and prolonged sadness.

Mother wasn't always like this. Mostly, it was on and off. After my father left, however, the numbing sadness she sometimes felt became far more persistent and intense. Sunlight or picnics or time spent with Hettie and me no longer helped.

Maybe that's why she always says she hates Father—because his absence hurt her more than his presence, and the news of his sudden death sent her spiraling out of control.

"She slept all day yesterday too," I finally say.

Hettie rips a clump of grass out of the ground and squishes it in her hand. "I'll draw her something."

I hold back my scoff. Drawing something won't help. Mother's dresser is cluttered with Hettie's cards and crayon-colored pictures, but it's done nothing. The sincerity in her voice, though, makes me feel bad for her.

"She'll like that," I say. Then I add, "But you have to draw me something too, okay?"

"I always draw you stuff, Ro."

"Yes, but you have to draw me *more* things."

Hettie's smile sparks a light in my heart, and I smile too.

"I'll draw you a bird," she says, her eyes flicking over to my tattoo. "A Rosella."

CHAPTER 2
THE GIRL AT THE DINER

Aunt Vivian's house is a quaint one-story farmhouse with a rustic air to it. Much like my aunt herself, there's something both quiet and pleasant about it.

It sits at the end of a makeshift court, which is nothing more than the crude outline of where a long dirt trail fades out. If you follow the trail, you'll pass a few houses—all spaced out evenly enough so that nobody really has any neighbors—a small, lonely farm, and what often seems like thousands of acres of fields. Although the trail branches off into a few smaller ones along the way, it's mostly a straight shot to downtown Larton. There's not much to do there other than eat at a few restaurants or shop at some clothing stores, but the people are nice and it's never very crowded, which suits me just fine.

I still miss my old home, though. I miss the cars that pass by at night and how their beams illuminate my bedroom. I miss the shopping center being only a ten-minute walk away. I miss my old school, as silly as that sounds, because at least I had friends there. At least I had things to do, people to see. Now, the only person I have to keep me company is Hettie.

Aunt Vivian says there are plenty of towns in Tennessee just like my old hometown, but it was her choice to live in a more rural area. Mother always commented on how Aunt Vivian enjoyed living in the quietest places possible. She used to tease her about it, but now I think she's grateful that Aunt Vivian lives alone and far away from people. It's less likely she'll have to interact with them that way, especially since socializing has become harder and harder for her lately.

Despite the unwanted changes these past few months have brought upon my family, I'm glad that we have Aunt Vivian. I've always liked her; she's hardworking, confident, and fiercely independent. She and Mother were raised solely by my grandfather, who passed when Aunt Vivian was eighteen and Mother was twenty-six. Instead of moving in with my mom and dad, who were married at the time, Aunt

Vivian moved to Tennessee, got into nursing school, and made a career for herself. Mother told me that she used to bug Aunt Vivian about finding a husband and settling down, to which my aunt would always reply, "I'm happier by myself." Those stories made me realize that Aunt Vivian is exactly the kind of person I want to be.

Although I've always admired my aunt, I've garnered a newfound respect for her these past few months. I know how much she loves her solitude and freedom, and yet when Mother needed her help, she didn't hesitate to let us move in. Without questions or complaints, she opened her home and welcomed us and all of our baggage with open arms. I don't think she'll ever know how grateful we are.

Mornings at Aunt Vivian's smell like coffee. She makes one for herself and sometimes one for me if I wake up early enough. After that, she leaves for work at the local hospital; "local" meaning thirty minutes from her house. She doesn't usually return until nine or ten at night depending on her workload.

Since it's summer, what to do during the day is up to Hettie and me. Sometimes we go outside and ride our bikes, other times we stay in all day, and every once in a while, like today, we make a trip downtown.

Hettie is awake when I find my way to the kitchen. She only looks up from her waffles to see that it's me, then continues to eat without saying a thing. I'm not surprised; when it comes to waffles, Hettie is head over heels.

I am surprised, though, to see Mother sitting next to her. She holds a ceramic mug of coffee between her hands as though it's winter and she's desperately trying to warm herself. Her hair is just as blond as mine, but long and straight instead of curly. People always ask where Hettie and I got our curls, to which Mother only shrugs in response. She never admits that we got them from our father.

I don't say anything as I sit down. She doesn't either, but she smiles at me—a strained smile that's all in her mouth but doesn't extend to her eyes.

"Did Aunt Vivian leave already?" I finally ask.

"About an hour ago," Mother says. Her voice is brittle.

Silence follows. I look to the edges of the kitchen, where neatly packed boxes have been stacked on top of and beside each other. We weren't able to bring everything from Oregon, but Mother insisted on packing enough moving boxes to make Aunt Vivian's kitchen look like a maze. The only place the boxes don't clutter is the corner of the room, where a mushroom-colored door leads out to the porch.

"Do you want waffles?" Mother asks me when my gaze returns to the table.

I shake my head. "I'll get something downtown. Hettie and I are going to bike down there in a bit."

Mother nods, then looks at the dress I'm wearing, which is one of the few I brought from home. Although I have an abundance of clothing back in Oregon—I have a penchant for shopping and I'm far too sentimental to give anything away—I was only able to fit a few outfits in my suitcases. As silly as it sounds, despite all the things I miss about Oregon, my closet is one of the things I miss most.

I expect Mother to compliment my dress, but the look she gives me is more skeptical than flattering.

"Are you going to bike in that?" she asks.

An unwanted sense of irritation rushes through me. I purse my lips and give her a curt nod.

Mother shrugs. "Just remember your helmet."

I loose a breath, feeling guilty with my touchiness toward her lately. I know she's struggling, but I often wonder if she realizes that Hettie and I are too.

"I will," I say.

"And be safe," Mother adds. She tells me this every time Hettie and I leave. "You remember what Aunt Vivian said about Larton."

"Mom, honestly, nothing is going to happen. We're only going downtown."

Mother nods in response. When we moved to Larton, Aunt Vivian mentioned that the rate of disappearance amongst children was higher than in most towns. She thought it had something to do with Larton being rural—there aren't as many people around to witness an abduction—but once Mother learned this, she wouldn't stop bringing it up.

Hettie finishes her last waffle quickly, and we're out the door without much conversation. The thought crosses my mind that maybe we should have stayed in with Mother since this is the first time in two days she's been out of her room, but I promised Hettie we'd go downtown and I need time out of the house.

Every time we leave, I think about the incident—what Hettie and I returned home to in April. I'm always worried that we'll come home to something similar again, but this time something worse. Although I want to move on with life, constant anxiety about Mother lingers at the back of my head. I don't know if it will ever go away, and that realization scares me the most.

I mount my bike after bugging Hettie about her helmet, and we start our descent down the road. Like always, she lags behind me, so I stop every so often and wait for her to catch up.

A couple of minutes down from the house and past Aunt Vivian's closest neighbor, the trail creates a fork. One way leads straight downtown, and the other acts as a little hiking path into the forest. I haven't gone that way yet.

I stop pedaling and lean onto the handles of my bike as I wait for Hettie to catch up. When she does, she's out of breath.

"Stop going so fast," she says.

"If I go any slower, I'll fall off."

"I don't go *that* slow."

"You're almost going in reverse." When she furrows her brow, I give a light laugh and remedy my comment with an, "I'm just kidding."

Hettie looks toward the forest. "Can we go that way?"

I squint in the sunlight as I look down the path. It runs parallel to a wide and empty field, and a few treks down, the landscape switches from a barren dirt road to thickets of green.

"Into the forest?"

Hettie nods. "We haven't explored there yet."

Since we've only lived here for a month, we haven't had time to scout all of Larton. Mother had insisted, despite everything, that we finish our school year before moving. Aunt Vivian put up a good fight but eventually conceded, granted that Mother called her every day.

"Besides, you always talk about how you miss the forest from home," Hettie adds.

"I do miss it. But let's go downtown first," I say. "I need something to eat. We can check it out on our way home."

Hettie nods and we continue on our way. The rest of the ride is silent; all I can hear is Hettie's deep breathing as she pedals behind me, trying to keep up. I make an effort to wait for her, and every so often, I look back to see her staring intently at the wheels of my bike, refusing to lift her eyes.

The trail eventually fades into the main road, and within two minutes we're downtown. Larton isn't particularly busy, even during the summer. I wonder where all the other kids are—the kids who will soon view me as the poster new student. When they ask me why I moved to Larton, what will I say? I've thought up stories to tell: my mother got a job here, my aunt needed help around the house...all of them result in more questions that will just end with me caught in a web of lies. But if I tell the truth—that my aunt forced us to move down here after my mother attempted to overdose on her sleeping pills—they'll probably be too disturbed to even try to get to know me. I absolutely will *not* tell anyone the truth.

Hettie and I dismount outside of a picturesque little diner that was built to resemble the style of the 1950s. The entirety of Larton has a traditional feel, almost like it's stuck in time while the outside world continues moving forward.

Meager lines of brownstone apartments close in on narrow streets, and a few shops and restaurants nestle close to one another here and there. A movie theater and gas station are closest to the freeway, which leads straight to the hospital where Aunt Vivian works.

"How's this one?" I ask Hettie, pointing at the diner. "We haven't tried here yet."

"Do you think they have waffles?"

"You just had a waffle," I say, poking her lightly. "But yes, I'm sure they do."

The diner smells like maple syrup and pancakes. Hettie and I take a booth by the window, and while Hettie picks at a strip of loose vinyl on her seat, a girl around my age greets us. Her dark hair is tied back in a bun, and thin, wispy strands fall in front of her eyes and face. I can tell she's a waitress by the apron she's wearing, but the pained look of boredom on her face is what really gives it away.

"Welcome, you two," she says, flashing us a well-rehearsed smile. "Have you dined here before?"

"It's our first time," I say, taking the menu she holds out to me. Hettie keeps her eyes on me, as she always does when someone new introduces themselves.

The girl nods and leans closer to me. "Well, don't order the ham omelet. It's crap."

I let out a surprised laugh.

"Seriously," she says, pushing a strand of hair behind her ear. "I ate it once and I swear to God, I almost threw up. Everything else is pretty good, though."

"Duly noted," I say, still a bit surprised and amused by her bluntness.

The girl grins and shifts her balance onto one foot. "I'm Ava," she says, tapping the nametag pinned onto her apron. "Ava Lim. Do you know what you want yet, or should I give you more time?"

I open my mouth to reply, but she speaks before I can.

"I haven't seen you two around here before," she says. "Are you visiting?"

"We just moved here, actually," I say, glancing at Hettie, whose eyes are now on her lap. I don't want Ava to ask me why we moved here, so I quickly add, "Do you live nearby?"

Ava nods. "I live in the apartment complex a few streets down, so it's a pretty short walk to work. That's one of the reasons my parents made me get a job here this summer while they went to visit my grandparents in Taiwan." She pauses, almost as though the thought annoys her. She shakes it off quickly, though, and shrugs. "I don't mind," she says, more to herself than to me. "We moved here last year, and I still haven't really gotten to know anyone yet. Working here gives me something to do. Why my parents picked to move to Tennessee of all places blows my mind, especially since we used to live in New York. Not to bash Larton or anything, but there was way more to do in New York. I didn't ask your name, by the way."

"I'm Ro," I say. "Short for Rosella. And this is my little sister, Hettie."

"Hey, Hettie," Ava says. She gets a small smile from Hettie, which is more than Hettie usually gives to unfamiliar people.

Ava shifts her balance again and grins. "Are you two going to the local schools?"

"Yeah, Hettie will be over at the elementary school, and I'll be at the high school." I almost add something about how I'm not looking forward to it, but I don't want to sound pessimistic.

"I'm at the high school too," Ava says. The excitement in her voice makes me smile. "What year?"

"Sophomore."

"No kidding! I'm going into sophomore year too. Maybe I'll see you around." She looks down at our menus and shakes her head. "Alright, I'll stop talking and let you decide what you want."

"Can you order for me?" Hettie whispers across the table. She points at the picture of waffles on the menu, and I notice Ava hold back a grin as she makes a little mark on her notepad.

"I already got it down," she says, giving Hettie a sweet smile. "Waffles for you, and…" She looks at me.

"I'll get the blueberry pancakes," I say.

"Smart choice," Ava says through a giggle. "Way better than the ham omelet." She takes our menus and, just as she is about to leave, looks down at my wrist and smiles. "Sweet tattoo," she says.

I grin as she walks away. This has been the first time in the past month that anyone my age in Larton has noticed me. Maybe living here won't be as boring as I thought.

CHAPTER 3
THE WELL

Hettie is an even slower eater than she is a biker. It takes an hour before we finally leave. When we do, I set aside a decent tip for Ava, and Hettie and I head back up out of town and to the fork in the trail that leads into the forest.

"Let's stay on the path for now," I remind my sister as we take the turn. We ride into the thicket of green, and I listen to the leaves rustle. It's the same sound I loved back in Oregon—the sound I escaped to whenever I could.

"Okay," Hettie says, pedaling a few yards behind me. "Can we..." She takes a deep breath. "Can we walk a little?"

I bring my foot down off my bike. "Yeah, sorry," I say. Sometimes it's hard for me to realize how fast I'm going.

Hettie stops as well and gently hops off her bike. "Let's leave them here," she says, pushing hers to the side of the trail and unclasping her helmet.

I lay my bike down next to Hettie's and look back. The tops of the trees lean toward each other, forming a tunnel that leads back out to the sunlit road.

I take my helmet off and rest it by my bike. "I don't want to walk too far into the forest, though, okay?" I tell Hettie, who nods. "Not until we know it a little better."

"Okay, just a *little* bit far," she says, nodding to herself this time. She takes my wrist and gingerly leads me into the gaping mouth of the forest.

I laugh. "Okay, only a little bit. We'll follow the trail, alright?"

The definition of the trail fades as we walk. I continually look back to make sure we haven't accidentally wandered off of it. The bright, artificial colors of our bikes grow smaller as we walk, and the world slowly becomes shrouded with trees that filter rays of sunlight through their spindly branches.

The forest evolves into patches of grass and dim light and then, abruptly, the trail stops. I guess not many people here enjoy hiking.

"Why did it stop?" Hettie asks, clearly disappointed. I don't blame her; exploring this forest must have seemed incredibly exciting, especially considering how dull the rest of Larton is.

I shrug. "I guess they decided this was the farthest they wanted to make the trail."

"Can we keep going?"

I tilt my head as I observe the labyrinth of trees and bushes before me. "I don't know, Hettie. I don't want to risk losing our path."

"We won't," Hettie says. "Not if we go straight. And we won't even go that far."

The persistence in her voice persuades me. That, and the fact that I'd like to explore a little more too.

"Okay, but we keep looking back so we know we aren't going too far. Deal?"

"Deal."

There are times when I think I'm too cautious. Despite being shy, Hettie has always been the type of kid to go down a slide headfirst or reach the tallest monkey bars without the fear of falling. I was never like that. I was never brave or bold; I was the kid who preferred reading at recess instead of playing. Even now, I rarely leave my comfort zone.

I suppose Hettie and I balance each other out. She pushes me to be okay with a little discomfort, and I make sure she doesn't get lost or hurt. The only problem is that Hettie doesn't always listen to me.

The summer leaves crunch beneath our feet as we step off of the trail. We continue straight—the way we would have gone if the trail continued—and I maintain a steady pace to ensure we haven't strayed too far. Or at least I try. I can't help but remember why I love forests. Perhaps it's because they remind me of home, or perhaps it's the feeling of being somewhere that has been, for the most part, untouched by anything but nature. The trees and leaves intermingle with one another unapologetically until they've become one—a coppice of green and brown that breathes and speaks all at the same time. Tiny aster flowers gather in clumps, and the smell of something sweet, like vanilla, lingers in the air.

"Ro, look!" Hettie says, pointing off to the left.

I turn my head away from the asters and follow her finger. The land slopes down into a grassy grove where the trees have formed a ring. Sunlight finds its way in easily. It's as if the trees made a silent pact with each other not to grow in this particular spot of land. And right in the middle of the ring, unobscured by the rest of the forest, sits a well. It's made of small gray and brown rocks stacked haphazardly on top of each other. Although it's pretty underwhelming, something about it is eerie as well. The way it sits alone in the center of the empty grove makes it look as though it's waiting for something.

"Do you have coins?" Hettie asks, turning to me.

"It may belong to someone, Hettie," I say. "They may not want people to throw coins into their well. Besides, I gave the rest of the money I had as a tip to Ava, remember?"

Hettie sighs loudly and dramatically. She wants me to know she's disappointed.

"I'm sure there are plenty of other wells in this world that you can throw coins into," I say. "Let's head back. We've gone farther than I wanted us to."

"Can we just go look into the well? I want to see how far down it goes."

I shake my head. "I told you, I don't know if it belongs to someone. People get their water from wells, and money is dirty."

"I didn't say I was going to throw coins in it."

"Still," I say. "Someone might own it. Let's go back."

"But *Rosella*," Hettie whines. She only ever uses my full name when she's upset or really wants something.

"It's just a well," I say, exhaling to relieve my suddenly tight chest. "I don't know why you're so obsessed."

"Just *one* look?"

"Christ, would you give it up?" I run my hand through my hair. My finger gets caught in a curl and I have to tug hard to free it, which annoys me even more. "It's rude to go onto someone's land uninvited."

"How do you know someone owns it?"

I pause. "I don't. But I don't want to risk it either. What if someone *does* own it and then they get angry with us for trespassing?"

"You're such a scaredy-cat," Hettie says.

"A scaredy-cat wouldn't have gone this far off the trail," I respond coolly.

"Rosella, *please*, just one look?"

Hettie's unfailing persistence will never cease to baffle me.

"If you shut up about it, maybe we can come back tomorrow," I say, trying to make it sound like I won't argue with her anymore. Something is making me nervous. I figure it must be the possibility that we're on private property.

"Tomorrow? Do you promise?"

"Sure, whatever. Tomorrow," I say. I just want to leave.

Hettie grins. It's a compromise she'll take.

Luckily, we hadn't gone too far. Relief washes over me when I see the trail and our bikes in the distance. The familiarity brings me comfort.

On the ride back to Aunt Vivian's house, I begin to regret telling Hettie that we'd return to the well. If someone owns it and gets mad at us for being on their property, I'm the one that will have to apologize and explain, not her. But now that I told her we would go back, I know she won't let it go.

Mother isn't in the kitchen when we return home. After securing our bikes in the garage, Hettie pulls out paper and crayons and busies herself at the kitchen table while I head down the narrow hallway to our room. I pass the laundry room next to the kitchen, and then the guest room, which Mother occupies. The door is shut, but I decide to check on her anyway. Slowly, so as not to make much noise, I crack open the door and peer inside. I can hardly see the bed or Mother because she's shut the blinds.

She's sleeping. Again. Something in my heart starts to ache, but I push the feeling away and pull the door shut.

I used to think that there was nothing worse than being hurt. Recently, though, I've come to realize that something even worse is watching someone you love hurt. When you're in pain, all you can focus on is yourself; you're blinded to the thoughts and feelings of others. But when someone you love is suffering, suddenly you don't know what to think or feel or say. Sometimes, all you can do is wait and hope that the misery stops.

I hear Hettie shuffle around the kitchen. She certainly doesn't need to watch Mother hurt, but I know she's not stupid either. She knows what's going on, and Mother isn't hiding anything from her by locking herself away.

I enter the bedroom that Hettie and I share, which is really only a small spare room with a large window and a single twin bed. Aunt Vivian bought a cot, which Hettie sleeps on, and we share the minimal closet space. I keep most of my belongings in my suitcases, but I know I'll probably have to unpack at some point. There's a tenacious part of me, though, that hopes all of this is temporary.

I lie on my bed facing the window and think about the girl I met at the diner. Maybe having a friend would be good; maybe it would get my mind off everything. Having some friends back in Oregon who call me every so often is one thing, but those friends are few and far between. Having a friend in Larton might improve my mood, even if only a little. Before I drift off to sleep, I decide that I'll visit the diner again with Hettie soon.

When I wake up, it's nine o'clock at night. This is what I get for refusing to set an alarm: six-hour naps that only make me more tired than I was before.

Hettie has moved all of her drawing supplies into our room. She sits on the hardwood floor in her pajamas, scribbling vigorously.

I sit up, feeling dazed and nowhere near as refreshed as I hoped I'd be.

"You took a nap for like ten years," Hettie says, not looking up from her paper.

"I certainly did," I say, grinning. "Have you been drawing the entire ten years I was asleep?"

"I didn't draw for *ten* years," she says, crinkling her nose. "But I drew a lot of pictures for Mommy and Aunt Vivian. I'm drawing one for you now, but Aunt Vivian just got home and told me it was time to get ready for bed, so I moved in here to draw."

"Did you brush your teeth?" I ask.

"I'm going to," Hettie says. She is probably not going to. I decide I'll nag her about it after I go greet Aunt Vivian.

"How about you finish drawing your picture for me, and then we'll get ready for bed?"

Hettie nods and pulls out a green crayon.

Halfway down the hallway, I can hear the voices of Mother and Aunt Vivian. It's clear they're trying to whisper, but the conversation has become heated. I stop before I reach the turn to the kitchen and hold my breath.

"This is important, Gianna," Aunt Vivian says. "Really important. We can't keep putting it off."

"We've been here less than a month," Mother says. I hear the legs of a chair drag across the floor before she sits. "I'm not ready to think about something this big. Not yet. I need time."

"When will you be ready, though?" I can imagine my aunt, sitting across from Mother—her blond hair tied back into a ponytail, still wearing her nursing uniform, staring at Mother intently with her blue eyes that are just as vibrant as Hettie's.

"Not now."

"Don't be hard. I'm trying to help."

"I know you are," Mother says. "And it means the world to me and the girls. But making a decision like this requires a lot more than just a quick 'yes' or 'no.' I can't just decide to sell the house in one night. Even if I did, can you imagine their reactions?"

"But were you ever really planning to go back?"

Silence. I pinch my lips together, trying not to make a sound.

"Honestly," Aunt Vivian says. Her voice is softer now, more sympathetic. "After what happened, I don't think it's right for you or the girls to return there. This house is big enough for all of us, and my being here is important. You know it is. The girls have already been enrolled in school here for one year. Do you really think they'll want to pack up and move again when it's over?"

"I haven't thought that far in advance," Mother says. Her voice is frail. "But I'm worried that selling our old house and leaving Oregon for good will crush them."

"So will having to deal with what happened to you in April again," Aunt Vivian says. She's always been blunt, but now she sounds more desperate than anything.

"That *won't* happen again. That was a mistake."

"Still," Aunt Vivian says. "Gianna, I love you, and I know you love Ro and Hettie. But you sleep all day—"

"It's better than bursting into tears in front of the girls," Mother snaps, heaving a great, shaky sigh. She's crying. I wonder how many times a day she cries.

"I know," Aunt Vivian whispers. "But regardless, your symptoms aren't getting any better. This isn't a cold or flu; you're not going to wake up one day and find that it's gone."

"Don't lecture me, Vivian," Mother says. I can tell she's struggling to hold back her anger. "I've dealt with this shit my whole life."

"But it's gotten *worse*," Aunt Vivian says. "Worse after Matthew died and worse still recently. You won't take medication and you won't see a therapist. You just suffer. And I know you can handle this shit...you've handled this shit your whole life. But it's not just you now. It's Rosella. It's Hettie. They can't depend on you when you're like this. They're losing their mom to this illness."

"God, I know, Vivian," Mother says. Her voice is stuffy; she's crying even harder. "I've let them down, and selling the house feels like I'm letting them down again."

"But you're not," Aunt Vivian says. "You're doing the opposite. You're helping them. You're helping yourself. You can't keep wasting money on a house you don't plan on living in again."

I look down at my feet and think of what a nuisance I'll be if I interrupt their conversation. But since I can't bear to hear it anymore either, I decide I'll greet Aunt Vivian tomorrow. For now, I need sleep. Despite my long naps and even longer nights, sleeping has become a welcome pastime for me recently as well. I've heard it's a symptom of depression, but I don't have that. I *can't* have that. Dealing with Mother having it is enough for me.

When I return to the room, I hear Hettie shuffling in the connecting bathroom. She turns the faucet on, and I smile despite everything, because she actually remembered to brush her teeth.

I approach my bed and find one of Hettie's drawings waiting for me. She's laid it on my pillow. I pick it up and observe it. As per her habit, she signed and dated her picture: *Hettie Gill, June 16, 1995.* Her attention to detail doesn't surprise me. What does surprise me, though, is that she didn't draw me a Rosella like she said she would. Instead, she drew a grassy grove shrouded with trees. And in the middle of the grove, she drew a well.

CHAPTER 4
SPIRAL STAIRCASE

Aunt Vivian is in the kitchen when I wake up. She beams at me as I sit down at the table, and I do my best to smile back. Although I know Aunt Vivian is trying to help, I can't help but scorn her for pushing Mother to sell our house. The hope within me—a flame that sputters to life one moment, then dies just as unpredictably—dreams of returning home. That sliver of hope has been the thing keeping me going, but now I feel like it's being stolen from me.

"Do you want a coffee?" she asks.

I nod. "You haven't left yet. It's almost noon."

"I'm going in a little later today," Aunt Vivian replies as she turns on the coffee maker. She runs her fingers through her hair, which looks exactly like Mother's. Sometimes, I think they could be twins if it weren't for the subtle differences in their faces. Aunt Vivian's nose is more pointed than Mother's, much like how my nose is more pointed than Hettie's, and her eyes are a few shades darker and a lot more present.

"Is Hettie up yet?" Aunt Vivian asks.

"She's been up for a bit, but she's occupied herself with her drawings, as usual," I say. I think of the picture she drew me last night. She clearly hasn't forgotten my promise that we'd return to the well today.

"Has she had breakfast?"

"She said she ate a bagel," I say, shrugging. "But we'll probably go downtown today, so I'll make sure she has something better to eat then."

Aunt Vivian raises her eyebrows. "Do you have money for that?"

I grin. "I may need a little bit."

Aunt Vivian chuckles and shuffles through her purse on the counter. "You're lucky I love you so much," she says, handing me a few dollar bills.

"Thank you for loving me," I tease as I stuff the money into my pocket.

The soft footsteps of Hettie entering the kitchen catch my attention. As soon as she sees me, she looks me dead in the eye and says, "Remember, you promised me we'd go see the well again today."

"A well?" Aunt Vivian eyes me quizzically.

"We biked into the forest yesterday and found it," I respond. "Hettie has become a bit obsessed." I throw my little sister a half-playful, half-disapproving look.

"The forest just a few minutes down?" Aunt Vivian asks, narrowing her eyebrows. When I nod, she says, "I've taken some walks there, but I never saw a well." She shrugs, dismissing the thought, and hands me a cup of coffee. "Leave it to me to be distracted," she adds.

"The problem is," I say, glancing at Hettie to gauge her reaction, "I have no idea if someone owns it. I told Hettie I was uncomfortable with the idea of possibly trespassing, but *someone* would rather risk it."

"You're just a scaredy-cat," Hettie responds, opening the freezer and grabbing a frozen waffle. She passes the toaster oven and sits down at the table, then takes a massive bite. Ice flakes that had formed on the waffle fall into her lap.

"First of all," I say, watching her as she gnaws at her frozen waffle, "that's disgusting." Hettie grins in response. "Second, I'm not a scaredy-cat, I'm just not looking to get into trouble. I don't want someone to yell at us for being on their land."

"I doubt you would get in trouble," Aunt Vivian says. I give her an unamused look. That wasn't the response I was looking for. She notices my expression and rubs me warmly on the back. "You worry too much, Ro," she says. "Even if someone does own it, they'd have to be an asshole to get angry with a teenager and her little sister." Realizing Hettie is in the room, she quickly corrects herself. "A *jerk*," she says. "They'd have to be a jerk."

I stifle a laugh. Aunt Vivian certainly has to watch her tongue a bit more now that a seven-year-old lives in her house.

"I say go for it," she continues. Her words are directed more at me than Hettie. "Go explore Larton. It's summer. You deserve to have some fun."

I don't respond. Maybe I *do* worry too much. But it isn't getting caught that scares me, I've realized. It's something else—a nameless anxiety I can't pinpoint.

Regardless, there's no use arguing with Hettie about it. If she wants to see the well, she'll bug me until she sees it. I might as well go with her. After all, it gives us something to do together. Maybe I'll save some change from breakfast and let Hettie toss coins like she wanted to.

I loosen up a little, and by the time Aunt Vivian leaves and Hettie and I make our way downtown, my restlessness has lifted.

We enter the same diner we ate at yesterday, and I get that familiar whiff of maple syrup. When I see Ava working some tables, I put a meek hand up to catch her attention. She quickly notices us and grins.

"You came back!" she says as she makes her way over to us. She has her arms wrapped around a few plates, which she sets down on an empty table. "I guess that means our food isn't terrible."

I laugh. "I'm not about to pass up some more blueberry pancakes."

"Right," Ava says. "And waffles for Hettie?"

When Hettie nods, Ava smiles proudly. "Not a bad memory, huh?"

"This kid lives on waffles," I say, gently poking Hettie.

Hettie crinkles her nose. "Not *only* waffles. I eat fruit sometimes."

"You're in luck, then," Ava says. "We offer a fruit plate, and sometimes they even let me assemble it."

She leads us to an empty booth, and within ten minutes she arrives back with our food. She hands Hettie the fruit plate, which she's arranged into a smiley-face with various bits of cantaloupe, grapes, and apples.

Hettie grins. "They do that in Oregon too!"

Ava chuckles. "Same with New York," she responds. "I guess it's a popular way to eat fruit. One time, I—"

She's cut off by the door of the diner, which swings open violently. Ava quickly turns around, and I strain to see who she's looking at.

It's a middle-aged man with unkempt brown hair, noticeable stubble, and baggy clothes. He walks slowly, as though his feet weigh too much—either that or he just has a bad hangover. His skin is ghostly white, which is fitting because he has a haunted look about himself, and he has a tall and stockier build despite seeming to have not eaten in days.

"Oh, Jesus Christ," Ava mutters to herself.

"What?" I say, following her eyes as she watches the man slump into a booth in a lonely corner of the diner.

"That guy is a mess. He comes here every other day or so, and he's always either drunk or hungover."

"Do you know what's wrong with him?"

Ava shrugs. "Nothing, I think. Just kind of weird. I think he likes it here because we're never very crowded. He's not into having conversations or anything."

I have a feeling that someone who isn't interested in conversations doesn't bode well for Ava. I don't blame her for feeling uneasy around him, though. He looks like he's about to vomit all over the tile.

"Guess that's part of the job," Ava says reluctantly. "You have to serve all types of people."

She sighs and makes her way over to his table. I watch as she smiles at him and asks what he'd like to eat. He rubs his temples and says something I can't hear.

"Is he sick?" Hettie whispers.

I shake my head. "Just hungover."

Hettie turns her attention back to her fruit plate, and I try not to seem obvious while I observe the man. Ava seems eager to take his order because she doesn't stay around and chat. Instead, she disappears into the diner kitchen and returns a few minutes later with a cup of coffee. After she hands it to him, she scurries back over to us.

"How'd it go?" I ask, still trying to discreetly peer over at the man as he slumps back in his booth.

Ava shrugs. "I've had worse," she says. "He's not a bad guy, just a bit out of it. He lives in my apartment complex, actually. I think his name is Wayne. Not that I ever really see him. He's a bit of a hermit. Honestly, whenever I *do* see him, I can't help but notice how sad he looks."

I glance again at the man, who is still slumped in his chair, one hand on his coffee mug, the other across his stomach. For a moment, I wonder if he has fallen asleep.

I could never be a waitress.

Ava shakes her head and changes the subject. "Speaking of my apartment," she says, "if you two ever find yourselves with nothing to do, you should come by. It's kind of lonely without my parents, and Larton gets really boring." She smiles nervously and adds, "If you guys want to, of course."

I grin. It seems I'm not the only person in Larton looking for a friend.

"That would be fun," I say. "We'd love to."

Hettie continues eating her waffle silently, but given that she's usually content to tag along wherever I go, I know she doesn't mind.

Ava lights up, and I quickly realize that she didn't expect my answer. I feel a bit bad for her; if her family is away and Larton is as boring for her as it has been for Hettie and me, I can't imagine her summer has been one for the books.

After exchanging phone numbers with Ava, Hettie and I make our way out of the diner.

The first thing Hettie says to me when we step outside is, "Can we go see the well now?"

"If you're really that excited about it."

"I *am* really excited about it."

I don't understand why, so I just shrug and we mount our bikes. After a few minutes of silent riding, we exit downtown Larton and start our way up the long, winding road that leads to Aunt Vivian's house. I stop every so often to wait for Hettie to catch up, and we take the turn into the forest in unison. The crisp leaves flit out of our way as we ride past them. This time, we continue riding into the forest.

Once the trail becomes so weak that we can hardly see it, we hop off our bikes and set them down next to a vivid patch of asters.

The grove isn't hard to find. The trees make such a definable circle around it that I'm surprised Hettie had to draw my attention to it the first time.

Whoever built the little well did a good job of making sure it sat right in the middle of the grove. From a bird's-eye view, I imagine it would look like a tiny circle within a much larger one, both spaced out perfectly.

Hettie lets out a little squeal of excitement.

"I honestly don't get why you're so excited about a well," I say, shaking my head. I reach into my pocket and produce a few coins I saved after paying for lunch. "But I kept these for you." I hand the coins to Hettie.

"I thought you said someone might get mad if we throw coins into their well," Hettie says. She smiles and takes them anyway.

"A few coins won't hurt." Besides, seeing how excited this makes Hettie is worth it.

I wish I were young enough to be amused by such small things. Maybe it's not a matter of age, though; maybe it's a matter of personality. Hettie has always been the kind of person to get excited about little things, like waffles or crayons or, in this case, an old well and a couple of coins.

I've never been like that, but I wish I were. Maybe seeing Hettie excited is what makes me happy.

I follow her down the slope of the grove and watch as she rushes to the well, coins in hand, her blond curls bobbing behind her as she runs. She grips the stone edge of the well and pauses. As soon as she does, the coins fall from her hand and into the grass.

"Um...Ro?" she says, looking over at me with a furrowed brow.

"Yeah?"

"Come look."

I pick up my pace, unsure of what to expect. The first thought that pops into my mind is that an animal got trapped down there. I hope it isn't injured—or worse. But when I approach Hettie and peer down into the hole of the well, I realize I was wrong. At first, I'm relieved we didn't come across a dead animal. But then, my relief is replaced with overwhelming confusion.

Starting at the edge of the well and descending into the hole in a tight spiral is a staircase.

CHAPTER 5
THE MOON

My toes curl in my shoes as I peer down the stairs, unsure of whether to be enthralled or afraid. The stairs are made of gray and brown rocks, much like the well itself. They wind downward so tightly that I can't see anything but rows and rows of stone stairs.

Of all the places to build a staircase, a well is the last place I would think of. Maybe it leads to a basement or a bunker, but why it would be built here perplexes me.

"What is it?" Hettie asks.

"I don't know," I say. I try to look farther down, but all I can see is stairs. "Whoever built this probably meant for it to be private. We should leave."

"But, Ro…"

"I'm serious this time. I was uncomfortable with the idea of trespassing in the first place. Now I'm sure this belongs to someone."

"Scaredy-cat," Hettie scoffs.

"Would you stop calling me that?"

Hettie shakes her head. "Wimp," she mutters.

"There's a difference between being a wimp and being smart," I say, but it's obvious that Hettie doesn't care. She continues to peer down into the hole, and she doesn't look up until I walk away.

"Rosella!"

"Hettie, come on," I say. My voice brooks no argument, but Hettie, being as she always is, argues with me anyway.

"Don't you want to see what's down there?" she asks.

"No," I say. It's kind of a lie. I *would* like to, but it feels wrong.

"We've never seen anything like this," Hettie says, still lingering eagerly at the side of the well. "There's nobody around…nobody will catch us."

"Unless someone lives down there," I say. I realize it sounds pretty stupid, but it's better to be safe than sorry.

Hettie groans.

"Hettie, let's go. I mean it. I'm done with you bugging me about this."

"I'm done with you acting like my mom."

For some reason, her response stings more than I would have expected it to.

"Keep getting on my nerves and I won't spend time with you at all," I bite back.

Hettie groans again, this time louder, and reluctantly leaves the side of the well. She trudges over to me and I start walking again. I look ahead at the entrance to the grove and listen to Hettie's footsteps behind me. They're soft in the grass, and I don't realize that she has completely turned around until I look over my shoulder.

"Hettie!" I yell.

She doesn't respond. Instead, she runs back over to the well and lifts herself up onto the edge. She doesn't even look at me as she drops down onto the first step of the staircase and begins her descent.

"Hettie, stop!" I yell again. She doesn't stop. I curse under my breath. This absolutely would not have happened if Mother or Aunt Vivian were here. It's as though she refuses to listen to me because I'm her sister, failing to realize that I take care of her the most.

I lunge forward and sprint over to the well. My stomach drops when I realize she's still descending the staircase.

Anger boils within me as I jump over the edge of the well. Although I know I'm only a couple of paces behind her, I can't see her because of how tightly wound the staircase is. Not being able to see her scares me more than it angers me, and I pick up my speed even more.

The staircase is lengthy and dark. As it descends into the well, the world above fades and a thousand thoughts pass through my mind. The first thought is how angry I am with Hettie and how she never stops until she gets what she wants. Then I think about the possibility that someone really does live down here in a bunker of some sort—the type of person who doesn't want to be bothered. I think of how long the staircase is and how I feel as though I'll never stop winding around in tight, compact spirals. It's as if I'm descending into the belly of a dark and cold cave. My senses are continually subdued as I step farther and farther down. The only things that guide me are the sounds of Hettie's distant footsteps, which reverberate dully off the walls of the well.

The thought that remains at the forefront of my mind, however, is the peculiarity of it all. How does one even build a staircase in a well? Where does it lead? And why in the world was it built in the first place? Perhaps this isn't a well at all—perhaps it's simply an entrance.

Finally, I take the last curve of the staircase. Something silver catches my eye, but I see Hettie first and grab her arm, spinning her so that she faces me.

"You're such a brat," I say. "Seriously, Hettie, this is dangerous."

I intend to keep scolding her, but I'm cut short by the sight of a small archway adorned with silver and gold ornaments. They twinkle despite the minimal light at the bottom of the staircase. And then, I hear water. Running water, but not from a faucet—it's more natural than that.

I release my grip on Hettie's arm and step forward. I realize that I'm shaking, whether in anger or fear I have no idea.

"What *is* this?" Hettie asks.

I don't answer her. Instead, I lean into the archway and take in my surroundings.

It isn't a bunker or a basement or a shed or anything like that.

It's a forest.

It isn't the forest from above, which is green and lush. This forest is small, shrouded in moonlight and filled with scattered trees. A few are decorated with tinsel, but the majority are bare; and yet, the towering trees with their spindled branches are more beautiful than they are eerie. To my right, a brook winds through the forest and leads to a larger lake that shimmers as its waters tap against the shore.

Despite my better judgment, I take a few steps forward and run my fingers over the silver tinsel that hangs from the tree closest to me. Like the others, it looks as though it was crafted, but by whom or what I can't tell. As I let the world around me sink in, I begin to think that the only normal parts of the trees are the trunks. Upon closer observation, however, I realize I'm wrong: carved into the bark of every tree is a face, but the craftsmanship is so remarkable that I wonder if it's even possible for a human or machine to have done something like this.

I dismiss the illogical thought and study the face on the tree I'm closest to, which is of a little girl. The edges of the bark outline her hair, and the wood is carved as such that I can see every freckle on her face. I reach my hand up to run my fingers over the carving. Hettie, who is just as surprised as I am, gently clutches the fabric of my shirt and pulls herself closer to me.

As my finger traces the carving of the girl, I feel the bumps of her nose and eyelids underneath my fingers. For a moment, I wonder if it's truly a tree I'm touching and not a real face. The girl has a soft complexion, and despite being only wood, she looks as though she's fallen into a deep, unyielding sleep.

My heart flutters in my chest as I approach another tree. It's almost identical to the one before, but this time the face is of a little boy with tousled hair. His nose is pointed and his lips are thin, and he too looks as though he is sleeping.

I've been to art galleries before, but I've never seen anything like this. The faces have been carved with a degree of precision and detail that I previously thought impossible. Whoever did this is incredibly talented. There must be at least a hundred trees, and a unique face has been carved on each of them.

"This is like a fairytale," Hettie says. "It's so pretty."

I nod, only because I'm too speechless to speak. Although a small part of me still wants to leave, it has been almost completely silenced.

I could understand someone creating the trees, but the rest of this little underground world leaves me with no explanation. It's as though we are outside, but I know we aren't because it's night here. I look up to see a cloud-covered sky, illuminated with oranges and pinks from a setting sun that doesn't exist. I can see the faint dots of stars here and there, but they're overpowered by what catches my eye most: the moon.

Despite being only a crescent, it's so bright and massive that I feel as though I can reach up and touch it. The craters I'm able to see are defined, and the beams of light that escape the moon cloak the little forest and the lake beyond in a perpetual glow.

This isn't the real moon; I know that for certain. Although it looks as real as the moon I know, there is no way a moon or a sky could be underground. And yet, it is. The whole world is underground, but the sky seems to go on forever. How can that be?

My attention turns to the stream that runs near the archway and leads out onto the lake. I squint to see farther, but the lake is as endless as the sky. The water sits still, gently running against the horizon, where the blurry silhouette of thousands of more trees paints the ethereal vista. They aren't connected to the spit of land Hettie and I are on, however. The lake wraps around us, creating an isolated island that houses the trees and the archway. I wonder if perhaps those faraway trees are real, or if it's simply a painting draped over some kind of massive wall. It's a silly thought, but I think it anyway.

Something deep down—a pull too enticing to ignore—beckons me to continue. The world is silent as Hettie and I walk farther into the forest; the only sounds I can hear are our footsteps in the grass and the gentle running of the stream.

I pass more trees, stopping at each one to observe the face carved into it. All of the faces are young; in fact, the oldest that I can see is perhaps only two or three years younger than me. The carvings all depict the children as though they are sleeping peacefully, unwilling to ever wake up. Since there is no more than one carving on each tree, every single one has a different personality—a different identity.

"What an interesting style of art," I whisper, half to Hettie, half to myself.

Again, I wonder who did this and if they might be coming back. The thought isn't enough to make me want to leave, though. Oddly enough, I want to *stay* more and more as I continue to observe the world around me.

I'm calm too—a welcome feeling that I had started to miss. The tranquility of the forest and the lake seeps into my body, and I realize that I would be content to stay here forever.

We continue walking parallel to the lake and past more trees. It dawns on me, quite suddenly, how small the island is. I look to the nearby archway, then pick up my pace, eager to see more.

Hettie and I move inward as we weave about the labyrinth of trees. A few yards in front of us, the forest thins out, making way for an ivory gazebo that stands stoutly at the edge of the water.

"It's like a dream," Hettie whispers.

"It's amazing." I can't believe I'm admitting it.

"Aren't you glad I decided to come down here?" Hettie asks, smirking.

I give her a gentle push, but I don't respond.

I approach the steps of the gazebo, which is massive compared to the little world around it. Clutching the nearest post, I lean to peer inside.

It's the most gorgeous thing I've ever seen. Tinsel hangs from the domed ceiling just like it does from the trees in the forest, and a garish crystal chandelier descends from the center. Moonlight bounces off the crystals and reflects onto the marble floor, dancing and twinkling playfully as I move inward. The lattice is decorated with golden flowers, which, like everything else, are shrouded in glitter. It's as though the moon continually gifts its light to the world below, waking the sleeping island with its silver.

I feel like I've entered a fairytale. The warmth inside me comes to a crescendo.

"Ro, look!" Hettie says from behind me.

When I turn around and follow Hettie's pointed finger, a lone deer catches my eye. It walks among the trees, nearing us on hesitant legs. Its body glows a soft silver, and the antlers on its head sparkle just like the crystals in the gazebo. My lips part in awe when I realize it's made entirely of glass. Like everything else in this strange place, the moonlight reflects off the stag's body; it's almost as though the touch of the light is what gives it life.

I don't protest when Hettie approaches it, because uncharacteristically, I'm not nervous. She reaches out her hand, and the glass deer lowers its nose to her palm. Gently and silently, it stays put, reassuring us that all is well.

Another movement catches my eye, and this time I see butterflies flitting seamlessly around the lattice of the gazebo. It isn't until one comes close to my face that I notice both its tiny body and fluttering wings are made of spun glass. Just like the deer, the butterfly reflects the moonlight that ricochets off the gazebo chandelier—awakened and revitalized by the ever-present silver beams.

"This is..." I can't find a word, because nothing will do this place justice. I settle on, "unreal."

"There's nobody else here," Hettie says, still watching the deer, which slowly walks away and grazes on a nearby patch of grass.

"I can't think of anyone who could have made this," I say, looking back up at the sky, which has begun to turn from the vibrant oranges and pinks of evening to a muted midnight blue. "There's no way a human can do any of this. The sky, the glass animals, the trees, the moon...it can't be man-made. It...it..."

"It's enchanted," Hettie says. "It has to be."

"But..." I cut myself off. I can argue all I like—I can muster up every bit of logic and every scientific explanation I've ever heard of—but this world will inevitably prove me wrong. I realize, quite to my discomfort, there *is* no way to explain this. But as much as the thought rattles me, it also intrigues me. What else is unable to be explained?

The question I find myself most drawn to, however, is if anyone else has ever seen this little wonderland. If they had, I would have seen it on the news. I would have watched as curious scientists, or perhaps even the entirety of the nation, attempted to uncover the mysteries of this underground world. There's absolutely no way a discovery like this would go unmentioned.

And yet, I've never heard of a strange well in the middle of rural Tennessee that leads to an underground forest. I've never heard of lifelike glass animals that move just like real ones. I've never heard of realistic faces carved into hundreds of tinsel-adorned trees. And I have certainly never heard of an endless sky and a moon that reside underground.

But what bugs me the most is that the well hadn't been hard to find. It stood out in the middle of the grove, close to the entrance of the forest—easy to spot and even easier to approach.

"How has this never been discovered?" I say aloud.

"Maybe it's a secret," Hettie says. "Maybe nobody else can see it."

I take a moment to register what she's said. "If that's the case," I finally say, "then why are *we* able to see it?"

Hettie shrugs. "I don't know."

"Right," I say. "It doesn't make sense. None of it does. Just think about it…there's no explanation." I bite my lip and repeat, "It doesn't make sense."

Hettie tilts her head. "Why does everything always have to make sense to you?"

I open my mouth slowly, only to find I don't have an answer. A tinge of irritation passes through me as I struggle to come up with a reply.

Hettie doesn't wait for my response. Instead, she scales the steps of the gazebo and does a little twirl on the marble tile. She giggles and runs over to the lattice edge, peering over the side and admiring the lake water that gently kisses the shore.

I follow her up the steps, simultaneously admiring the world and continuing to wonder how it could possibly exist.

Though I can hardly choose which part of this hidden place is the most beautiful, it's the moon that mesmerizes me most. Its presence is everywhere. Its light seeps into the gazebo, through the strange trees, and reflects off the lake. It touches every inch of the tinsel and crystals, exerting its unrelenting authority.

But the strangest part is that it calms me—more so than the lake or the forest or the celestial way the crystals reflect the light. Upon looking at it longer, all of my questions begin to flit away like the butterflies with glass wings.

When I tell Hettie that we should get back home, she looks at me with disappointment.

"Will we come back?" she asks, tracing her finger across the side of the gazebo.

I look back up at the moon.

"Definitely," I say.

CHAPTER 6
MOTHER

I make Hettie promise she won't tell Mother or Aunt Vivian what we found. Though I'm usually uncomfortable keeping secrets, this is different. Something within me feels that it's best to keep this quiet, lest someone finds out and doesn't let us go back. And if there's one thing I know, it's that I desperately want to go back.

It's hard to leave, but deciding to return the next day makes it easier. Hettie and I ride home in silence, and as soon as we get inside, Hettie runs to our room and takes out some paper.

"What are you doing?" I ask her as she eagerly dumps her box of crayons onto the floor.

"Drawing it," she says. "So I don't forget."

I sit on my bed, gently feeling the fabric of my comforter to convince myself I'm not dreaming. I'm still trying to take everything in, but I'm not sure it's possible.

"Just remember not to tell anyone," I say.

Hettie grins. "That's how I know this must be special," she says. "You don't want to put an end to it."

I don't argue with her. She's right, after all; most new or different things set me off balance and make me want to return to what I know is safe. But not this. I want to keep this—to protect this secret world at all costs and make sure nobody ruins it.

I lie back and try to fathom a feasible explanation for how it may have come to be, but I can't. And yet, the mystery of this place is part of what makes it so intriguing. It's wholly untouched by the world above—uncorrupted and pure.

That evening, after dinner, I walk outside and look up at the moon. It's so far away compared to the underground moon, and it isn't a crescent either. I sit on the porch steps and spend a while just looking up, enjoying the silence and the space my solitude gives me to think.

I'm so lost in thought that the sound of the door opening behind me makes me jump. I turn around quickly. It isn't Hettie—it's Mother.

"Hey there, Ro," she says. "What are you doing?"

I shrug. "Just thinking."

To my surprise, Mother sits down next to me. Despite the stifling Tennessee heat, she's wrapped herself in a shawl, which she tightens around her body as she sits down.

I study her face, which is strikingly similar to my own. It's delicate, elfin, and holds a sense of impassivity to it—a quiet, introspective detachment.

"About what?" she asks.

"I don't know," I say. It's not entirely a lie. "Do you know what kind of moon that is?"

Mother chuckles. "A waning gibbous, I think. I can't believe I still remember that. I learned about moon phases years ago."

I bring my knees up to my chest and rest my arms on them.

After a few moments of silence, Mother asks, "What did you and Hettie do today?"

"We went downtown," I say, still staring up at the moon. "I met a girl named Ava yesterday. She goes to the high school. She's in my grade."

"That's great," Mother says. She smiles, but I can't decipher how genuine it is.

"What did *you* do today?" I ask, not sure if I want to hear the answer.

"Oh, you know," Mother says. This time it's her who shrugs. "Not much."

That's another way of saying she slept all day. I look down at my shoes.

Though the question makes me uncomfortable, I decide to ask it anyway. "How are you feeling?"

Mother gives me a brittle smile. "I'm okay, honey," she says. Then she repeats it, more to herself than me. "I'm okay." She turns in toward me. "Thank you for always letting Hettie tag along. She has so much fun with you. I'm sure she appreciates it."

"I have fun with her," I say, surprised that Mother thinks it's a chore for me. "She's one of the only people I know here."

"I know," Mother says through a sigh. "It's been a tough few months. You've been a trooper. I don't say it enough."

"You don't need to," I say. "I'm just glad we can be out here with Aunt Vivian." I don't know if I'm lying or telling the truth. While Aunt Vivian's presence brings me comfort, my heart sinks when I think of never returning to Oregon. Although I want to, I don't bring up the conversation I overheard the other night. After all, maybe it won't end up being a reality. Maybe Mother will get well soon and we'll be able to move back. The sliver of hope, despite how minute it is, makes me feel a little better.

"Having a sister is a blessing," Mother says. She smiles at me, this time with warmth in her eyes. "I'm so glad I got to have two girls who can share the kind of bond I have with Vivian."

I look back up at the moon, still thinking about the one underground. All of the sudden, I want to tell Mother what Hettie and I found earlier today. I want to tell her about the well and the world that is hidden underneath. But I keep my mouth shut. Perhaps I'll tell her in the future, but tonight, I still have things I need to think about.

"Mom?" Hettie's voice sounds from behind me. I turn around to see her lingering at the door, her little body nestled in the crack Mother left open. My heart flutters nervously and I bite down on my lip, praying she doesn't spill our secret. "Where's my doll? The one with the pink hair?"

I feel myself loose a breath after she finishes.

Mother stands up. "I don't know," she says. "Have you looked in your suitcase?"

Hettie nods and Mother shakes her head. She touches my shoulder gently and goes back inside. Hettie's voice echoes from the kitchen as she tries to explain what her doll looks like.

I turn my attention back to the world around me. For a while, I think about Mother, and then I think about Hettie.

Inevitably, my thoughts return to the well, and I sit silently, not really thinking about anything—just picturing the way the world looked. Ten minutes pass, then twenty more, and all the while I think about returning and seeing that crescent moon again. Maybe going back will give me some answers.

I must have stayed outside for over an hour. When Hettie comes out, she clutches her pink-haired doll in her hand. She walks over to me and sits down.

"You found your doll," I say, grinning. "Did Mom help?"

Hettie shrugs. "Kind of. She got tired so I kept looking. I found Teresa in my backpack. That's her name, just so you know. Teresa Autumn Gill. She has our last name."

I try to seem interested, but unease settles in my stomach as I look back at the half-opened door. "Did Mom go to sleep?"

"I think so," Hettie says. She runs her fingers through the tangled locks of hair on her doll. Then, she puts it down next to her and sighs. "I miss her," she says.

I raise an eyebrow. "Who?"

"Mommy."

I utter a confused laugh. "You were just speaking with her."

"I know," Hettie says, gently tapping her foot against the wooden porch steps. "But I miss her anyway."

CHAPTER 7
SPINNING WHEEL

Before we go to bed, Hettie shuffles through her suitcase and pulls out a poorly bound book of fairytales that she's had since before she could walk.

"Do you know what that underground world reminded me of?" she asks, handing me the book.

I grin. "A fairytale?"

Hettie nods. "You should read me one."

I shoot her a half-smile. "How about you read me one? It's good practice."

She shrugs and climbs up onto my bed. I know the story she'll pick; it's the same one she picks every time she wants to read this book.

As if the location is embedded in her memory, Hettie flips to *Sleeping Beauty*. She reads quickly—so quickly that the unsuspecting listener would think she has the prowess of someone five times her age, when in reality she's simply memorized the entire story. She knows every word, every picture, and every tiny way the plot progresses, but when she finishes, she still asks me the same questions she always does.

"Why does the princess touch the spinning wheel if it's evil?" she asks, shaking her head as though she's scolding a young child.

"She doesn't know it's evil," I say. "She's in a trance. The witch makes her think she needs to touch the spinning wheel, but she's tricking her. That way, the princess will prick her finger and fall into a deep sleep."

Hettie scrunches her nose. "Do you think you would know the spinning wheel was bad if you were the princess?"

I look at the picture on the last page before I respond. The princess, with her long and gold-spun hair, looks ever so much like Hettie.

"I don't know," I say, shrugging. "Probably not if I was in a trance. Do you think *you* would?"

Hettie closes the book after admiring the final image of the princess in her ball gown, then says confidently, "I think I would know."

"If only the princess was as smart as you," I say. "Then she wouldn't need the prince."

Hettie gets up and shoves the book back into her suitcase with surprising strength, burying it under her jumbled clothes and shoes. No wonder it's falling apart.

"Princes are stupid," she says. "Sisters are way better. Would you save me if I was going to prick my finger on a spinning wheel?"

The question makes me grin. "Of course I would."

The next morning, after a quick breakfast, Hettie and I rush out the door and mount our bikes. Hettie rides faster than usual; in fact, she manages to keep up with me. We decide to skip visiting downtown today and go straight to the well.

It sits in the middle of the grove as if it's waiting for us. I try not to seem too eager, but I quicken my pace as I approach it. Part of me is worried that I'll look down the well and see nothing but a dark hole filled with water. I hold my breath as I grip the edge and peer over, sighing in relief when I see the stairs.

Although I'm tired—I fell asleep later than usual—I'm so entranced by this otherworldly place that I hardly mind. Hettie and I descend the spiraling staircase in bounds, and I feel like I used to years ago on Christmas morning.

The underground world greets us with the silver archway and tinsel-covered trees. I look around at first to make sure we're alone. When all I hear is running water from the stream and small swells from the lake tapping against the shore, I feel all the more liberated.

Hettie and I weave about the trees, and I take a few moments to observe the faces on them. But the gazebo is what pulls me forward. It shines brighter than it did last time. The moon is brighter too; its beams make the flowers on the lattice shimmer even more intensely than before. Hettie and I scale the steps, then lean onto the edge of the gazebo and look out at the lake.

"I don't see the glass deer this time," Hettie says. She leaves my side and walks to the center of the gazebo.

I open my mouth to respond but close it promptly when something orange flashes in the water. At first, I think it's a reflection of the clouds above, but when I see it again, brighter, I realize that it came from something underwater.

"Hettie, look," I say, motioning for her to come back to me. "I think there's something under the water."

Hettie walks over to me and looks out at the lake.

This time, I see something red. It's slightly closer to us, but its light dies down as soon as I notice it.

"That!" I say as I point out onto the lake.

Hettie stands on her tiptoes. "Where?"

"It went away," I say, impatience brimming within me. "Just give it a second, it may come back."

Then, in response, two more lights begin to shine in the water. This time, I'm able to see what they are.

"Stingrays!" I point so Hettie can see.

She gasps when she notices. The stingrays glide beneath the surface of the water, each one glowing a different color. As one comes to life, so does another, until there are far too many to count. What was once a sleeping lake has evolved into a kaleidoscope of color that mirrors the clouds above, and even when I think there are no more colors left to add, more stingrays come—each one a new and distinct shade.

I stand with my eyes wide and my fingers tightly gripping the rail of the gazebo as I watch the stingrays entwine about each other. They float throughout the water with the same effortlessness of the glass butterflies that once flitted around the gazebo. It's almost as though they're welcoming us with this show of colors—as though they're glad we came back.

Hettie squeals in delight as the stingrays continue their spellbinding dance. The lake fills with even more light and color until it seems like the water can no longer contain it. Bursts of reds, greens, yellows, and blues echo off the surface and onto our faces. Even the crystals on the chandelier overflow with color, changing in response to the movements of the stingrays.

I don't know how long the show, or whatever it is, lasts. Perhaps fifteen minutes, maybe longer. And then, as quickly as the colors came to life, they fade away. The lake goes from rainbow back to blue within seconds, and the stingrays disappear completely.

"That was *amazing*," Hettie says.

I don't know whether I should laugh or cry.

"It was like a disco," she says, grabbing me by the arm. "Don't you think it was like a disco?"

"It was better than a disco."

Hettie utters another excited squeal. "Have you ever seen rainbow stingrays?"

"I don't think there's such a thing as rainbow stingrays." I pause and add, "At least, not where we're from."

"This place is a thousand times better than where we're from," Hettie says.

I grin. Though we often differ in opinions, this time I wholeheartedly agree with her.

We spend a while longer staring off at the lake and the faraway hills that surround it. The stingrays don't return, but the way the moon shines on the water captivates me just as much.

"Imagine if someone held a ball here," Hettie says after a few minutes of silence. She moves toward the center of the gazebo and looks up at the chandelier. Even from where

I'm standing, I can see the lights from the crystals twinkle in her eyes. "This would be the perfect place to dance. I would wear the most beautiful ball gown ever."

"We can hold our own ball," I say as I approach her. "Besides, aren't we planning on moving into a castle together when we grow up?"

"We should move *here*," Hettie says. "This is better than any castle."

"I think so too," I say. "But what about Mom and Aunt Vivian?"

"They can come," Hettie says. "Then Mommy would have to be happy."

"It would be hard not to be." Then, more seriously, I say, "But you can't tell them about this, remember? If they find out, they may try to stop us from coming back."

"*You* almost tried to stop me," Hettie says.

"That's because I didn't know what we would find." I look around at the gazebo and the little forest directly outside of it. "But now that we know, you better not blabber about it to anyone."

"I don't blabber," Hettie protests. "I didn't even say anything last night."

"I know. I'm just reminding you."

Although I don't want to admit it, the thought of never returning upsets me more than it reasonably should.

Hettie and I spend an hour in the gazebo and another half-hour meandering about the tinsel forest. I take more time to observe the faces on the trees. I wonder why they're here, what they mean, and why they're all so young. Mostly, I wonder who or what is responsible for the carvings. But just like last time, I can't come up with any explanations.

Oddly enough, the lack of knowledge doesn't bother me—not like it did before. Instead, I'm utterly entranced and intrigued. It's a bizarre change of heart, but I welcome it regardless.

When Hettie and I finally leave, all I can think about is when we'll come back.

CHAPTER 8
AN EMERALD PENDANT

That night, I dream of silver forests and moonlit lakes, and the underground moon resides above it all. I wake up more refreshed than I've felt in a long while. Even Aunt Vivian comments on how early I woke up as she's about to leave.

"I haven't seen you up and about before noon in quite some time," she teases me as she makes her coffee. "Aren't teenagers supposed to hate mornings?"

"I slept well," I say. "Really well, actually."

"I'm glad. There's nothing quite like a good night's sleep." Once she's poured her coffee, she leans against the counter, stirring her drink with a spoon. She's in her nursing uniform, which is a light and sterile blue with little accents around the sleeves. "Did you and Hettie end up going back to that well?" she asks.

The question catches me off guard. I had expected her to forget about our conversation.

As casually as I can, I shrug. "Yeah," I say, focusing on the kitchen table. "It was cute."

"And I'm guessing nobody owned it?" she asks. I know what she's trying to do—she's trying to prove to me that my incessant worrying is often unwarranted.

I decide to appease her. "Nobody owned it," I say. "Not that we know of. I shouldn't have worried so much about it. It's just a well."

Aunt Vivian laughs. "That's my Ro," she says. "Always worrying about little things. I'm glad you two got to check it out. Larton can be boring, but it makes the small things that much more interesting."

"Have you seen Mom this morning?" I ask her, trying to change the subject.

"She was up an hour ago when I got up," Aunt Vivian says. "Is Hettie still asleep?"

I nod.

"When you see her, give her a hug for me," Aunt Vivian says. She kisses the top of my head and grabs her purse. "Have fun today, love."

"I will." I smile at her as she leaves.

Once I hear her car back out, I audibly exhale in relief. I don't know why the thought of accidentally slipping and telling her what we found makes me worry so much.

When I was Hettie's age—a year or so before she was born—Mother bought an expensive china set and told me over and over again not to touch it. I did, of course, and ended up dropping a gorgeous plate, shattering it into hundreds of pieces. It was a total cliché; all I could do was think about how stupid I'd been. I decided not to tell her, hoping that she would think I had nothing to do with it. She figured it out quickly, but I remember the way I felt when I was keeping the secret. It's the same way I feel now. Although I think it's the best thing to do, I feel guilty about it. I'm in a constant state of wanting to tell someone and convincing myself to stay quiet.

Hettie trudges into the kitchen. Her hair is a mess.

"You look like you got caught in a tornado," I tease her as she sits down at the table.

"I didn't brush my hair yet," she says groggily.

"Do you want toast?" I ask her. "I'm going to make myself some."

Hettie nods, staring at the table. When I put her plate down in front of her, she hardly reacts.

"Are you feeling okay?" I ask.

"Yeah," she says.

"You sure?" I ask again. She hasn't even started eating yet. "Do you feel sick?"

Hettie shakes her head. "I'm good."

I watch her while I eat. She doesn't even pick up her toast. She just stares at it, as if she's in a daze.

"Hettie?"

No reaction.

I lean over and nudge her. "Hettie?"

"What?"

"Would you rather have waffles?"

Hettie nods. She could have just told me.

I take her toast for myself and stick waffles in the toaster, observing her while I wait for them to finish. I don't want to annoy her, but she's off and it bugs me.

When I put her waffles in front of her, I rest my hand against her forehead. She feels fine. She must just be tired.

It relieves me when she starts eating. Maybe waffles were what she needed. It is Hettie, after all. She hardly eats anything else.

"So," I say as Hettie finishes her last couple of bites, "what do you say we visit the well again today? We can pretend to be princesses and hold a ball in the gazebo."

As soon as I say it, Hettie's entire demeanor changes. Her eyes twinkle and her face lights up as she nods rapidly in response.

After we get dressed and I force Hettie to brush her hair—which she makes clear she doesn't want to do, but concedes when I offer to tie a ribbon in her hair—we hop on our bikes and make our way back to the well.

Mother was in the kitchen making her own breakfast when we left, but she didn't ask us where we were going. She only told us to be back by evening, and I promised her we would. I'm glad she didn't pry for details. I don't want to have to lie.

We toss our bikes off to the side of the grove as soon as we arrive and, to my delight, the stairs are waiting for us. Eagerly, we hop over the edge of the well and rush down. A trill of excitement rises in my chest as we re-enter the beautiful forest.

The first thing I see is the moon. It's bigger—still a crescent, but brighter and slightly fuller.

I wonder if this moon has phases too, much like the real one. I picture what it's like when it's full, reveling in how magnificent it must look—even more magnificent than the moon above. Perhaps it becomes as bright as the sun, but silver instead of searing white.

Today, there are no glass animals or rainbow-colored stingrays. Instead, dripping like dewdrops from the twisted branches of the trees are hundreds of necklaces, bracelets, and rings. Hettie and I gasp.

"It's for our ball!" Hettie shrieks in excitement as she rushes over to the tree closest to us and pulls down a blue and gold pearl necklace. "This one's mine," she says. She strings it around her neck and twirls. "I'm a princess!"

I approach another tree. This one has a carving of a little girl's face on the trunk. She has bangs that fall in front of her eyes and tiny dimples at the sides of her mouth.

I reach my hand up to where the tinsel and jewelry hang parallel to each other. Gently, so as not to disturb the tree, I pluck a diamond bracelet from its gnarled branch. I study the gems in the incoming moonlight, then slip the bracelet onto my wrist and admire how perfectly it fits.

Hettie comes up behind me wearing another five or so necklaces and bracelets all the way up her arms. She giggles when I look her way, then does a little curtsey.

I grin. "You look like you're ready for our ball."

"And *you* need more jewelry," Hettie says. She jumps up and pulls a golden necklace from the tree we're standing by. It's only a few yards away from the archway, not quite on the outskirts of the forest, but not concealed in the middle either. The necklace has an emerald pendant at the end that glitters as Hettie turns it in her hands. "This one's for you," she says, handing it to me. "It matches your eyes."

I study the tree she took the necklace from. This carving is of a girl around Hettie's age. She has long, pin-straight hair, thin eyebrows, and a slightly upturned nose that is sprinkled with freckles. She looks like a fairy—ever so delicate and pure.

I bend down and let Hettie slip the necklace over my head. As soon as I stand upright, soft echoes of music enter the atmosphere, piquing my attention.

Hettie looks in the direction of the music. We share a curious look when we realize that the sounds are coming from the gazebo.

Hettie takes my hand as we make our way hastily through the forest. Every tree is adorned with hundreds upon hundreds of bracelets, necklaces, and rings, and they are all just as lavish as the ones we wear. I wonder if the gems and pearls are real. I can't help but think about how much they're worth.

The music grows louder as we approach the gazebo. It's a mix of piano and violin—that much I can tell, but I don't know where it's coming from. Upon our entering the gazebo, the tune comes to a crescendo, leaving my heart in a flutter as I look around for the source of the music. I don't see it.

Hettie releases her grip on my hand and begins to twirl sloppily in the center of the gazebo. Her shoes squeak as they scuff against the marble. The music continues in an ethereal, haunting kind of way that makes me feel as though

I've gone back in time—back to when music was made of pure emotion and sweet, poignant symphonies. The melody ebbs and flows like a gentle river, and by the time the song stops, I've grown very still, entranced by the peace inducing effect of the music. When another song begins, it plays even louder. The sound reverberates above my head, and I, too, start to dance with Hettie.

I'm a terrible dancer, but I don't mind. I find that the music moves me of its own accord. The tempos adjust to our bodies as Hettie and I grasp each other's hands, flailing around in circles as we dance our own ballet, guided by the sound of echoing piano and otherworldly violin. The intangibility of the music slowly becomes corporeal as we dance, and I can feel it pass through my body like rushes of cool water. I let it calm and move me, and though I'd usually resist, I let it bring tears to my eyes.

I don't know how long we dance, but the music never stops playing. I feel as though I've entered Heaven; my worries have no place here. I pull Hettie in, who giggles as I spin her around. My pesky, lingering thoughts about Mother, the new school year, and how much I miss Oregon dissipate with every swell of the music. In this moment, I'm as free as I've ever been and ever will be.

CHAPTER 9
THE HAUNTED MAN

I'm in a daze when we finally decide to leave. Hettie and I return our jewelry to the trees, bidding a sad goodbye to the music and promising both ourselves and this little world that we'll come back.

I'm so enthralled with it all that I don't snap out of my giddiness until we climb back out of the well and see a man standing in the grove a few feet away.

I stop dead in my tracks. It's the same man we saw at the diner days ago, only he doesn't look nearly as drunk.

His eyes widen when he sees us. Hettie stands closer to me than usual, and I feel her hair tickle my arm as she presses against me.

The well, which stands stubbornly between us and the man, makes a dull creaking sound. If I didn't know any better, I would think it felt the tension in the air.

"Do you...do you own this?" I ask when I find my voice.

The man shakes his head. "No, I don't," he says. His voice oscillates between being raucous and meek, making it impossible to tell what he's thinking.

I take a few moments to observe him now that he stands before me. He seems far more stable than he did the other day, but he's still disheveled. His face is gaunt and his eyes are dark; it looks like he hasn't slept in days. What's most arrestive, however, is the haunted air he carries. It's an air rooted deep in his eyes—so deep that no amount of sleep could cure it. I noticed it when I saw him in the diner, and it's even stronger now that he stands before me.

I'm not sure what to say. I have a thousand questions for him, but I can't decide which one to ask.

I don't end up deciding. The man shakes his head, puts his hand up pleadingly, and says in a low, stern whisper, "Don't go back down there."

It takes me a moment to find my voice. "Why?" I finally ask. The happiness I felt only moments ago has dissipated entirely. I decide to ask again, "Does this belong to you?"

"I said it doesn't," he snaps. Hettie and I look at each other. I take her hand in my own and give it a squeeze. "If you have any sense at all, you'll stop going down there." For a painful moment, he waivers, lips quivering and eyebrows raised, before shaking his head again and turning around.

No—he can't leave. Not after saying that.

"Why?" I ask, this time louder.

He whirls around. "Jesus Christ, girl, just take a bit of advice."

"Have you seen what's down there?"

He doesn't respond. Instead, he walks past the well and over to me. Before I can react, he grabs my shoulders and bends down so we're face-to-face with each other. Hettie whimpers and gets behind me.

"Just. Don't. Go. Back. Down. There," he says. He reeks of liquor and cigarettes.

He releases me and turns away, briskly walking out of the grove and refusing to look back. I'm so stunned that I don't move, and it takes Hettie pulling on the sleeve of my shirt to bring me back.

"Why was he so angry?" she asks, her voice wobbling. "Was he mad at us? We didn't do anything..."

I shake my head. "I don't know what his problem is."

I feel sick. Irritated with myself for being in such a daze, I grab Hettie's hand and we hurry to our bikes.

"What are you going to do?" she asks.

"*We* are going to go home."

"That's it? Are you gonna tell Aunt Vivian or Mommy?"

I shake my head. "No. And neither are you. Not yet, at least. I need time to think."

Hettie nods and chooses not to ask any more questions. We ride home quickly, and once there, we rush inside and to our room. I shut the door behind us.

"Ro, I'm scared," Hettie says.

"Me too." I take a moment to myself to think. "Maybe we shouldn't go back."

Hettie freezes. "What?"

"I don't want that to happen again," I say.

"But...don't you want to go back?"

I do. More than anything, I do. I want to see the gazebo and the forest and the lake. I want to gaze at the moon and feel calm, if only for a few moments. I want to forget everything and dance with Hettie to the otherworldly music and feel as though nothing bad can touch me.

"Maybe he won't come back," Hettie says. "Maybe we can go back and he won't even know."

I bite my lip. "It's not him I'm worried about," I say. After his warning, or whatever it was, the thought of simply returning makes me feel uneasy.

"But Ro..."

"Give me a while to think about it," I say firmly. "I need to process everything."

Hettie sits down on her cot and picks at a bit of thread coming loose from her sheets.

I lie back on my bed, using the coolness of my pillow to ground myself. I close my eyes and think about everything: the well, the world, the moon, the lake, the gazebo, and the man. I remember Ava saying his name was Wayne.

Sudden curiosity overtakes me, beckoning me to leave the room. Aunt Vivian keeps a phone book in her office, which I find immediately under her desk. I pull it out and sit on the floor, eagerly skimming the pages.

The phone book for Larton is larger than I expected it to be, but I don't stop until I've found two people by the name of Wayne. Only one lives in the apartment complex: Wayne Reyes.

Although I definitely don't want to call him, seeing his address gives me an idea.

I check the clock. It's past two in the afternoon, which means Ava is off of work. If I ask to hang out at her place, I may be able to get more information about Wayne. But I have to be careful about it. I don't want to seem weird, and I certainly don't want to tell her what's going on.

I dial her number and lean against the wall, feeling butterflies in my stomach as I hear it ring.

"Hello?"

I breathe a sharp sigh of relief upon hearing her voice.

"Hey, Ava," I say, steadying myself. "It's Ro."

"Oh my gosh, Ro!" Her voice has gone up about five octaves in excitement. "What's up?"

"I just wanted to call and see if you're up to hang out today," I say. I feel a little guilty, but I convince myself I'm not only using this as an opportunity to find out about Wayne; I want to get to know Ava as well.

"Of course!" Ava says. "Do you want to meet me at my apartment complex?"

"That sounds good," I say, pleasantly surprised that she actually wants to hang out. "I should be about twenty minutes if you're cool with me coming over right now."

"Yes, I'm absolutely cool with that! I'm doing nothing right now." She laughs nervously. "They lock the entryway, so I'll meet you at the front and let you in."

"Okay, great," I say. "I can't wait. Do you mind if Hettie comes?"

"Of course," Ava says. "She's totally welcome."

"She'll be happy to hear that," I say. "Twenty minutes it is."

I hang up, feeling some semblance of relief rush over me. I hurry back over to our room. Hettie is lying on her cot, staring up at the ceiling.

"Hettie?"

I don't get much more than a murmur in response.

"Do you want to come with me to hang out with Ava?"

Hettie slowly sits up. "I thought you were going to think about the well," she says. "Can we go back?"

"I'm still thinking about it," I say. The response doesn't thrill her. She crosses her arms and pouts. "Let's take a break and go have fun," I add. "We'll feel a little less stressed later tonight, okay?" And, hopefully, I'll know more about Wayne.

"You can go," Hettie says.

"Are you sure?"

Hettie nods. "I want to stay here and draw."

"Oh," I say. I'm a little disappointed, and more than that, I'm confused. Hettie almost always wants to tag along with me. "Are you sure?"

"I'm sure."

I linger by the door a while longer, waiting for her to change her mind, but she doesn't. Maybe it's best; after all, I probably shouldn't question Ava about Wayne with Hettie there. She may accidentally tell Ava about the well, and that would make this a bigger mess than it needs to be.

The late afternoon breeze brushes across my face as I ride downtown. My mind feels particularly numb and resists any thoughts that try to enter, so I keep my eyes on the road and do my best not to look worried when I arrive at Ava's apartment complex.

She's leaning against the entryway gate when I pull up, fiddling with a strand of her hair. She brightens when she sees me.

"Hey, Ro!" she beams. Her eyes dart behind me and she raises her eyebrows inquisitively. "Where's Hettie?"

"She's tired today," I respond, shrugging and trying to sound nonchalant. "She wanted to stay home and draw, so I figured maybe she could tag along another time."

"I get that," Ava says, smiling as she unlocks the gate. "I liked drawing as a kid too. I'd spend hours doing nothing but making pictures for my family."

"That sounds like Hettie," I say. I follow her through the little entryway with mailboxes on the walls and we take the stairs up to the third floor. Although I'm burning with questions about Wayne, I hold my tongue and wait for the right moment.

Ava's apartment is small and quaint. She's opened every curtain so that sunlight makes its way through the windows freely, brightening the space and bringing about a cheery ambience.

"I bet it's awesome being able to live alone for a while," I say. "Do your parents ever get worried?"

Ava shrugs and puts the key on her kitchen table. "Not really," she says. "My mom likes to call every other night or so to check in and ask me about my day, but I don't think my parents get too nervous. They're pretty hands-off when it comes to...well, everything, I guess."

"That's kind of cool," I say.

Ava giggles nervously. "Yeah, I guess," she says, though it doesn't sound like she agrees. "What about you? Do your parents let you stay home alone while they travel?"

I shake my head. Father would have let me; he left me alone in the house a few times when I was even younger than Hettie. Mother was furious. Sometimes I wonder if she realizes that her actions have been similar as of late.

"My mom is kind of uptight about that stuff," I say. "I think it's mostly because Hettie is so young."

"That makes sense," Ava says. She gestures for me to follow her and leads me to her room. It's small and clean, with not much more than a bed, desk, beanbag chair, and armoire. Her wall, though, is another story. She's covered every inch with vivid and colorful paintings, leaving no space for her wallpaper to show.

"Did you do this?" I ask, looking at a realistic painting of a girl on a hill, who gazes out onto a valley of deep greens and blues.

Ava nods.

"I thought you said you drew as a kid!" I say, my surprise growing as I admire each painting. She's amazing—the type of artist Hettie always says she'll grow up to be.

"I draw now too," Ava laughs. "Well, I paint. My parents make me go outside to do it when they're home, but since they're gone and can't nag me about it, I just use the kitchen." She pauses and grins. "I've gotten paint on the floor a few times, but they don't need to know that."

"You're really talented," I say. "Hettie will want you to give her lessons."

"I'd love to," Ava says. When she smiles, dimples form by her mouth. She reminds me a bit of the little girl I saw carved into one of the underground trees, and suddenly, I begin to feel anxious. Though it's tempting, I don't ask Ava about Wayne. I need to wait for the right moment.

"Actually," Ava continues, "painting kind of kept me sane last year in school."

I crinkle my nose. "Was it that bad?"

"Not the school itself." She grins reassuringly. "Don't worry, you'll be fine. I just made some bad decisions. It's my fault. You can sit on my bed, by the way."

Ava falls back into the fuzzy beanbag on her carpet and I sit on her bed, smoothing the evergreen comforter beneath my fingers.

"What happened?" I ask.

Ava shrugs and plays with a strand of her hair. "I..." She pauses and tries to search for the words. "Well, I kind of made a group of people hate me. That's why I don't have anyone to hang out with this summer…or at school." She clamps her lips shut and winces. "I hope that doesn't make you want to leave or anything," she says, adding a light laugh to the end of her sentence. The nervousness in her eyes is obvious.

"Of course not," I say as she noticeably exhales in relief. I lie back on her bed and turn to look at her. "High school kids are total idiots, for the most part. I can't stand them on a good day."

"You can say that again," Ava says. "Although, I'm guilty of also being an idiot. I was dating this guy, but I kind of fell in love with his best friend, who was probably the most popular person at school. I made the stupid decision to break it off with my boyfriend and tell his friend how I felt. It didn't end well."

"Yikes," I say. "I'm guessing you didn't end up dating the other guy?"

Ava lowers her head a little and purses her lips. "It was a girl," she says softly. "Her name was Paige."

"Oh," I say. We're quiet for a few moments. "Was she at least polite about it?"

Ava gives me a thin, uncomfortable smile. "Not at all. She kind of freaked out and turned all of her friends against me, which sucked because I was the new kid and I didn't know anyone else. I spent most of my lunches alone after that." She wrings her hands together nervously. "I really hope that doesn't make you want to leave," she repeats, forcing another laugh.

"Why in the world would I want to leave?" I give her what I hope will be a comforting smile, but I'm not sure if it works. "You were brave to tell that girl how you felt, even if she ended up being an asshole about it. At least she showed her true colors."

I see a little bit of warmth in Ava's eyes as she smiles back at me. Then, to rid herself of the thought, she shakes her head and asks, "What about you? Have you ever made any stupid decisions?"

I laugh and roll up my sleeve, showing her my tattoo. "I forced my dad to give me this tattoo when I was nine. My mom was pissed."

"Well, he did a good job," Ava says. "I thought you had it done professionally."

"Yeah, he made his living that way for a while," I say, "until he just decided to stop working."

"Does he work now?"

I bite my lip, wondering if I should lie, but after how open Ava was with me, I decide to try to be the same with her.

"He's dead," I say. Immediately after I say it, I recoil, hesitant of her reaction.

"Oh, shit, Ro, I'm so sorry," Ava says. She looks as though she regrets her question.

"Don't be," I say. "Honestly, he had it coming for a while. He was making some really bad choices. It was years ago, anyway."

"Is that why you moved to Tennessee?"

"No," I say. "We just decided to live with my aunt for a bit." Although I'm comfortable telling Ava some things, my family's reason for moving will remain a secret.

"Well, I know Larton is boring," Ava says. "But I have some cool video games if you want to play."

"I'd love to," I say. I decide I'll ask about Wayne later.

We move into the living room and Ava pulls out some obscure game I've never heard of, but it actually ends up being fun. I wish I could focus on it, though. Instead, my thoughts keep going back to Wayne and the way he cornered Hettie and me—the way he told us not to go back to the well. At first, I thought he was angry, but now I'm starting to think he was scared.

Being with Ava helps my nerves more than I would have expected it to, however. While we play, we talk about all sorts of things—our favorite animals, where we used to live, what we like to do best—and I realize that getting to know someone new gives me a little more hope about the lingering school year. I thought I was dreading school, but

Ava seems to be dreading it even more. She tells me about the teachers and the campus, but mostly, she tells me about her own experience, which was an accumulation of distant parents and nasty teenage girls.

"I wish I had a sister," she says. "You and Hettie seem to really get along."

"For the most part. She drives me crazy sometimes, but I don't think she'd be a normal seven-year-old if she didn't."

"Just imagine how much she'll look to you for advice when she's in high school," Ava says. "Wouldn't it feel like such an honor to be the big sister who has all the answers? She'll think of you as the perfect role model."

I laugh. "I don't know. Hettie and I are different. She's always been more outgoing than me. Something tells me she'll have a different experience in school."

"How so?"

"I think she'll make more friends, for one," I say. "I had some friends, but I never really considered them to be super close. But the odd thing is, it never bugged me. I've always been able to occupy myself."

"I wish I were like that," Ava says. "Back in New York I felt really comfortable because I knew people...I had friends. But then, out of the blue, my dad told me we were moving. He hardly gave me an explanation as to why. He said he got a job opportunity. That's it. Next thing I knew,

I was in the middle of some rural town with hardly anything to do. Other than painting or playing video games, I haven't found much else to do."

"Moving is tough," I say. I pause for a moment and smile, thinking of Oregon. "There was a forest right outside our backyard at my old place, and I'd spend hours just walking through it and thinking. My favorite thing to do was to go outside at night when the moonlight made the trees look silver."

Silver, like the trees in the underground forest. An unwanted tremor shoots through my body.

"That sounds beautiful," Ava says. "I can't imagine living next to a forest. I lived next to a shoe store."

I grin in response, but my thoughts have inevitably wandered elsewhere: back to the underground moon. Back to Wayne.

"Do you remember that guy you served the other day?" I venture slowly. Ava doesn't take her eyes off the television screen, but she nods.

"Yeah, the drunk one," she says. "Why?"

"Did you say his name was Wayne?"

Ava nods again. This time, though, she looks at me and tilts her head. "How come?"

"Oh, I don't know," I say, trying to sound apathetic. "I was just wondering who he is and if he's okay."

"I don't know much about him," Ava says. "I think he's okay, though. Sane enough. Just an alcoholic."

"Do you know anything else about him?"

Ava puts the game on pause. "No," she says. She looks skeptical.

Great. I don't know how to be casual about this. I wring my hands together as I try to come up with a story.

"I'm just curious," I say. "He confronted Hettie and me downtown today and he seemed drunk." It's a crappy lie, but it's the best one I've got.

"Oh," Ava says. Now she looks less skeptical and more worried. "He didn't hurt you guys or anything, right?"

I shake my head and rest my game controller on my leg. "Oh God, no. Not at all. He was just drunk. It made me a little curious, that's all."

"All I know is that he lives on the fourth floor," Ava says. "But he rarely comes out. Not unless he wants a coffee at the diner, but that's only a few times a week. Other than that, I think he just holes himself up. I don't even know if he has a job. Sometimes I wonder if he's agoraphobic or if he just really dislikes people. I've talked to him a couple times when I was working, but even then, it's only been to take his order. I tried to make small talk once, but he straight up ignored me and I haven't tried since. I guess he seems harmless enough. I'm surprised you two ran into him."

"It was a quick encounter," I say.

I can't think of any other questions to ask—not that Ava can answer, at least—so I pick my game controller back up. Ava, however, sets hers down.

"I'm hungry," she says. "We have some microwaveable pizza if you want any. Very fancy stuff."

I grin and put my controller down as well. "Sounds delicious."

The rest of the evening goes by quickly. I lose track of time as Ava and I talk and eat. She's sarcastic and witty, and by the end of our makeshift dinner, we're laughing so hard that our sides hurt.

I leave around nine o'clock, surprised that I stayed with her that long. I'm glad I did, though. I needed a distraction, and now I'm ready to think clearly.

That being said, I still haven't made my decision about whether or not to return to the well. Despite Wayne's warning and my better judgment, the urge to return is so strong that even thinking about never going back makes me feel sick to my stomach.

I know it's stupid and childish and all the things I usually scorn, but I can't help how much I want to see the moon and the forest again. Besides, I hardly know Wayne. From what Ava seems to think, he's a hermit and a drunk. Why in the world would I listen to him?

I feel as though I'm in a constant state of both rejecting and accepting my feelings. A part of me tells me I'm wrong —that I'm an idiot to return. But another part of me doesn't care.

Aunt Vivian is home when I return. She sits with Mother at the kitchen table, both of them silently looking down at their hands.

I feel awkward, like I'm intruding on something.

"Hey, Ro," Aunt Vivian says. I can't tell what she's thinking. Mother's face is easier to decipher. Her eyes are blank, as though they've lost all feeling. Still, she manages to greet me with a weak smile.

"How are you?" Though I ask the question to both of them, it's directed more toward Mother.

"I'm okay," Mother says. That's all she ever says when I ask her how she's doing.

"I hung out with Ava today," I say, hoping it will cheer her up a little. "She's really nice. I think you'd like her."

"That's great, sweetie," Mother says. Aunt Vivian smiles at me.

I'd usually expand, but I decide not to. I leave the kitchen, and instead of staying behind to try to hear what they're talking about, I go straight to my and Hettie's room.

Hettie sits motionless on her cot when I enter, and she doesn't turn around at the sound of me shutting the door.

She's staring out the window by her bed. I look around to see if she's drawn any pictures, but I don't see anything.

"Hettie?"

Nothing—just like at breakfast.

I walk on hesitant feet over to her side and put my hand on her shoulder. That gets her attention.

"Hi," she says in no more than a meek whisper.

"Are you okay?" I ask, sitting down next to her.

Hettie nods absentmindedly.

"Did you draw anything today?"

She looks down at her hands and shakes her head.

"You were like this at breakfast too. Are you sure you're not getting sick?"

She doesn't answer me.

"Did you eat dinner?"

She shakes her head again, still not saying anything.

I'm at a loss for what to do. I try to tell her something that I think will interest her. "Did you know Ava likes art, just like you?" I say. "She said she can teach you to paint. She's really good."

Hettie smiles, but it isn't her normal one. It's a tired, emotionless smile that makes me even more worried.

"Are we going to go back tomorrow?" she asks me. I immediately know what she's talking about.

"I don't know, Hettie..."

"Ro, *please*," Hettie says. This isn't her usual, whiny voice she uses when she wants something. She's begging me, just like Wayne did when he said *not* to go back down. I don't know what to say, or do, or think. I take in Hettie's face and think of Mother and Aunt Vivian out in the kitchen. I wonder how long they've been sitting there. Has anyone even been paying attention to Hettie while I was gone?

A rush of anger enters my body. Though I feel guilty and would never admit it out loud, I resent Mother for being so absent, and I'm annoyed with Aunt Vivian for not noticing how odd Hettie's been acting today. I know it isn't Mother's fault, and Aunt Vivian is the last person I want to be angry with considering how much she's done for us, but I can't help my feelings. I'm upset with both of them for expecting me to be doing it all. Most fifteen-year-olds can go hang out with a friend and not worry about their little sister being left alone.

On top of it all, the well and the world beneath it are the only things that make Hettie and me genuinely excited. That is far too precious to give up.

Without answering Hettie, I spin around and march down the hallway, back to the kitchen where Mother and Aunt Vivian are still sitting. They must have sensed my irritation when I walked in, because they both stop speaking and look up at me.

"Have either of you noticed that Hettie's been unlike herself today?" I ask. It's a rhetorical question; I know what the answer is.

"No," Aunt Vivian says. She looks worried, which pleases me. I want her to be worried. She *should* be worried.

"I'm sure Hettie will be fine," I say. "She doesn't seem like she has a fever, but I'm surprised neither of you took the time to notice." I hate being like this, but I can't help it.

When I don't get a response, I put my hands on my hips and scoff. "I go out to see a friend for a few hours and I come back to Hettie completely alone, staring out her window, acting like a neglected child," I say. Now that I've started, I can't stop. "She hasn't eaten dinner, she barely touched her breakfast this morning until I gave her a waffle, she turned down coming with me to Ava's, and now she's acting like this. And the worst part is I have no idea how long she's been alone. The entire time I was gone? Or did you at least check in with her and see how she was?"

"Ro," Aunt Vivian says. "I just got home from work. I assumed Hettie was drawing. She never told us that she was feeling weird."

"She shouldn't have to," I say. Then I look at Mother, who wasn't at work and could have spent the whole time I was gone with Hettie. "What about *you*?" I snap.

"Ro..." Mother says. Her voice cracks a little bit.

"You know what? Never mind," I say. "She's fine. I learned my lesson. I won't leave her alone that long again. It seems like I'm the only person here who acts like her parent."

"Ro," Aunt Vivian says. She's lowered her voice, but I can tell she isn't used to acting stern. "That's not fair to assume. We're here for Hettie too, and we certainly don't expect you to be doing it all."

The fact that she even has to justify herself makes me fume. I turn around without listening to whatever else she has to say and hurry back to our room. I shut the door behind me and look at Hettie. I'm not sure if she overheard the conversation, but she's staring at me with those big blue eyes, and I feel like I want to cry.

"The answer is yes," I say. "We'll go back to the well."

CHAPTER 10
ROSELLA

Aunt Vivian is already gone when Hettie and I wake up, and Mother is still sleeping.

Hettie seems a bit more present. I make her scrambled eggs and fruit for breakfast, which she eats. Happy with myself for getting her to eat something healthier than waffles, I go a step further and blend a smoothie for us to share. Hettie finishes her half quickly. I try to be silent when I sigh in relief.

"You seem like you're feeling a little bit better today," I say.

Hettie nods. "I'm feeling fine."

"Good. Do you think you were just tired?"

Hettie shrugs. "Yeah, a little." She slides off her chair and heads toward the door to the porch. "Are you ready to go?"

I swallow and nod. My decision to go back to the well was rasher than I had intended it to be, but I'm going to stick to it.

Hettie rides faster than me today, which is a surprising change. It's partially because I'm hanging back, trying to buy time. I don't know what I'm waiting for, though. I made my decision in anger, and now I have to accept it.

Ava said that Wayne was an alcoholic, and from what I saw and smelled of him, I don't think she's wrong. If that's the case, whatever advice he has to give to Hettie and me probably isn't worth much. Maybe he was drunk when he confronted us. Maybe he doesn't know what he's talking about.

I know it's weak reassurance and even weaker reasoning, but I want to believe it so badly that I do. When Hettie and I reach the well, I take a moment to look around for Wayne. I don't see him, which relieves me, and I gesture for Hettie to follow me. We descend the staircase just as quickly and eagerly as we did yesterday.

The world greets us with twinkles of silver and gold. Upon stepping into the archway, I feel a warmth inside of me, which I'm drawn to. I walk farther—past the trees, toward the lake, and into the gazebo. The water is calm tonight and even brighter than it was before.

I look up at the moon, as I always do. Once again, it has grown bigger and brighter. It's no longer a crescent, but it's not half full yet either.

"Did you notice the moon?" I ask Hettie.

Hettie looks up. "It's pretty."

"It's grown bigger," I say. "Bigger than the last three times."

"Oh," Hettie says. "I didn't notice."

"It started out small, but it looks different now."

"Cool." Her tone is marked by utter indifference.

I shift to lean against a post that borders part of the gazebo. The moon is more than pretty; it's stunning. Not even the real moon can compare. Something is wrong, though. I don't know what it is, but despite the warmth I feel and how content Hettie seems to be here, something within me isn't what it used to be.

"Ro," Hettie whispers. She points to the lake.

I look away from the moon, expecting to see the rainbow stingrays. But instead, I see a dolphin—a gorgeous dolphin that's a mix of light gray and blue. It squeaks playfully as it nears the shore.

Hettie gasps and rushes down the steps of the gazebo to the edge of the lake. Once I've reached her side, two more have appeared. They swim around each other in circles and whistle when they jump in the air.

"They're beautiful!" Hettie's eyes have completely lit up.

I watch in awe as the dolphins spin in the air and dive back into the water, only to reappear moments later while Hettie squeals in delight.

Then, I hear something different—soft flapping near my head. I turn to my side and see a bird. It looks like a parrot, with deep crimson and blue feathers and a long tail. It flies around my head, flaunting its beauty and mirroring the movements of my eyes. Slowly, I reach my arm out, and the bird stills its wings and lands on my forearm. It's gentle and friendly, and I can't help but laugh. It looks familiar too.

Hettie begins to run up and down a stretch of the shore while the dolphins in the lake follow her. They mirror her movements, which excites her even more. I think back to that conversation we had when we were watching the fireflies a few nights ago. I remember how Hettie said that if she were an animal, she would be a dolphin. It fits her; like a dolphin, Hettie is playful and carefree. She skips along the shore as the dolphins skim across the water. They look one and the same.

Then I remember what animal I said I would be. I look back at the parrot, which still rests on my arm. I observe its gentle talons and, instinctively, I flick my eyes toward my wrist where my tattoo is. I look back up at the bird, then over at Hettie and the dolphins.

And then, something in me clicks.

The bird on my arm is a Rosella.

CHAPTER 11

GRAVES

There are certain things that, despite their beauty, are marked with danger. Foxglove flowers are gorgeous, but if you ingest too many, you'll die. Jellyfish flit about the sea with elegance, but if you find yourself near a certain type, you may suffer a fatal sting.

Even once we return home, I can't shake the feeling that the dolphins and the Rosella aren't as innocent as they seem. I knew the world was enchanted—that much was beyond dispute—but the animals that appeared to Hettie and me today were no coincidence. What perplexes me the most, however, is how the world could have known something that Hettie and I never mentioned down there.

"Do you remember that conversation we had the other day when we were watching the fireflies?" I ask Hettie that night.

"Which one?"

"The conversation when you told me that if you were an animal, you'd be a dolphin," I say, "and I said I would be a Rosella."

"Yeah, I remember."

"Don't you think it's a little weird that dolphins and a Rosella were in the underground world today?" Part of me fears asking the question out loud. What if the world can still hear me, even up above?

"Wasn't that amazing?" Hettie beams. "It was like the world *knew*."

I raise an eyebrow. "I thought it was odd."

"How come?"

"I just..." I try to find the right words. "I just felt like it was too strange to be a coincidence. We never had that conversation down there, but it knew anyway."

"But it's magic."

I open my mouth, then shut it just as quickly.

Oddly enough, despite all the words I would have used to describe the underground world Hettie and I found, magic didn't make the list. Magic is fairytales and princess stories. It's something I've always dismissed as a trivial thing kids believe in and disregard once they've grown up. And yet, perhaps magic isn't such a bad descriptor. After all, what other words could be used to so accurately describe what we found?

As much as I want to think of magic as a good thing, though, I can't. Not in this case.

Wayne's warning made me think, but I still returned to the well. The Rosella and the dolphins, however, have caused me to change my course completely.

I don't want to go back now. Something is wrong, and I'm ashamed I didn't notice it before.

It's as if the underground world understood Hettie and me—as if it took the time to observe us, and beyond that, as if it knew things about us that it shouldn't have known. Why else would the bird and the dolphins show up?

I don't know why Hettie doesn't share my unease.

"You don't think it's weird at all?" I ask her.

"No," she says.

I feel as though a rock is in my stomach.

That night, I dream of the underground forest. It isn't like my previous dream, though, with silver lakes that reflect the light of the moon. Instead, I dream of the trees with the carvings of children's faces. I float throughout the forest, not entirely myself, just watching. I see the familiar face of the girl with dimples and the thin boy, and I continue until I reach the gazebo.

Two new trees have grown near it, closer than the others. The face on one is that of a young girl with long hair that falls around her face in ringlets. The other is a teenage girl, with short hair that's a mix between frizzy and curly, a pointed nose, and waif-like features. Like the rest, both faces are carved with their eyes closed, as though they're in a deep, eternal sleep.

Then, I realize two things. One, the faces depicted on the trees belong to Hettie and me. Two, the trees are not trees at all. They're graves.

CHAPTER 12
A GOOD SISTER

I wake up the next morning in a cold sweat. Aunt Vivian notices how disgruntled I am when I walk into the kitchen, and she silently sets a cup of coffee down in front of me as though it's a peace offering for the argument that we had the other night.

That's the last thing on my mind, though. As much as I still feel angry with her and Mother for leaving Hettie alone for so long, my dream is what really has me in a funk. I can't shake the image of the trees—the carvings of Hettie and me—and the realization of what they really are.

"How are you feeling, Ro?" Aunt Vivian asks me. Her voice is gentle.

I try to collect my thoughts, but it doesn't work.

"Fine," I respond curtly.

"Are you really?"

I nod.

"I'm about to get going," Aunt Vivian says. "I know we haven't really talked about the other night."

"Honestly, Aunt Vivian, it's fine," I say. "I made a big deal out of nothing."

"No, you didn't," she says. She leans against the counter and takes a sip of her coffee. "I may not be used to having anyone else around and I may work long hours, but that's no excuse. And I want you to know how proud I am of you for taking care of Hettie. I promise we're going to work everything out."

I look down at my coffee mug and drum my fingers against it.

"I'm going to look into getting some hours off," Aunt Vivian continues. "I want you to be able to hang out with your new friend and not worry about Hettie all the time."

I stare at my cup for a long moment as I try to figure out what to say. Finally, I whisper, "She's been acting weird, Aunt Vivian. And not just the other day."

It's the first time I've admitted it to anyone.

"I don't think she's sick," I continue, "but she's *off*. She gets into these weird moods where she's absent-minded and out of it, and I don't know what to think. She's only done it a few times, but it's been enough for me to notice."

Now it's Aunt Vivian's turn to be silent. "Was she alright last night?" she finally asks.

I nod.

"Okay," Aunt Vivian says slowly. "Let's keep an eye on her. She could be tired or fighting a bug. She may also be adjusting."

"What do you mean?"

Aunt Vivian smiles sadly. "Adjusting to being here, to your mom...it's been a tough few months. I'm sure Hettie has absorbed a fair amount of stress."

It sounds like a logical explanation—it really does. But I don't believe it. A deep-seated part of me knows it's something else.

I nod at Aunt Vivian anyway. "I know."

"We'll keep an eye on her," she says. Then, reassuringly, she adds, "All of us."

Before she leaves, she kisses the top of my head and whispers, "Hettie is lucky she has such a good big sister."

I fight back my tears until after she leaves, and then I start to cry—silently, so that Mother or Hettie don't hear me.

I'm not crying because of my conversation with Aunt Vivian or my guilt about being angry with Mother. I'm crying because of Hettie—because of the well and the trees and the moon. It's not right. If Wayne didn't make me believe it, the Rosella did.

I wipe away my tears, ashamed with myself for not having realized something was wrong earlier. The fact that I believed something so perfect was free of bad intentions angers me. How could I have been so blindly naive?

A good sister wouldn't have put Hettie in a situation like that. It's my lack of judgment that got us into this situation in the first place.

I think back to my dream. Pitying myself for poor choices will do nothing. If anything, I need to find Wayne; I need to figure out what he knows about this underground world. Maybe I'll meet up with Ava again tomorrow and see if I can find a way to "accidentally" make my way up to the fourth floor. It's a crappy plan, but right now it seems like it's my best one.

"Ro?"

Hettie slinks into the kitchen and nears me on quiet feet. She sits feebly in the kitchen chair across from me.

"How are you doing?" I ask her, hoping my face doesn't look too red or teary.

Hettie shrugs.

"Do you want a waffle?"

She shrugs again. "Not really."

"How about toast?"

"No. Can we go back today?"

My body seizes up. "Not today, Hettie. Maybe later."

"What? Why?"

"I don't feel like it." I say it gently; I'm worried my response will upset her.

I'm right. Hettie furrows her eyebrows. "I don't get it," she says. "You wanted to go yesterday."

"That was yesterday. Let's skip it today."

"But...don't you want to go back?" Hettie's eyes well up with tears.

I shake my head and bite down on my lip.

"That's not fair," Hettie says. "I don't get it."

"Hettie, I..." I rub my temples. "I'm tired today and I don't want to go. We'll go another time." I hope my lie may calm her down a little bit, but it doesn't.

"You're being bossy," she says.

When I don't react or respond, she gets even angrier.

"You're being mean," she says, her eyes narrowed. "You think you're the boss of everyone."

I cross my arms. "I'm not going to argue with you."

Hettie pushes herself up from her chair with far more vigor than I would have expected.

"You're a bitch!" she yells, so loudly that I worry she may have woken Mother up. I clamp my mouth shut for a moment and glance to the hallway, listening for Mother's footsteps. When I don't hear them, I turn back to Hettie.

"What the hell was that for?" She's never used that word before. I didn't even know she knew it. "That's really rude to say."

"I don't care," Hettie says. "I hate you. You're a liar and you think you can control everything. I don't care if you never go back to the well. I'm going back."

My heart almost stops. "No, you absolutely are not. I won't let you."

"Yes, I am," she says through gritted teeth. "I need it."

"You *need* it? Christ, Hettie..."

"I don't need you to tell me what to do."

This is not Hettie. This has never been Hettie. She's pushy, yes, but not like this. My head starts to spin.

"Yeah, you do," I say.

"You keep acting like my mom when you're not!"

Something in me snaps. I lean over to her. "No, I'm not your mom," I say in a low voice. "Do you know where your mom is? She's sleeping. She's been sleeping since yesterday. And when she wakes up, she'll spend another few hours in her room, before roaming around like a ghost and repeating the cycle all over again. Do you know why?" I hate how cruel I'm being, but I can't stop. "Because Mom is sick. And Aunt Vivian needs to work. So I'm all you've got, and if I say we aren't going back to the well, we are *not* going back to the well."

Hettie's face twists into an unreadable expression and her eyes grow even more watery. She reaches out and grabs my arm, pinching it hard.

I slap her hand away in shock, but before I can say anything, Hettie whirls around and runs back to our room in tears. I fall back into the kitchen chair and put my head in my hands to stop myself from crying.

Though I wish I could wonder why Hettie is acting the way she is, the writing is on the wall. It's time I stop ignoring it.

I can't talk to Wayne tomorrow. I need to talk to him today.

CHAPTER 13
A PLEA FOR ANSWERS

It's an hour before noon, which means Ava still has three hours before she's off work. I can't get into her apartment without a key, and I can't get her key without making her suspicious. I decide I'll visit her at the diner anyway and see what I can ask her.

Hettie has locked herself in our room, but I don't care. I rush outside and mount my bike, ignoring my helmet because it will just take up more of my time. I pedal faster than I'm comfortable with, but I end up getting to the diner in a little over ten minutes. I leave my bike on the curb instead of locking it up, and I walk straight into the diner and look around for Ava.

She sees me before I see her. She's serving an elderly couple, and when I finally look her way, she smiles. I put up a hesitant hand to greet her and stand awkwardly by the entrance. Before she finishes, however, I see a familiar man sitting alone in the corner of the diner.

Wayne.

I remember Ava saying he came to the diner every few days, but I didn't think I'd get this lucky. My heart skips a few beats. I don't take any time to decide the best way to go about this; instead, I stride straight over to the booth Wayne sits slumped over at and sit down across from him.

He slowly looks up at me.

"Hi," I say. I can feel Ava looking at me from across the diner. I'll make something up to appease her later.

Wayne crosses his arms. "What do you want?"

"You remember me, don't you?"

He grunts. "Yeah, I remember you."

"Good," I say. "I need answers. You told my little sister and me not to go back into the well, which means you know what's down there. So tell me. What's wrong with it?"

Wayne shifts in his seat. "Have you ever heard of just taking advice?" he asks. His tone is condescending and uncouth. "Or does the concept of simply being grateful that someone goes out of their way to help you not make sense to you?"

Though I can sense his derision, I don't give up. "My sister is seven," I say. "She's acting weird, and I know it has something to do with the well and what's underneath it. I *know* it. I need an explanation, and it seems like only you can give me one."

Wayne eyes me for a moment, then takes a prolonged sip of coffee. It's as if he's testing me to see how much patience I have. "She'll be fine if you don't go back down there," he finally says. "Easy as that, kid. Happy now?"

"No, not at all," I say. My manners have no place in this conversation; I'm desperate. "Why is she acting strange? Can anyone else see what's underneath the well? Do you know what made the trees and the carvings?"

"First of all," Wayne whispers, "lower your voice. You can ask questions without screaming."

"I'm not screaming."

"Second of all, I'll tell you this, and then you need to leave me alone: no, not everyone can see what's under there. Not people my age, anyway. Only young people can see it. More specifically, young people who *need* it. It likes that. It feeds off your need for comfort. But it's a trap. Do yourself and your sister a favor and stay away from it."

"It? What's *it*?" Now I have a thousand more questions. "And if people your age can't see it, why can you? And what's *it* feeding off of?"

"I'm done answering questions," Wayne says. "Get up, go back home, keep an eye on your sister, and don't go back to the well. Don't make me regret helping you."

I shake my head. "No. You need to tell me more."

Wayne groans. "This is why I hate being in public," he says. I can't tell if he's talking to himself or me. "Listen, kid—"

"Rosella," I say.

"Whatever. If there's one thing I *don't* need to do, it's tell you more. You, however, need to stop acting entitled to answers."

He slams a couple of dollars down on the table and gets up to leave.

"No!" I nearly grab his arm but quickly stop myself. If he leaves now, I may not be able to find him again. I'm not going to let this stroke of luck go to waste. Instead, I clear my throat and whisper, "Wayne Reyes."

That catches him off guard. He freezes in his spot. "Who told you my name?"

"Please, Wayne. I need an explanation," I plead.

"Screw off."

This time, he leaves before I can figure out what to say or do.

I sit back in the booth, utterly defeated, as the door of the diner closes behind him.

After what he just said, how in the world can he expect me to simply stop asking questions?

A few moments go by as I stare off into space, thinking of nothing and everything all at once. Ava interrupts my thoughts.

"Hey there, Ro," she says quietly—skeptically.

I acknowledge her with a forced smile. "Hey."

"Do you mind if I ask what just happened?"

I exhale loudly. "I needed to ask him something," I say, "but he didn't want to answer."

Ava lingers next to me, uncharacteristically quiet for a moment. "What...what did you need to ask him?"

I put my elbows on the table and rest my head in my hands. "It's a long story."

I can tell she doesn't want to pry but that she's also curious.

"Tell you what," I say, looking back up at her. "When you're off, we can meet up if you're free. I can explain then."

Ava grins mischievously. "What if I get off now?"

"I thought you got off at two o'clock."

"One of the perks of this job is that my manager is only a few years older than me and he's an absolute idiot. If I sweet talk him and act like it's *such a big emergency*," the exaggerated sarcasm drips from her tone, "then he'll give in. Meet you outside in ten?"

"Are you sure?"

Ava shrugs. "I come to work every single day and stay my entire shift. It's fine."

"I mean…if you're sure."

Ava nods affirmatively and tucks an empty plate underneath her arm. "Outside in ten," she says.

I have no clue what I'm going to tell her, but having a friend takes a little bit of stress off me.

Ava stays true to her word. Within ten minutes, she meets me outside by my bike.

"Geez, you weren't joking around," I say.

"Yeah, he's a pretty easy person to fool," Ava says lightheartedly. "I kind of feel bad for the guy, but I don't really see any problem in taking advantage of his gullibility during desperate times."

Her joke is ironic; she doesn't realize how desperate my situation really is.

"So what's up?" she asks.

"I don't even know where to begin," I say. Furthermore, I'm tired of making up lies and excuses. "Do you want to walk with me back up to my aunt's house? I have my bike, but I won't ride it. I'll explain on the way."

Ava shrugs. "Sure."

We walk in silence for a few blocks until we reach the dirt road.

"So are you going to tell me what's going on?" Ava asks. "And why you confronted Wayne about something?"

I exhale, trying my best not to sound frazzled. Then, in less than a whisper, I say, "Hettie's been acting weird. *Really* weird. It started a few days ago, and I'm worried about her."

"Is she sick?"

I shake my head. "No. Not really."

More silence. Finally, Ava speaks up. "But what does that have to do with Wayne?"

"I..." my voice trails off. There's no way to explain this situation to her. "I think Wayne knows something about why Hettie might be acting weird, so I was trying to get him to give me some answers. He ended up just confusing me more, though, and he seemed angry that I wanted to speak to him."

Lines form around Ava's eyebrows and she tilts her head. "I don't understand," she says.

"I'll show you when we get back to my aunt's house. Hettie has been going through these weird phases where she just stares off into space. Today, she blew up at me out of nowhere."

"Sounds like she reached her teenage years early," Ava jokes lightly.

Though the remark makes a grin spread across my face, I feel far too sick and disoriented to laugh.

We walk the rest of the way quietly. I would normally worry about the awkward silence, but right now, I'm too consumed by my thoughts to care. Ava kicks a little pebble in front of her for a while as we walk, and once we reach the house, I don't even bother to put my bike back in the garage. Instead, I have Ava follow me straight through the porch door and into the kitchen.

Mother is sitting at the table when we get inside. A pang of nervousness twists around my stomach. I really hope Hettie didn't tell her we got into an argument. The last thing I need right now is Mother interrogating or scolding me about it.

"Hey, Mom," I say.

Ava smiles nervously from behind me.

Mother sets down a book and smiles her usual empty smile, but this time I can see she's a bit surprised by Ava's company.

"Hi there," she says. She isn't used to anyone but Aunt Vivian, Hettie, and me, and I can see it in her face. She does her best to put forth a cheery demeanor, something she hasn't had to do in months. I can tell when she's doing it, though; something about her seems masked and vacant.

"Hi," Ava says. "I'm Ava Lim. Nice to meet you."

"Nice to meet you too," Mother says. "Ro told me she met a new friend a few days ago."

"Have you seen Hettie today?" I ask.

"Briefly, a little less than an hour ago. I made her some food and she went back to the bedroom to draw."

She ate. Thank goodness, she finally ate something.

My relief that she must be feeling better, however, comes second to my relief that she didn't tell Mother about our fight. Maybe she's feeling a little more like herself.

"I took a half-hour nap afterward and the bedroom door was still closed when I woke up, so I decided not to disturb her," Mother continues, finishing with another forced smile.

I nod. "Well, it sounds like she's occupying herself," I say. "Ava and I will go hang out with her."

"That sounds good, honey," Mother says. "It was nice to meet you, Ava."

Ava responds with a smile and a "you too," then follows me down the hallway. To my relief, the bedroom door is unlocked. I open it slowly. My breath lingers in my throat as I pray that Hettie is in a better mood.

"Hettie? Ava came to hang out with us," I say.

There's no response. I enter the room with Ava trailing hesitantly behind me.

My heart stops mid-beat when I see a ferociously scribbled drawing on her bedside table. Hettie was clearly upset when she drew it. The lines are pressed hard into the paper and the tips of her scattered crayons are smushed.

I approach the drawing and utter a sharp gasp when I realize that she drew a moon—a half full moon that lingers above a forest.

The worst part, however, is that Hettie isn't here with it.

CHAPTER 14
HETTIE AND THE MOON

"Where is she?" Ava asks me.

I know where she is—where she went when Mother was sleeping. What I don't know, however, is who to be angrier with: Mother for not keeping an eye on Hettie, Hettie for disobeying me, or myself for leaving after we fought. A dizzying wave of nausea floods over me as I turn to face Ava.

"I need to tell you something," I say, inhaling deeply to curb the churning sensation in my stomach. "It's not going to make any sense, though." *Calm...I need to stay calm.* "Hettie and I found something weird. Something really weird. But I can't explain it without showing it to you."

Now Ava looks worried. "What is it?"

"It's a well," I say, struggling to repress the compulsion to vomit. I can't help but admonish myself for taking such a risky leap of faith. "Hettie must have snuck out when my mom was sleeping. I need to go get her. I understand if you don't want to come, but I'm not going to be able to explain any of this to you if you don't see it for yourself."

"You're sure that's where she is?" Ava asks. When I nod, she smiles. "I'll come," she says, hardly giving the situation any thought. Her response surprises me; I expected her to have more questions. Her invariable outgoingness reminds me of Hettie. Although the realization would usually make me happy, right now all I want to do is cry.

"I don't want to force you..."

"You're not forcing me, Ro," Ava says. "I can see it on your face. You're bent up about something. So let's go."

I take a deep breath to steady myself. "Here's what I need you to do," I say. "When we go back into the kitchen, act like nothing's wrong. Pretend like we're heading back downtown or something. My mom can't know Hettie is gone. I'll explain why I don't want to tell her later."

Ava nods. It's obvious that she's unsure about what to expect, but the fact that she's agreed to go with me anyway makes me admire her even more. If I'm being honest with myself, I'm not sure I would do the same.

I shut the bedroom door behind us so Mother still thinks Hettie is home, and we walk to the kitchen trying our best to seem casual.

"We're going to go hang out downtown," I say when Mother looks up from her book.

"Okay," she says. "Is Hettie coming with you?"

I shake my head. "She's busy drawing."

Mother gives me a curt nod. "Remember, Ro, be safe downtown."

"I know," I say. My breathing is getting more difficult to control, so I quickly slip out the door before Mother notices. Once outside, I don't even grab my bike. Instead, I bolt over to the road. Ava manages to keep up with me, and it doesn't take long to get to the forest.

"Where are we going?" Ava asks once we've reached the tunnel-like entrance. She stops for a moment to catch her breath.

"The well," I say. "I know she's there."

"Right," Ava says between breaths. "The well."

I can't fathom how she'll react when she sees the staircase...*if* she sees it.

Then I remember what Wayne said—that only young people who need it can see what's underneath. What does that even mean? What if Ava can't see the staircase? She'll think I'm either a liar or crazy...

I've never felt my heart pound so hard against my chest before. As we continue through the forest and finally reach the grove and the well, I think it may fall out.

I run over to the edge of the well and grip the stone sides with so much power that my fingers begin to hurt. Ava follows close behind me, and we both look down into the hole.

Oh God, what if she can't see it? I think. *Then what will I do? I'll seem crazy.*

"Holy shit," Ava whispers.

"You see it?" I ask, feeling lightheaded.

"Yeah," Ava says. Her voice is distant as she stares down the spiraling staircase. "I see it."

"She's down there," I say.

"What...what's down there?"

My explanation will do no justice. In fact, I'm not even sure I *can* explain.

"Have you been down there before?" Ava asks. Her previous assuredness has deserted her, and the hesitancy on her face is as clear as day.

"Four times," I say. "You don't have to come down if you don't want to."

"No, it's okay. I'll come down," Ava says in a slow, modulated voice, as though she's telling herself and not me. She repeats it softly to herself. "I'll come down."

"We can't spend much time down there, though," I say. "I want to find Hettie and get the hell out of there as quickly as possible."

"Why?"

"Because I think it's dangerous."

Ava lingers at the edge of the well.

"You really don't need to come," I say. "You can wait up here."

"I'll come," Ava says. "But I'll be honest...I don't know what to expect."

I try to breathe. "If it makes you feel any better," I say, "I don't either."

Then, together, we descend. Ava is slow as she finds her way in the dark. I feel bad keeping such a brisk pace, but I need to find Hettie.

As I listen to Ava behind me, I start to think it was a bad idea to bring her down with me. What if she gets attached to the world just like Hettie—like I used to be? What if she wants to keep returning?

I certainly can't turn her away now, though. She already knows the staircase exists, and I don't think Ava is the type of person to walk away from something like this without figuring out as much as she can. I continue down the stairs as she follows me, and when we finally reach the archway, I observe her expression turn from confusion to awe.

"Oh my God...Ro, what is this?"

"I know, it's crazy," I say, hardly processing her question. My eyes dart around for Hettie. I don't see her.

Ava stands motionless on the threshold, looking out at the forest and lake. I see the silver glint in her dark eyes as she takes it all in.

"I've painted so much," she says in less than a whisper, "and yet I don't think I could ever paint this."

I'm torn between my enduring reverence for this place and my newfound fear of it.

"The moon is amazing," Ava continues, stepping out from under the archway to get a better look. "Is that the real one?"

I shake my head. "It's underground. All of this is."

"An underground moon," Ava whispers. She nervously runs her fingers through her hair. "This is...this is a lot to take in."

I don't respond. Instead, I look up at the moon. It's bigger—half full, maybe more. All I can think about is how much I want to find Hettie.

I motion for Ava to follow me through the trees. I can tell she wants to stay behind and observe the carvings and the tinsel, but she keeps up with me.

I make my way straight toward the gazebo, but Hettie isn't there. Instead, she's sitting on the shore by the lake, which is completely motionless. There are no dolphins, no stingrays, no glass animals, and no Rosella birds. It's only Hettie and the moon.

"Hettie!"

Hettie whirls around and stands up. The silver of the moonlight makes her curls look even livelier than usual.

"Ro?"

I make a beeline straight to her and grab her by the shoulders. My emotions are in a whirlwind. "What in the world were you thinking? I told you not to come back." Although I want to yell at her, I speak in a low voice. A small but primal intuition worries that the world is listening.

"I'm sorry," Hettie says. She blinks rapidly, as though she's straining to snap out of a daze. "Mommy went to sleep and I couldn't stop thinking about it. I wanted to come here again because I was sad. I would close my eyes and I'd only think about this world, and...and..."

"It's okay," I say. I don't want her to react like she did this morning—not right now. "It's fine."

I no longer feel the same blind delight I felt the first few times Hettie and I visited this place. Now the only thing I feel is unrelenting anxiety. All I want to do is leave.

"Let's go, Hettie."

"But..."

"*Hettie,*" I whisper through gritted teeth.

She doesn't argue with me this time. Instead, she follows Ava and me back through the forest. Ava remains quiet; I can tell it takes willpower for her to leave without exploring more, but she does anyway.

I take one last look at the moon as we reach the archway. Something about it seems hungry, but perhaps I'm just paranoid. If I didn't know any better, I would think it disliked me for making Hettie leave.

Ava is quiet on the walk home. When we finally get back, I thank my lucky stars that Mother had left the kitchen and won't question us about where we were and why Hettie is suddenly with us. I quickly motion for Ava and Hettie to follow me back to the bedroom.

As soon as I shut the door, I let out a loud, relieved sigh. Hettie is home. She's safe here. Now I need to worry about Ava—about explaining all of this to her, if I even can.

"I still feel like that wasn't real," Ava whispers as she sits at the foot of my bed. Hettie lingers by her cot and doesn't say anything. For a fleeting moment, I feel like a bit of a hypocrite. I told Hettie not to tell anyone about the well, but I brought Ava down there.

It was an emergency, I think. *After all, maybe Ava can help me with Wayne. Maybe it was a good thing I showed her.*

"How did you two find that place?" she asks me.

"It was an accident, really," I say. "We were exploring and Hettie spotted it. After that, she begged me to take her back, and..." my voice trails off. *She begged me to take her back.* I had wondered why Hettie was so obsessed with the idea of going back. I'd thought it was odd, but I'd given in anyway. "And then we came across the stairs," I finish, more to myself than Ava.

The pull I felt to return to the underground world after Hettie and I came across it wasn't like me. I disregarded logic and after a while, I hardly worried about being in any danger. I just *wanted*—wanted to see the forest, the lake, the gazebo, and the moon. It was a want so deep within me that ignoring it was impossible until Wayne ran into us and woke my dormant worries—until I saw the Rosella and realized how cognizant whatever's down there really is.

Perhaps Hettie had felt that pull before we even discovered the staircase and the world below. I remember what Wayne said to me today about young people—how it chooses to make itself known to children who need it. Though the comment made me more confused than I was before, I think I'm starting to understand. Perhaps it recognized that Hettie needed it, for whatever reason. Maybe she needed the comfort of a sanctuary. Maybe we both did.

Hettie and I have been different since finding the underground world. The image of the moon, and the way it grew brighter and fuller with each visit, is seared into my mind.

And then I remember how Ava told me about her struggles in school—her constant loneliness and dejection. Maybe it sensed she needed it too.

"I need to speak to Wayne," I tell Ava.

"Right, that's another question I have," Ava says. "What does Wayne have to do with this?"

"He knows about the well," I say. "That's what I was questioning him about today at the diner. Hettie and I ran into him one day after we left the well, and he told us never to go back down there. He seemed really freaked out about it. When I saw him today, I couldn't pass up the opportunity to ask him what he knows. I had to confront him and see if I could get more answers."

"Did he tell you anything?"

"Hardly. He told me to screw off."

"He sounds pleasant," Ava says.

"He's an asshole, but I know he has information— information I *need*." I look over at Hettie, who hasn't moved much at all. "How are you feeling?" I ask her.

Hettie shrugs.

I eye Ava and purse my lips.

I move closer to Hettie and sit down on her cot so I'm beside her. "I'm sorry about our fight today," I say.

"I'm sorry too," Hettie whispers. She rests her eyes on her feet. "I shouldn't have called you bad names."

"I said some mean things too," I say. "I said them because I was worried, but I shouldn't have said them at all."

"What were you worried about?" Hettie asks quietly.

"About the well," I say. "About the underground world. I think it might be bad, Hettie. That's why I didn't want to go back."

"It's not bad," she says. "It's the best thing in the whole entire world."

I don't know how to respond to that because on the outside, it is.

It's a trap. Wayne's words ring in my ears.

"I don't think it is, though," I say. "I think it's pretending to be the best thing in the world so it can trap us."

"But it *won't* trap us," Hettie says. "It's good...it's better than anything." Her eyes are wet and she rubs angrily at them.

My chest tightens. I don't know if I'll ever be able to say anything that will make her believe me.

"This is why I need to talk to Wayne," I say, turning back to Ava.

Ava pulls on a strand of her hair nervously. We're both quiet until she says, "Maybe I can find his apartment number."

"How?"

Ava shakes her head. "I don't know yet. But I'll figure it out. I already know he lives on the fourth floor. I'll ask around or something."

"I can help," I say.

"You should stay here with Hettie," she says. "At least for tonight. Let's meet up tomorrow after my shift, and if I haven't figured anything out, we can try together."

I wonder why she's so willing to help me, especially with something as weird and potentially dangerous as this.

"Thank you," I say.

"Don't worry about it. You don't expect me to walk away after everything I've just seen, do you?"

"Just don't tell anyone," I say. "The fewer people who know, the better. That's why I haven't told my mom or my aunt...it may just make things worse. I don't know how either of them would react, and I can't deal with them right now. This is too serious."

That, and the fact that Mother struggles to get through every single day. I know that telling her about a magical underground world wouldn't do well for her at all. Not right now, at least.

Ava laughs. "Don't worry, Ro," she says. "I don't really have anyone to tell."

Though her manner is lighthearted, it's obvious that the joke was not.

CHAPTER 15
RED AND BLUE

The last thing I tell Ava before she leaves is to not go back to the well, no matter how much she wants to. Making sure she knows to stay away eases my nerves, if only minimally. She promises me she won't return and that she'll let me know if she's discovered anything about Wayne's apartment number when we meet up tomorrow.

The rest of the afternoon and evening, I try my best to keep Hettie busy. I offer to draw with her or play whatever game she wants, but she turns me down. Her thoughts are on the underground world and nothing but that.

Dinner is quiet, and although Mother helps me make it, she doesn't seem interested in entertaining conversation.

After Hettie clears her plate, she leaves the table without saying a word. I wonder if Mother notices how different she's been acting. I wonder how much of anything she notices at all.

Hettie falls asleep early, and although I can hear Aunt Vivian's car pull into the driveway, I don't feel like going out to greet her. I shut the bedroom door and listen to Hettie as she stirs in her sleep.

Though I try to think about how I'll get Wayne to talk to me and how I'll convince him to tell me what he knows, my mind wanders to something else—to a very painful and recent memory that I've tried my best to bury.

I think about April, and what happened that night. It was cool out, the way Oregon usually is, especially compared to Tennessee. Mother had been acting oddly withdrawn and despondent, so I decided to bring Hettie with me to get our nails done. She had picked red. I'd picked blue.

I thought I was doing the right thing to get Hettie out of the house. When we returned, it was early evening, and we had been giggling the whole way home. Hettie was telling me about how she would be the only girl in second grade with professionally painted nails, and how everyone would be jealous because nobody else had an older sister who would take them to a nail salon. Nobody else was as lucky as *she* was.

I had felt a swell of pride in that moment—that I was the older sister who took her sibling out to do fun things. We talked and laughed, and for a while, I genuinely believed that whatever was going on with Mother would soon be a thing of the past. I told Hettie that evening, "One day, things will go back to normal. One day, Mother will beat her illness and all three of us will get our nails done together." How incredibly naive I'd been.

When we returned home, the house was quiet in an unusual and cold sort of way. And when Hettie went upstairs and into the bathroom, she found Mother.

The way she screamed my name sent raw, unbridled fear throughout my body. It was as though needles had pierced my skin and made their way so deep inside of me that every breath I took was accompanied by pain. My adrenaline was primitive; I didn't tell myself to run, I just did. I took the stairs three at a time, running toward the light of the bathroom and the figure of Mother on the floor, blurred by my tears. I knew what had happened as soon as I'd heard Hettie scream. It wasn't an accident.

Whatever I was feeling and thinking didn't matter. Fear, anger, sadness, hurt, betrayal...what good would any of those emotions do for me—for Mother and Hettie? As soon as I was upstairs, I was back downstairs, phone in my hand, dialing 911 with shaking fingers, trying to tell the call-taker what had happened and trying even harder to understand it myself.

My mom may be dead. She's not breathing. I don't know what she took. I think she still has a pulse...I don't know, I didn't take the time to check. My little sister is with her. My little sister saw it. She's only seven years old. We need help. My mom is going to die.

And then, sirens—red and blue ones like the colors on my and Hettie's nails. After that, I don't remember much at all.

Everything became hazy in the days that followed. Who knew shock could last for so long? Aunt Vivian flew out and met us in the hospital. She was crying when she saw us. Then she spoke with Mother, who had already voluntarily admitted herself to a psychiatric unit. A week or so later, Mother was discharged. A month after that, we moved to Tennessee.

I roll over in bed, trying to rid myself of the terrible memory. I hear a soft splat as a tear drips onto my pillow. I rest my fingertip on the spot where my tear landed, then scratch at it, as if I'm willing it to go away—just like the harrowing feelings that accompany it. I'm not sure the hurt and the fear will ever really go away, regardless of how much I try to forget.

If the underground world truly does reveal itself to young people who need it, as Wayne had mentioned, then the only thing I have no questions about is why it chose Hettie and me.

My head is foggy when I wake up. The feeling finally goes away after I eat breakfast. I notice that Hettie is still withdrawn. I can't tell if she's angry with me or just upset that I think the underground world is dangerous.

Mother, as always, is less difficult to decipher. She's the same way she was at dinner last night.

After Hettie leaves the room, I sit back in the kitchen chair and pick at a few remaining bits of oatmeal. I observe Mother's face; her blank expression is somewhat present and somewhat far off. Her portion size is tiny, and even then, she's barely touched it.

"Mom?"

She looks up and smiles at me with her usual empty expression. "Yeah?"

"Have you ever thought of trying medication?"

The question just kind of comes out. I know she doesn't like to talk about it, but she's been so distant and tired that the need to ask is overwhelming. I feel trapped in the middle of two withdrawn people who I love and care for so much. Although I know Hettie's behavior comes from something else entirely—something I'll deal with as soon as I can get into contact with Wayne—I hate to see Mother suffer when she may be able to do something about it.

"I've thought about it, hon'. I'm not sure it's the right thing for me."

"Why not?" I ask. "It may help you feel less terrible...less like this."

The memory of the sirens—those vivid, fluorescent colors—pops back into my head.

Mother stares at her spoon and doesn't answer me.

"Even if you're not comfortable with medication, maybe seeing someone will help."

"That's all very expensive, Ro," she says.

"Maybe it'll be worth it."

She shakes her head. "I don't know."

"But how can you know if you've never tried it?"

Silence. Again.

"Anything must be better than this," I say softly.

"I'm dealing, Ro."

"Yes, but...how well are you dealing?" I don't like this conversation, but I need to have it.

"Well enough."

The irritation I've tried so hard to suppress springs to life. "Well *enough*?"

"I don't want this to be something you worry about," Mother says quietly. "Aunt Vivian and I will deal with it.

You're doing such a good job keeping Hettie occupied, Ro, you really are. And—"

"No, I'm not," I say. "She notices. *I* notice. And all you can say is you're dealing with it well *enough*?"

"Rosella, I'm not in the mood."

"You'll *never* be in the mood," I say. "Not until you get help. Why are you so against getting help?"

"I'm not against it at all," Mother says. Now she seems irritated, but the presence of her emotion delights me. Any emotion, even a negative one, is better than nothing but deep, empty despondency.

"If you're not against it, then why not try it out?" I say. "I'm not trying to annoy you, Mom, but you need to know that as much as you don't want this to affect Hettie and me, it does."

Mother purses her lips and inhales slowly. "I need to give this time right now. If I don't improve, maybe I'll consider seeking help."

"That's what you said months ago," I whisper.

Her eyes shift across the room as if she just now realizes Hettie isn't here.

"It takes time," she says.

"I know it does. But maybe it will take less time if you reach out to someone who can help you. Aunt Vivian tries her best, but she works such long hours and she isn't a psychiatrist. And I just..." my voice fades out, and it takes considerable energy to regain it. "I just don't know what to do."

"Ro, I really do appreciate you caring about me, but this is a decision *I* need to make."

"That's not exactly fair to say given the circumstances," I snap. "I understand that it's your decision, but it seems like you've hardly thought about the impact *not* getting help has had on Hettie and me. What if April happens again?"

Mother makes a muted, disparaging noise. "It won't."

"Even so, you aren't present anymore. Have you noticed how different Hettie has been acting?"

When she doesn't respond, I disregard my filter and say, "What about *me*, Mom? Have you noticed that I've been struggling? I miss you, and more than that, I hate seeing you in pain all the time."

"I know," Mother says. Her eyes fill with tears and she rests her forehead in her hands. "I know, Rosella."

"Do you?" I ask. "Do you really? Because you still do nothing to at least *try* to get help. Sleeping all day won't do it, Mom. You have to know that."

"It's just...hard," she says, her voice cracking. "I'm really trying to get through the days—to be there for you and Hettie. But I feel as if this *weight* is on me and I can't shake it off, and it makes me so exhausted and foggy. Sometimes even moving is hard. And I feel this terrible guilt...for you and Hettie...for not being there. And I'm so sorry."

Trying my hardest not to cry, I lean forward and gently touch her wrist to pull it away from her face. "I know, Mom," I whisper. Anything louder will provoke more tears. "I understand. I know it takes time. And I'm not asking you to get help for my sake, or Aunt Vivian's, or Hettie's. I'm asking for *your* sake. I see how much you're suffering and I just...I just know there are options."

Through her tears, she smiles at me. "I know."

I realize that as much as I want to persuade her, my words will do nothing right now.

"It's just something I've been wanting to bring up," I say.

She doesn't respond. I swallow hard and slowly get to my feet.

At least I gave it a shot.

When I leave the room, I don't look at her. It will only make things worse.

CHAPTER 16
WAITING

Waiting until two o'clock to meet up with Ava is hard. Hettie is unresponsive to any jokes I try to make, and after a while, I give up entirely.

Before I leave, I ask her if she would like to come with me—mostly because I'd feel more comfortable if I could keep an eye on her—but she declines my offer.

I know that forcing her won't do anything, and I don't trust Mother to keep an eye on her after what happened last time I left her alone, so before I leave, I make Hettie promise me over and over again that she won't return to the well. I can tell it annoys her, but I don't care. I need to make sure she knows how serious I am.

"No matter what you feel," I say, "and no matter what you want to do, don't go back. If you feel like you're going to break your promise, what do you do?"

"I draw," she says.

"Yes, or anything that keeps you occupied. Play with dolls, read, dress-up, watch television...whatever you want. You can do *anything* except go back to the well. I'll be back soon."

"I still don't understand why you think it's so bad," she says.

"I just know it is, Hettie. You need to trust me right now."

Despite making her promise me a hundred more times, I still feel uneasy when I leave. I'm desperate to speak to Wayne, though. I need to know not only what is going on with Hettie, but also what this underground world truly is. I can't keep seeing my sister like this.

Ava is waiting outside the apartment complex for me when I arrive.

The first thing I say is, "Did you figure out Wayne's apartment number?"

Ava sighs and shakes her head. "I tried," she says. "But I couldn't find anyone who knew. I'm so sorry, Ro."

I try to conceal my disappointment, but the look on Ava's face tells me I'm not doing well.

"I know for sure he lives on the fourth floor," she says. "I was thinking that if you have time, we could just wait in the hallway for someone to come out and ask them. I'm sure they'd know. They'd have to have seen him coming in and out."

"Of course I have time," I say. "That's a really good idea, but what do we do if someone questions us?"

Ava shrugs. "We improvise."

I follow her inside the complex—we make a pit stop at her apartment and she grabs a box of Oreos for us to eat—and then we make our way up to the fourth floor and find a particularly bare wall to lean against while we wait. The hallway is dimly lit with no windows and a carpet that has a white-turned-beige hue to it. The whole building looks like it has been around for ages.

"I hope someone comes out soon," I say as I fiddle with the hem of my skirt. "I hate leaving Hettie alone."

"You could have brought her with you, you know," Ava says, taking the top off her Oreo and licking the filling.

"I asked her to come, but she wanted to stay home," I say. "She's been so unlike herself lately. I know it has something to do with...that place." I lower my voice to a whisper. I'm worried someone will hear me, even though there's nobody in the hallway. "That's why I need to speak with Wayne. It's more than just curiosity. I know something is wrong with Hettie, with the underground world...with all of this."

Ava takes a moment to respond. "It's odd," she says. "I spent a lot of time thinking about the underground world last night. I mean...I've never seen anything like it. Never. Not even close. Even now, I can't fully comprehend it. If it weren't for you being so afraid of it, I may have thought to go back."

"I know," I say. "I went back three times before Wayne confronted Hettie and me, and another before I finally realized something was up."

"It's like a sedative," Ava says. "Even when we were down there, and even though I was confused, I was calm."

A shiver runs up my spine and down to the tips of my fingers. "That's the problem with it," I say. "You don't question it. Hettie and I spent hours there every time we went, and I never really thought to step back and ask myself about what was going on. I was..." I pause and think of Hettie. "I was like a kid."

"What made you realize?"

My eyes move down to my tattoo. I take a deep, long breath before I whisper, "A Rosella landed on my arm."

Ava raises an eyebrow, puzzled.

I bite down on my lip. The spot on my forearm where the bird landed feels cold, as though the remnants of its talons stayed behind to remind me that the underground world still exists even if I refuse to go back.

"A few days before we found the well," I say, "Hettie and I were talking about the animals we thought we were most like. She said she would be a dolphin and I said that I'd be a Rosella."

Ava half-smiles. "That's not very creative of you," she teases.

I try to laugh, but my nerves suppress it and it ends up being more of a worried giggle. "Every time we visited the underground world, something new would be there," I continue. "Animals, jewelry...as if they were there for *us*. But the fourth time we went, there were dolphins. I didn't remember the conversation Hettie and I'd had until the Rosella showed up."

Even telling Ava makes the knot in my stomach grow. "It was as if the world knew us," I say. "It knew what we liked and what we wanted. It took me a while to realize—I even ignored Wayne's first warning—but the Rosella did the trick. It knew something that we'd never discussed down there...that it *shouldn't* have known."

Ava noticeably shudders.

"But it hasn't seemed to click for Hettie," I say.

"She's seven, isn't she?" Ava asks, and I nod. "Well, if I were seven, I don't think I would realize how strange the whole thing is either. I'd be too entranced by the moonlight and the forest to wonder if something was wrong."

I pick an Oreo out of the box and run my finger over the indents on the top half. "But now, Hettie is acting odd. Distant...like she's no longer herself. All she can think about is going back." My stomach does a flip. "When I talked to Wayne in the diner, he told me that the world was a trap. He's the only person who may have the answers about this place that I need."

Ava pops another Oreo into her mouth. "That's why we're waiting," she says. "To get you those answers."

CHAPTER 17
A FRIEND

The apartment complex is quiet, more so than I thought it would be. When Ava and I don't speak, I can hear every creak in the walls as the building settles, and the sound of the air conditioner is amplified in the silence.

I can't think of conversation to make, mostly because all I can focus on is the nervousness that resides in my stomach and chest.

After a few minutes of quiet, Ava decides to bring up a different topic, no doubt to get my mind off of how I feel.

"So, tell me," she says. "Did you ever date anyone back in Oregon? Hopefully you didn't make any shitty decisions like I did."

I bring my knees up to my chest and lean back against the wall. "No way," I shake my head. "I've never been into any of that."

Ava shrugs. "To each their own," she says. "You'll probably have to deal with a lot less stress, I'll tell you that. I was always that kid who wanted to watch princess movies and dreamed of living a life like that."

"The more you talk, the more you sound like Hettie," I say as I tug nervously on my shoelace. "I was never like that. My mom always said it was because I was too anxious and that I'd withdraw in those situations. But I don't think it's that. I think I'm just the type of person who's happy being on her own."

"Well, I think that's admirable," Ava says. "If I were like that, I wouldn't have gotten into all the trouble I'm in now." She smiles sadly at me. "I'm glad to know I'll have a friend this coming school year."

I return her smile. "Me too. Maybe once we get our driver's licenses, we can go off campus for lunch and get away from the school for a little bit."

"That would be amazing," Ava says. "They have the cutest coffee place that's only a minute from campus. I've been dying to go there."

"Coffee it is, then," I say, grinning.

After a few more moments of silence, I turn toward her.

"I really appreciate all your help with this mess, Ava," I say. "I think most people would have freaked out by now and run off."

Ava shakes her head. "You don't need to thank me," she says. "I've always entertained the idea of magic anyway."

"Really?"

Ava nods. "Yeah, I think so. This is still a lot to grasp, but it's certainly a cool thing to have discovered."

I laugh nervously. I'm not so sure I agree with her.

"Whatever's going on...whatever I saw down there," she says, "I'm glad you trusted me enough to show me." She crosses her legs and runs her finger across a dark patch of carpet. "Besides," she adds, "I don't think you know how much it meant when you listened to me that first day we hung out. After I told you about my whole debacle last year, you didn't judge me. You accepted me without hesitation. I don't even think my own parents would have done that." I can tell that saying it out loud makes her sad.

"I was so lonely for such a long time, especially after moving from New York," she continues. "On top of that, things are different here...the people are different. I used to live in the middle of a city, and now I live in Larton, which is such a culture shift. And then you came along, and not only did you become my friend, but you showed me a freaking magical underground world." She laughs anxiously, then shakes her head and shifts back to a serious tone. "I mean, I know it's not exactly a *good* magic underground world, but geez...magic, an underground moon and forest...I never thought I'd be a part of something like this. My life has gone from being boring and lonely to being crazy and filled with adventure in a matter of days."

Ava takes the top off of another Oreo and licks the filling before eating the rest of the cookie. "But magic and craziness aside," she says, "what mattered the most to me was how accepting you were. After I told you about my liking girls—not to mention my poor taste in certain girls, apparently—and all that crap I had gone through last year in school, I regretted it. I thought I had confided too much in such a short period of time. But then I realized it's not something for me to worry about, not if I have a friend I can trust. And if I can trust you, you should be able to trust me. *That's* why I'm helping you."

The knot in my stomach unravels just a little bit, but it's enough to make me feel some semblance of both relief and warmth.

"I think that's about the sweetest thing anyone has ever said to me," I say, grinning.

"I mean it, though." She pauses and adds, "And to think, this is all because I warned you against getting some shitty ham omelet."

This time, I'm able to laugh. "I'm sure you didn't expect that to lead you *here*."

Ava smiles with only one side of her mouth. "I think expecting things is overrated."

We're interrupted by the sound of a door at the end of the hallway opening. My head moves toward the sound; I desperately hope it's Wayne. It's not.

An elderly woman with thin hair and glasses that make her eyes look bigger than they really are shuffles down the hall with a few shopping bags in hand. She stops to smile at us as she passes.

"Are you two Girl Scouts?" she asks, peering at the box of Oreo cookies. Her voice is light and airy, and I can tell she's the type of person who enjoys making conversation.

Ava grins and stuffs a cookie into her mouth, but before she can answer, I take the opportunity.

"Actually, we are," I say. "We're delivering to someone by the name of Wayne Reyes, but we don't know where he lives."

The elderly woman laughs. She looks confused. "Wayne Reyes?" she asks. "You're sure?"

I nod. "Positive."

She shrugs and adjusts the shopping bags on her arm. "Well, you're on the right floor. He's apartment 427," she says. "Not that I ever see him outside of it. But I suppose cookies delight even the most morose of folks. Are you still selling?"

Ava looks down at the half-eaten box of Oreos. "This is our last one, sadly," she says. "But next season we will be."

The woman shakes her head. "Shame," she says. "You're selling him only half a box?"

As much as I appreciate her giving us Wayne's apartment number, I really want her to leave right now.

"He only paid for half," Ava says, subtly shrugging to me.

The woman scoffs. "I wish I were surprised," she says. "My only encounters with him have been not up to par if I say so myself."

"Well, thank you for your help," I say, trying to smile. All I want to do is see if Wayne is home, but I need to wait until she leaves. Ava notices my impatience. She stands up and smiles sweetly at the old woman.

"Do you want help with your bags?" she asks. "I can walk with you to your car if you like."

"Well, aren't you just a darling?" the woman says. "How can I turn down such a sweet offer?"

Ava gives me a thin-lipped smile and takes some of the woman's bags. "You go sell those cookies to him, Ro," she says as she and the woman start walking down the hall. The woman is still talking Ava's ear off as they turn the corner, and in that moment, I have never been more thankful for someone as I am for Ava.

Leaving the Oreos on the ground, I take one more look around the hallway to ensure nobody else is there. I'm alone. The thought brings me comfort—as much comfort as I'm able to feel right now, at least.

On light feet, trying my best to breathe and calm my nerves, I approach 427. The longer I stand around and think, the more likely it is I'll doubt myself, so I promptly knock on the door and hold my breath.

Nothing.

I knock again, this time louder.

Come on.

Before I raise my fist to knock for a third time, the door opens.

I'm actually a bit shocked to see Wayne, despite my persistence in finding him. Part of me had expected him to refuse to answer the door for anyone.

When he sees me, a look of both anger and fear manifest on his gaunt face.

"Jesus Christ, girl," he says, pressing his teeth together so hard I'm surprised they don't shatter. "Do I need to call the police?"

"What you need to do is answer my questions," I say.

"Who the hell gave you my apartment number?"

"Who cares? We need to discuss something way more important than how I figured out where you live. I wouldn't be here if I wasn't desperate."

"I told you, if you and your sister don't go back there, she'll be fine," he says. He starts to shut his door, but I shove my foot into the threshold. I hold back a wince as it hits the side of my foot harder than I'd expected.

"She's *not* fine, though," I say. "All she can talk about is going back. She even went back there when I wasn't home. She's obsessed. Why is she so obsessed? Why am I afraid of this place and she isn't?"

"Because she's a kid," Wayne says sharply. "And kids are idiots. They never realize things until it's too late."

Something in me snaps and I grab the edge of the door he's holding, trying my best to push it open. I don't get very far, though. His grip is stronger and more persistent than mine.

"Kids are not idiots," I say. My voice cracks as if I'm about to cry. "Hettie is not an idiot. She's seven, for God's sake. This place has done something to her. Why are you so against telling me what's going on?"

Wayne lets his hands fall to his side. The door to his apartment is still cracked only half-open, but he isn't as intent to close it anymore. I don't move my foot, though. I want him to know I don't plan on leaving.

"I've told you everything I know," he says. His voice is less than a whisper.

"Somehow, I highly doubt that," I say. "Why were you at the well that day you ran into Hettie and me? You were scared. I saw it on your face. You've been down there, haven't you?"

Wayne leans forward and tries to look around the hallway to make sure that nobody is there.

"All you need to know is that the well and what's beneath it is dangerous," he says, ignoring my question. "It has made over twenty years of my life nothing but misery and regret. I warned you and your sister against returning. How much more do you want from me?"

"I want information," I say. "I want what you know. How difficult is that?"

Wayne looks long and hard at me. "More difficult than you'd think."

I return his stare, but I don't say anything. Honestly, I don't know what to say.

Both of us are persistent. We're so persistent that I don't notice Ava when she appears behind me.

"Who the hell is this?" Wayne says. His hand is back on the edge of his door, and I put my hand up in defense. I can feel Ava recoil.

"A friend," I say. "Her name is Ava. She's seen it too."

"For Christ's sake, have you shown all of Tennessee?"

"Only her and Hettie," I say. "That's it. They haven't told anyone. How many more people know what's down there?"

"Nobody else," he says. Then, after a moment's thought, he adds, "I hope."

"Please," I say. "I need you to tell me what's going on."

Wayne pinches the bridge of his nose with his fingers and shakes his head. He lets his hand fall to his side once again but rests the other cautiously on the door frame. Seeing how eager he is to turn us away only makes my grip on his door tighten. I twist my free hand behind my back and clutch the jamb in defiance.

"Fine," he says. "You get two questions."

My sudden relief dies quicker than it sprang to life, and dismay takes its place.

"Two questions?" I say, trying not to scoff. "Is this a game to you?"

"Two or zero," he says stonily. "I'd prefer the latter, but I'm being generous." He scratches his chin and adds, "I don't play games."

I side-eye Ava. From what I can see of her face, she dislikes him just as much as I do.

"Can we at least come inside?" I ask.

Wayne shakes his head again. "No."

I don't just dislike him. I *hate* him. I hate the way he refuses to help, the way he makes me bargain for answers that may save my little sister. But my hatred won't make him give me the answers I seek, so I conceal my anger and do my best to sound confident.

"Fine," I say. "Why is my sister acting so weird? It's like she's sick...like she's in a daze and the only thing that makes her happy is visiting the well."

"Your sister is young," Wayne says. His eyes don't meet my face or Ava's. Instead, they dart around, anxious that someone else is listening. "That world is like poison. The younger and smaller a person is, the more damage the poison will do. That's why your sister is acting differently. It's gotten inside of her and altered her thinking. But it isn't permanent. If you don't go back, over time she'll return to normal."

"Over time? How long?"

"I don't know. Are you finished?"

"I get one more question."

"You asked two already."

Ava lets out a derisive laugh.

"My second one didn't count," I argue. "You didn't know the answer."

"I don't know as much as you seem to think I do," Wayne says in a low voice.

The more I study his face, the more I realize how dead he looks. His ghostly figure and dark eyes depict a man deprived of health—the type of person who watches the world go by, not participating, not reacting, just watching. But despite how removed he seems, a part of him that is far too large to hide is haunted, yet I don't know by what. The image of the trees—the graves—with my face and Hettie's carved onto them pops into my head.

"What are the carvings of?" I ask. Though this question swirls amidst thousands of others, it seems the most important. "The carvings on the trees...what—*who*—are they?"

"They're children," Wayne says. "Children like you, your sister, and your friend. Children like I once was. But unlike you, they didn't get a warning and they continued going back until the poison became too much and it devoured them whole."

I don't speak, but Ava does. "What does that mean?" she asks.

"It means that if you stay away, you'll be safe," he says. The haunted look in his eyes has grown and become something more than just misery rooted in the past. It consumes the present too, and it's directed at Ava and me. It's as if our very presence pains him. "I warned you that day at the well because I don't want it to win again," he says, finally looking me in the face. "It lures you in and traps you. It makes you think everything is perfect until it's too late to turn back. It likes children best...children younger than you. Children like your sister. *That* is why I warned you. The least you can do is stop asking me questions. Stop making me relive this. I'm sorry I can't do more for you."

He doesn't give us time to react before he shuts the door. I move my foot just before it slams into place.

Ava and I stare at the closed door in silence. After a few moments, Ava gingerly takes my wrist and leads me down the hallway.

"I can't," I say in a broken whisper. "I can't just leave."

"He's not going to answer any more questions right now, Ro," she says gently. "He said so himself. Maybe you can try another day."

I shake my head and feel hot tears prick the corners of my eyes. "I knew that was why Hettie was acting differently, but for some reason, hearing it from Wayne made me feel worse. I thought that if I could get more answers, I'd be able to figure out how to help Hettie. But I couldn't even do that."

Ava doesn't respond. I don't blame her; if I were in her situation, I wouldn't know what to say either.

"He said it likes children," I say. "And when I spoke to him at the diner, he told me that it only shows itself to young people who *need* it. So clearly not everyone can see it. My aunt told me that she hikes near where the well is, but she said she's never seen it."

"You told her about it?"

"No," I say. "Not about what's beneath it, at least. But before Hettie and I found the staircase, I mentioned the well to her."

Ava nods. "If what Wayne said is true, and it really does only show up for people who need it, maybe it tries to find people who are hurting."

"But...what's *it*?"

"I don't know. Maybe the underground world is *it*."

I slump against the wall near the stairway. Even the thought of descending to the third floor makes me feel exhausted. I just want to sit on the carpet of the hallway and stare into nothingness, if only for a little bit.

"Can I ask you something, Ro?"

I tilt my head, then nod.

"Let's say this place really does pick and choose who it shows up for, and that it picks children who are hurting. You know why I'm hurting. I told you what happened to me last year, how my parents are never here for me, how I was isolated at school...all of that." She pauses and searches for the right words to her question. "But why do you think you and Hettie can see it?"

I bite my lip. I know the answer, but I'm not so sure I want to say it.

"My mom," I finally say. "She's the reason we moved to Larton to be with my Aunt Vivian. In April, she tried to overdose on her sleeping pills and it didn't work."

Ava blinks back her shock.

"Everything kind of led up to that moment," I continue. "She'd been different for a few years and just kept getting worse. Then *that* happened, and staying in Oregon just didn't seem reasonable anymore." I inhale and look down the hall to prevent myself from having to observe Ava's reaction. "Hettie and I have been bystanders to my mom's depression for a long time. I think after a while, being a bystander makes you feel like you're part of the problem."

Ava leans against the wall and exhales slowly before she speaks. "I'm so sorry, Ro," she says after a moment.

"Well," I say, doing my best to smile ironically, "at least I have one question completely cleared up: why we're able to see it."

Ava wraps her arms around her stomach. "And you're sure he's right about all of this?"

I shake my head. "No. But he seems like the best bet."

"Are you going to try to force him to answer more of your questions?" When I don't respond, she turns to face me. "You could try to show your aunt the well," she says, "as a test to see if what Wayne is saying is true. If she truly can't see what we've seen, then you know he's right, and maybe forcing him to speak to you again will be worth it."

"Don't you think she'd be suspicious?"

"You're a good improviser," Ava says, poking my arm lightly. "That whole lie about the Girl Scout cookies? Brilliant. I didn't even think of that."

Her reassurance doesn't make me feel any better.

"Or maybe I should just give up on Wayne," I say. "Something about answering these questions upsets him, and I'm worried that no amount of knowledge will keep Hettie from acting the way she is. Maybe I just need to wait it out and keep an eye on Hettie until she goes back to normal."

Ava looks down at her shoes. "Maybe," she says. "And if that's what you decide to do, then I'll support that. But that well will always be there, which means there is always a possibility she'll go back." The thought makes me want to wither away into oblivion, and Ava notices. She puts a gentle hand on my shoulder. "I know you don't want to hear that, Ro," she says. "But you know it's true. I saw how taken up Hettie was with that place when I went with you, and Wayne said that younger children are more affected by its poison."

Even though she says the last word quietly, a cold shiver snakes up my spine.

"So you think I should try to get more information out of Wayne?" I ask.

Ava nods. "But not now. He clearly doesn't want to talk to you. Eventually, though, I think you should try again."

She's right, I know she is. If I refuse to seek Wayne's help simply because he turned me away, then I'll remain just as much of a bystander to Hettie as I am to Mother. Every day I'll live in fear that Hettie is still entranced with this underground world and that she'll end up as nothing more than another face carved into a tree.

I can't simply wait around for her to grow out of it, because at the back of my mind, pressing anxiety will always linger. And what's more is that it isn't fair for Hettie to have to live like this any longer. Although she may not notice it, she's miserable. How much time will it take for her to stop acting the way she is now? A month? A year?

Aunt Vivian told me I was a good sister. A good sister wouldn't let her little sister continue suffering, even if only for a minute, if there was a way she could get answers that may lead to a solution.

"Wayne can still see the well," I say. "But I don't understand why. He said it only shows itself to young people...young people who need it."

Ava looks away from her shoes and back up at me, then shrugs. "Maybe he used to need it."

CHAPTER 18
GONE

The first thing I do when I get back is check on Hettie. When I see her in our bedroom, the relief I feel is incomparable to all my other muddled emotions. She's safe...she's home. After a few moments of appreciating how it feels to have an invisible weight lifted off my shoulders— one I hadn't fully recognized was there to begin with—my observations bring me crashing back down to reality.

I approach Hettie slowly. She isn't sitting on her cot, or drawing, or doing much of anything at all. She's opened the little window in our room, which she stands motionless in front of.

"I'm back," I say.

Nothing. Oh God, not again. How long has she been like this?

"I'm back," I repeat, this time louder. "Hettie?"

I touch her shoulder gently. That usually gets her to snap out of it.

When she does nothing, my heart drops and my stomach starts to roil.

I position myself next to her, hoping that seeing me will bring her back. Her eyes are as dead as Wayne's, perhaps even more so.

She stares out the window in a vacant, dazed sort of way, looking at nothing at all. Her eyes are glossy and no longer a vibrant blue. Instead, they're dark gray, the way clouds look before a storm. I blink back my shock. This is the worst she's ever been.

"Hettie," I say. I grab her shoulders and turn her to face me. When she still doesn't come out of her daze, I snap my fingers in front of her eyes. She doesn't even blink.

Now my heart is pounding.

I should get Mother. But what would she do? I can't tell her why Hettie is acting like this, and even if I did—even if I told her about the well and what we found—she wouldn't believe me. And if what Wayne told me was true, then showing her wouldn't do anything either.

"Hettie, look at me. Look at my face."

I bend down so my face is right in front of hers. Although her eyes meet mine, I know she doesn't see me; her mind is far away.

I take her face in my hands, smoothing her curls as I do my best to speak without bursting into tears.

"Hettie, come back," I beg. My voice cracks as I lose control of it, and I make a strangled noise that is halfway between crying and groaning.

"Ro." Her voice is weak, but it delights me nonetheless.

"Oh my God, Hettie," I say, pulling her into a tight hug. I repeat myself three, maybe four times. "Oh my God, I thought I'd lost you."

"Lost me?" She blinks. Her eyes finally recognize my own.

"What were you doing?" I ask.

"Nothing," she says.

"Yes, I could see that. But I meant...did you not see me when I came in?"

"I thought you went to see Ava."

"I already did."

"But you just left."

"I..." My mouth closes as promptly as it opens. "Hettie, I've been gone for a few hours."

Hettie furrows her eyebrows. Does she truly not realize how much time has passed?

"What did you do after I left?" I ask. "What do you remember?"

Hettie shrugs. "I went to the kitchen and saw Mommy."

"What about after that?"

"I don't know."

"Just try your best."

Hettie tilts her head inquisitively. "She was tired and sad, and so she went to sleep. And then I got sad...I wanted to go back, but you told me not to, so I didn't."

I remember the conversation I had earlier with Mother and feel a pang of guilt run through me. Maybe she wouldn't have been so upset if I'd stopped bugging her about medication—if I'd just let the subject be.

"Yes," I say, refusing to let my arms leave Hettie's sides. "I'm so proud of you. What happened after?"

"Nothing," she says. "You came back."

That's not possible. I've been gone for three hours, maybe longer.

"You don't remember doing anything after Mom went back to sleep?"

Hettie shakes her head.

Suddenly, I feel nauseous. Though I'm relieved that Hettie didn't return to the well, my realization that her trance left her unaware of both her surroundings and time snuffs out any respite I feel.

If she spent three hours oblivious to her surroundings and her actions, then she had no mind to make any conscious choices. And if this happens again, what if she returns to the well unconsciously?

"How are you feeling right now?" I ask, looking into her eyes and silently rejoicing when I see that the blue has returned.

"Fine," Hettie says. "I'm good. Why are you asking me all of these questions?"

I shake my head, more to myself than Hettie, and sit on her cot.

"Do you think you're acting weird?" I ask her.

"I'm acting fine," she says. "When are we going to go back?"

I need to get my thoughts straight. Right now, they're swirling at a thousand miles a minute, and it won't do Hettie or me any good if I'm not in the right frame of mind. More than that, I need answers—more answers than Wayne gave me today.

I'm going to see him again soon, I tell myself, *and I'm not going to let him turn me away. Not anymore.*

I remember what Ava said about showing Aunt Vivian the well—about seeing whether or not she can see what I see. But Aunt Vivian isn't home; she probably won't be for another few hours, and I'm not in the mood to wait around.

I stand up and gather a pile of spare paper lying on the floor by Hettie's suitcase. Then I grab her box of crayons and hand them to her.

"I want you to draw me a picture."

"When are we going back to the well?"

I shake my head. "First, I want a picture." This may be the only thing to keep her occupied—to keep her from entering another daze.

Hettie takes the crayons and paper from me. "Of what?"

"Of anything," I say. "Of us...of that castle I always tell you we're going to live in when we're older. You can draw us as princesses in beautiful ballgowns."

"Why?"

"It'll make me happy to get another one of your amazing pictures," I say. "Take your time, and when I come back, you can show it to me, okay?"

"Where are you going?"

"I'm going to be right back. But you have to stay here and draw a picture for me. I need something to hang up by my bed, and you always draw the best pictures."

Hettie smiles. It's the first genuine smile she has given me in a few days, but I don't let it fool me. She's still not completely right.

"Okay," she says. "After I finish, will we go to the well?"

"The picture, Hettie," I say. "Focus on the picture."

To my relief, she doesn't question me again. Instead, she lowers herself to the floor and places a blank sheet of paper in front of her.

When I've convinced myself she'll stay put, I hurry down the hall to Mother's room. I'm not careful about opening the door quietly. I want her to hear me.

To my surprise, she's not sleeping. She sits on the edge of her bed, rubbing her temples as if she just woke up.

"Hey there, sweetie," she says when she sees me.

I nod a "hello" to her. "Do you want to go for a walk with me?" I ask.

Mother stands up, slower than a normal person would. It's as if something invisible tethers her to her bed, and moving away from it is an ordeal that requires the strength of ten men. Still, she stands and straightens herself, no doubt to appear stronger than she feels.

"I don't know, hon'," she says. "My energy is zapped today."

"A walk will help," I say. "We'll only take a short one."

Mother purses her lips and takes a moment to think.

"What about Hettie?" she asks after a long moment.

"Hettie's preoccupied," I say. "She's drawing."

"I don't want to leave her home alone."

That's convenient, I think, *because you have no problem leaving her unattended while you sleep during the day.*

As always, my thought is accompanied by guilt. It's not her fault. And yet, the way Hettie looked when I came home—emotionless and absent to the world—makes me want to reproach Mother for never checking on her.

"A short walk," I say. "We'll only be gone for a little bit. Besides, this is the safest place she can be."

"How about another time?"

I shake my head. "Mom, I really need this."

Now she looks concerned. "Are you alright?"

"I just want to spend some time with you. It's beautiful outside today...really sunny. Besides, I think a walk will do us both some good."

That, and I need to test if Wayne's theory is true so I know whether or not to return to him for more answers.

"Hettie's seven," I continue. "And she's not going to go anywhere right now. She's very busy with her drawing."

Mother sighs. "A quick walk, okay? I'm low on energy."

I can't believe she actually agreed to come along.

"That's fine, it'll be really short, just enough to get us some fresh air," I say as my chest tightens. I really hope I sound nonchalant, but I'm not sure I do.

Though Mother is still hesitant about leaving Hettie home, my constant reassurance that we're not walking far eases her mind. She's slow and sluggish in the beginning, but the summer air helps with her energy.

For a fleeting moment, I wonder what would happen if I told her everything. It's a thought that, although tempting, is too risky to become a decision. First, I need to see what she sees, just like Ava suggested.

"Hettie and I ride down here almost every day," I say, trying to make conversation.

Mother stays quiet for a moment, and I listen to the sound of the loose gravel crunch beneath our shoes.

"We've been exploring downtown Larton. That's where we met Ava," I add.

"I'm glad you two have found things to do," Mother says. She pauses and takes a moment for herself, letting the world around her—the world she's hardly seen in the past few months—settle in. "Larton isn't too bad, is it?"

I shake my head. "No, it's not. It's kind of nice."

My comment seems to comfort her, but I can't be sure. I feel like I've become worse at reading her emotions lately. Either that or she's gotten better at hiding them.

"Of course, I don't like that whole statistic about the rates of missing children, but it really is a cute town," she adds after a moment.

"Honestly, Mom, I've never felt unsafe downtown."

Mother gives me a nervous smile. Regardless of any emotions she feels—or doesn't feel—she will always be a worrier. We're a lot alike in that way.

"Well," she says, "it certainly is a cozy place to live."

I nod in response. Then, cautiously, hoping that I'm as good of an improviser as Ava seems to think I am, I say, "Do you want to see something Hettie and I found?" Even asking makes my stomach do a flip. "It's close," I continue. "It's the cutest thing—a little well."

I really hope this is a good idea.

"How close?" Mother asks, quickly glancing back in the direction of Aunt Vivian's house.

"A few minutes," I respond.

"Alright," Mother says, nodding to me. "Lead the way."

I don't know whether to feel overjoyed that she's agreed to accompany me or worried about what she'll see, so I try my best not to feel anything at all.

Once we reach the fork in the road leading to the forest, I quicken my pace. I just want to get this over with.

"How far off the trail?" Mother asks when she realizes I intend to go farther into the forest.

"Not far," I say. "Don't worry."

My heart flutters faster the closer we get to the grove. What if it *knows* I'm close? What if it understands my intentions? I can't possibly predict what we'll see when we get to the well, and it's the unknown that bothers me the most. If she does see the well—the staircase—what then? Do I tell her everything? Perhaps it will be best. I can finally unburden myself and confide in someone other than Ava. But what if she doesn't see it? Then what? I'm not sure which option I prefer.

My eyes fall to the tattoo on my wrist as I remember the Rosella that landed on my arm. It knew me, just like the dolphins knew Hettie and how the world knew what we wanted. The gazebo, the jewelry, the animals...all of them enticed us by appealing to what we liked.

Mother notices where I'm looking.

"Every time I see your tattoo," she says softly, "I remember how angry I got at your father when you showed me what he did."

I try to smile. It doesn't work.

"But," she continues, "I also remember how much he made you laugh as a kid. He used to make me laugh too, if you'd believe it."

"He did?"

Mother nods. "All the time."

"I don't remember that," I say.

Silence follows. A light breeze makes leaves on the forest floor drift across the surface. Some gently scuff our shoes as they pass by. It reminds me of summers in Oregon.

"I don't think I've ever told you this," I venture slowly, "but Dad only gave me that tattoo because I begged him to. It wasn't his idea. It was mine."

I study her face to gauge her reaction, but she only smiles gently. "I know," she says.

"Then why were you so mad at him?"

"Because he should have said no."

Despite how anxious I feel, I'm finally able to manage a genuine smile. "Since when did you know Dad to ever say no?"

This time, when Mother smiles, it isn't as empty as it usually is. "Never," she admits.

We walk in silence for a bit longer, but it's comfortable instead of strained. We must be approaching the grove, but I don't see it yet.

"You know," says Mother in less than a whisper, "I used to get so angry with your father for being an absent parent. I would nag him all the time about being more responsible. About being there for you and Hettie." She pauses and exhales. I can tell she's ashamed. "And now I realize I'm being the same as he was."

"You're not." I'm not sure I completely believe what I'm saying, but I want to make her feel better.

"No," she says. "I am. Maybe for different reasons than your dad..."

"More important reasons."

"Still. What do reasons matter when the consequences are the same?"

"They matter." I bite my lip nervously. "It's not your fault. You're ill and he wasn't. He was just irresponsible."

"Maybe," Mother says. "I've been thinking a lot about our conversation this morning. Vivian has told me the same thing over and over again, but it was different coming from you...coming from my own daughter."

"Did you change your mind?"

Mother makes a movement with her head, but I can't tell if it's a nod. "How much farther are you planning to go?" she asks.

I stop walking, suddenly realizing how far we've gone. Why haven't we passed the grove? It wasn't hard to miss when I was here with Hettie or Ava.

"I don't...I don't see it," I mumble to myself. My heart rate increases.

We must have missed it. I turn around and walk away from Mother, peering through the trees and seeing nothing but acres of shrubs and tree trunks. There's no parting in the forest that makes a circle around a grove. It's as if the well was never there to begin with.

When my hands begin shaking, I try hard to consciously still them so Mother doesn't notice.

"It's not here," I say. "It's...it's gone."

"What do you mean?"

"I thought..."

I hadn't known what to expect, and yet I hadn't needed to expect anything at all. The well and the grove are gone, concealed by something I can't fathom. Is it even here anymore? Has it disappeared entirely?

I look back at Mother again, who waits for me to say something.

"I guess I forgot where it was," I say, trying to shrug casually. "I don't know my way around this forest like I did back home in Oregon."

Mother raises an eyebrow, but doesn't seem skeptical. "That's okay," she says. "I'd like to get back to Hettie, anyway. We've been gone a bit longer than I thought we would be."

I nod, my throat dry. "Yeah," I say. "Good idea." Then, so as not to seem suspicious, I add, "Maybe when I learn my way around here better, I'll show it to you. I think you'd like it."

Mother nods. "I'm sure I will."

She must notice that I look a bit distraught because she puts her hand on my shoulder. "The walk was nice," she says, "even if we didn't find the well you wanted to show me. We should go on more together."

"Yeah," I say. "I like that idea."

We head back to the house, once again in silence. Though getting Mother outside with me would usually be somewhat of a victory, I don't have the mind to celebrate. Instead, my thoughts wander to Hettie—to her sleep-like trances, to the well, and to the world beneath it that chooses the people it reveals itself to. I think of the underground moon, and how perhaps it isn't a moon at all, but instead a watchful eye that knows what it wants and how to get it.

Though my emotions are conflicted, I do know one thing for certain: Wayne was telling the truth.

CHAPTER 19
THE OPEN WINDOW

That evening, Aunt Vivian comes home a little earlier, and we all eat dinner together. Hettie seems normal, much to my surprise. She talks about her drawings and eats a fair amount, and after dinner, she shows me the picture of the castle that she drew for me. I hang it above my bed, which delights her. It seems, if only for a moment, that things have gone back to normal. She hasn't asked about the well again, and blind hope reassures me that perhaps she forgot.

As per my inherent nature, though, I'm not entirely optimistic. I still worry that I'll wake the next morning and find her in another daze, or that she'll bring up returning to the well again and I'll be unable to persuade her otherwise.

Before I fall asleep, I decide that regardless of how Hettie is acting, I need to see Wayne again. Whether or not he tries to kick me out won't matter because he won't succeed. When I see him next, I won't leave until every question I have has been answered.

I don't realize how tired I am until I get into bed. Worrying nonstop for the past few days has made my whole body heavy, and I fall asleep to the gentle breeze coming in through the open window of our bedroom.

When I wake up, it's three in the morning. For a moment, I lie staring at the clock on my bedside table, wondering why I woke so suddenly.

Then, I feel it.

It's as though someone crammed both hands down through the top of my skull, forcing my neck and chest apart from within. Bony claws wind their way through my body, and with one nerve-shattering wrench tear me inside out, shredding me apart, turning my raw and tender nerves to the air.

I lie back on my pillow, but its softness has been transformed into rasp-like points. I'm like the pillowcase itself, turned inside out—exposed, as though I've been stripped of my skin, left squirming in pain as the air pricks my every muscle and vein. Everything in the room is the same, yet nothing is on its proper side; nothing is where I expect it to be. It's like stepping through a mirror and being at home, yet in an unfamiliar house.

I stare into the semi-darkness, the doorway throbbing with each beat of my pounding heart. With every pulse, it recedes, and as it gets smaller, it pulls me toward it. I close my eyes and will the pulling to stop, but I open them again in a flash.

The specter behind my lids is even more unreal than the nightmarish situation in which I've found myself.

It's the underground moon, or perhaps only a projection of it. It is both above and within me, beckoning me with every glint of white light. It's full this time too, and something is wrong. It's not a beautiful full moon like the real one—it's sinister and menacing, and it wants something desperately. It wants to devour. To take. Something silvery oozes from its craters, and then the moon flickers off, like a dying light bulb.

The curtain flaps at the window Hettie left open. I tense, expecting the breeze to sear across my body. Instead, a mist of silence settles over me, and my feelings fade into nothingness. The curtain still flaps, but noiselessly, uselessly. No breeze moves through it. I watch the door through half-closed eyes. I can't wake myself up, not entirely. I'm stuck between sleep and wake, wondering if I'm acting at all of my own accord.

The edges of my vision blur and fade, leaving the doorway as a focal point. I try to look away, but the doorway twists slowly to the left, pulling the intersecting lines of the ceiling and walls with it. Like the spiral of a whirlpool, it pulls.

I try to reach out for the head of my bed to hold myself back, but I can't be sure if I'm really reaching back at all. The pull on my feet increases. It feels so real—not at all like a dream. I try to scream, but no noise escapes my throat. Perhaps it's futile to resist, but the thought of what lies beyond evokes such a primal fear in me that I can't help but lash out.

Finally, my hand touches the headboard. I clench my fingers around it, holding on with the strength of my rage.

Something shatters faintly in the distance. The pull lessens slightly, and I blink at the doorway. Slowly—almost in surrender—it rights itself, untwisting the walls and the ceiling. Objects begin to take their place in the order of the room like a pattern of crumpled cloth smoothed by unseen hands.

I reach out tentatively and touch my head. I feel my hair beneath my fingers and realize that I haven't been cut in half at all.

I'm awake now, this time for real. I'm okay. I spread out my hand and lay it on my chest, feeling my heart rate steadily decrease.

I turn my head to Hettie's cot and hear her stir in her sleep. Everything is back to normal. I'm too frightened to sit up, though, so I continue to stare at Hettie's silhouette, my body rigid and my eyes wide.

The curtain flaps again, shifting my attention. In my half-sleep-induced, half-terrified state, I realize that no breeze has entered the open window.

CHAPTER 20
SISTERS DON'T LIE

The world knows. The underground moon knows.

It knows who I am; it has shown me that much. But after my dream, which was far too lucid to really be a dream at all, I suspect it knows much more than I previously thought. It knows what I intend to do. It knows I want answers— that I will protect Hettie at all costs. Most of all, it knows how much I fear it.

But not all is lost. I know what it wants too. It wants more trees—more graves—this time with new faces. It wants a moon that is fuller and brighter than ever before. It wants Hettie, and it's angry with me that I'm trying to keep her from it.

There are some things that only the intuition knows. Although I've always found solace in logic, it doesn't belong here. I can writhe in my discomfort and spend every waking moment watching over Hettie, making sure she doesn't return or fall into another daze, or I can get the answers I need.

Hettie is gone when I wake up. Fear courses through my body when I realize. I quickly get out of bed and rush to the kitchen, praying that I'll find her there. Is this what my life is going to be like from now on? Always worrying that it will successfully lure her? Never truly resting when she's not with me?

When I see her sitting with Mother and Aunt Vivian, the fear releases its hold on me. I focus on suppressing my conflating emotions as I sit down so that I don't get any questions. I think I'm doing a good job until Aunt Vivian raises an eyebrow.

"Feeling okay, Ro?" she asks.

"Good," I say. "Yes. Fine. Just tired."

She passes me her coffee cup. "I only took a sip," she says.

I inhale the bitter warmth of the coffee but pass it back to her. The thought of drinking or eating anything right now makes me nauseous.

"I'm okay," I say. "But thanks."

She looks surprised, but takes the cup back anyway.

"Where is Ro?" she teases. "You're the last person I'd think would refuse coffee."

"I know." I try to grin. "Guess I'm just not feeling it today."

Aunt Vivian shrugs but doesn't say anything else.

Mother shifts in her seat nervously, clasping her hands together. For a moment, she's silent. I can tell that she's searching for the right words to say whatever is on her mind. I observe her slow, yet restless movements. Finally, she speaks.

"I've decided to sell our house back in Oregon."

I hadn't expected that. I'm silent for a moment, and then I look over at Hettie, whose face is just as blank as my own.

"Why?" I ask. It's a stupid question. I know why, of course. I heard the conversation Mother and Aunt Vivian had a few nights ago. But I want to hear it from Mother.

"It's unreasonable to keep it," Mother says. "Aunt Vivian and I have been talking about it. With everything that has happened, I think staying here is the best option."

"I just..." my words fade in and out. "I...I just thought that we'd go back, at least eventually."

Mother looks down at her hands. Instead of focusing on her, I glance over at Hettie, who is still emotionless.

Aunt Vivian notices too. "Hettie, hon? Did you hear?"

Hettie nods.

"Do you feel okay with that?"

She nods again. "I don't care."

I stare at her for a moment. That wasn't the reaction I thought she'd have, even with how odd she's been acting.

What makes Hettie's indifference even worse is how upset *I* feel about the news. I always hoped that, in time, when Mother got better, we would go back—that our time in Tennessee was temporary and soon the Oregon forest I love so much would be mine to return to. But the worst part is that now I know how close the well and its underground world will always be. Now I know for certain that I can't escape it—that Hettie can't escape it. Not by moving away, at least.

My nightmare from last night creeps back into my mind. The moon—the full moon with its silvery craters and its insidious presence—hovers right in front of me. It's only a memory, but it's very real too.

"Ro?"

The words are muffled.

"Ro."

I blink and look over at Aunt Vivian.

"Did you hear me?" she asks.

I shake my head numbly and try to swallow, but I can't. Something both within my ears and very far off rings.

"I said, in a few weeks, all of us will fly to Oregon to get your belongings or things you'd like to take back here with you."

"And then we'll never get to see it again?"

Aunt Vivian tucks a strand of hair behind her ear. "What do you mean?"

"Just like that," I say, "we'll leave Oregon and never go back. Is that what you mean?"

Aunt Vivian sighs. "We can always visit if you want."

I curl my lip. It's not the same.

There are a thousand things I want to say, but somehow none of them come out. Instead, I shrug. "Okay."

"I know it's tough," Aunt Vivian says gently. "I know Oregon was familiar and Tennessee is not. I know—"

"It's fine," I snap. Hot tears prick the corner of my eyes, threatening to spill out. That sliver of hope I so often search for has deserted me entirely. I look at Mother, but it doesn't seem like she's going to say anything. Then, I shift my attention to Hettie, who picks at her food absentmindedly.

I stand abruptly. "I'm going to go see Ava."

Aunt Vivian smiles at me, but it's a weak smile that is hesitant of my reaction. She nods and says, "Are you sure you don't want breakfast?"

"I'll eat there," I say. It's a lie, of course. I'm not going to see Ava at all. She's working and I don't want to wait for her to get off. Instead, I'm going to see Wayne—to get into the complex somehow and force him to talk to me.

If my nightmare hadn't convinced me that seeing Wayne was paramount, Mother's news did. Now that I know the plan is to stay in Tennessee indefinitely, close to the well and its hungry underground world, I'm desperate. I don't know exactly what it is I want besides answers, but I suppose it's as good a place as any to start.

When I return to my bedroom to get dressed, I take a moment to observe my surroundings. The permanence of it all slowly settles in, but Hettie's soft footsteps behind me snap me out of my growing self-pity.

When she enters the room, she shuts the door behind her and stares at me for a moment.

"What, Hettie?" I say. My tone is tinged with irritation, and I feel a bit guilty.

"Are you mad?"

I shake my head as Hettie climbs onto her cot. I tense, bracing myself for the moment she asks me about going back to the well, but it doesn't come.

"When are you coming back?" she asks.

I shrug as I pull on my clothes. "I'll try to be home before evening," I say as I smooth my wrinkled shirt. When I realize my hands are shaking, I drop them to my sides and try to still them. "What are you planning to do today?"

Hettie plays with the seam of her comforter. "I don't know," she says. "Wait for you, maybe."

My heart sinks. I hesitate before putting on my shoes. Maybe I shouldn't leave, especially now that she's acting a little more normal.

"What about drawing?" I ask. "You'll be so busy that you'll forget I'm even gone."

"That's all I ever do," she says.

"But you love drawing."

Hettie shrugs. "It's okay."

I sit across from her on my bed. "Just okay?"

When she doesn't answer, I bite my lip, trying to ignore the knot in my stomach. "I don't have to go," I say. "I can stay here with you."

Hettie doesn't respond. For a moment, she looks at me with a blank expression, then gets up and sits at the foot of my bed.

"I had a dream last night," she mumbles after a moment.

I feel the blood drain from my face as my vision slowly blurs. As quietly as I can, I ask, "About what?"

"About *it*," she says. "About the world."

I'm not sure if it's adrenaline or something else that courses through my body, but I suddenly feel very dizzy and weak.

"Do you remember what happened?" I ask.

I don't bother to compose myself. My nightmare has returned to me in full force, and I wonder if the room really is spinning or if it's just me.

"It was the best dream I've ever had," Hettie says. "The moon was in our room, and it was full. It was brighter than the sun and it made me feel happier than I've ever felt before. It told me that everything will be okay."

My breathing turns shallow. I lower my voice even further as I say, "I had a dream about the moon too. But it wasn't a good dream."

Hettie narrows her eyebrows. "Why not?"

"Because the moon is evil, Hettie," I say, hating how this world has gotten into both of our heads—hating how it's fooling Hettie and taunting me at the same time. "It wants to hurt us...to hurt *you*. Do you remember that man we ran into that day after we danced in the gazebo? The one who was angry?"

Hettie nods.

"He knows about the world," I say. "And he told me it was bad. He told me it feeds on kids. Kids like you and me."

"He was lying, then," Hettie says. "I know he was lying."

"How in the world can you know he was lying?" I feel my fear turning into anger; those two emotions dance about each other and mold into an overpowering medley of hate and hopelessness.

"Because the moon told me that the world was good," Hettie says. "In my dream, the moon said that the world loved me and that it has everything we'll ever need. It has dolphins and birds and music and jewelry for fancy balls. And it misses us. It misses both of us...because *you* won't let us return."

Her face twists into an unreadable expression, and I can't tell if she is about to cry or yell at me. "And *I* miss it, Ro," she says. "I miss it so much, but I don't go back because you told me not to. But then you leave me alone in this room and all I can do is draw and pretend like I've gone back to the well."

"Hettie," I say in a strangled whisper. "You know I would never lie to you about anything. I've never lied to you before. I'm not lying now."

"But you *have* lied to me before," she says.

Something inside of me shrivels up. "When?"

"That night you told me about Mommy getting better," she says. "You said that she would get better and we would all paint our nails together. And...and then we came back home and she was *not* better."

"I wasn't lying," I say, choking on my own words. "I was just wrong."

"You're wrong now too," she snaps. "You're wrong about the world and the moon and *everything*."

"I'm not wrong, Hettie," I say. "I've never been surer about anything in my life. I know it sounds crazy, but it wants you to not believe me. It wants you to think it's good and that it loves you and wants you to come back. But it's lying."

Hettie shakes her head but doesn't say anything.

"I lied about going to see Ava," I whisper, hating myself for admitting to yet another lie that Hettie can hold against me. "I'm going to see Wayne. That's the name of the man we met. He has answers and he's going to give them to me. When I come home, I'll tell you everything I've learned. We'll work through this together."

I watch a tear fall down Hettie's cheek and onto my bed. I take her hands in my own, look straight into her eyes, and firmly say, "You're my sister. And I'm yours. And sisters don't lie to each other. I would never lie to you."

"You *just* said you lied about going to see Ava."

I hold back a groan. "Yes, I know, but that was for a good reason." I purse my lips and do my best to hide my conflating emotions. "Sometimes I may be wrong and sometimes you may think I'm being mean or bossy, but right now, you need to trust me," I say. "You're doing so well—not telling Mom or Aunt Vivian, staying here and listening to me...I know it's hard. But sometimes, you have to do things you don't like doing in order to stay safe."

Hettie lets go of my hands and wipes at her eyes. "I thought that maybe when Mommy said we were going to stay in Tennessee, you would change your mind about everything."

I stay quiet for a moment. It seems that no matter how hard I try, Hettie's love for and infatuation with the underground world will always surpass any arguments I make.

"Do you remember *Sleeping Beauty*?" I ask after a few more moments of silence. It's a rhetorical question, of course, but I wait for Hettie to nod before I continue. "Do you remember the spinning wheel and how the witch made the princess fall into a trance so that she would prick her finger, even though the wheel was evil?"

"Yes," Hettie says between sniffles.

"Everybody else knew the spinning wheel was bad, but the princess didn't. She wasn't herself...she was in a trance and she wasn't thinking correctly, so she pricked her finger and fell into a deep sleep."

"I remember," Hettie says.

"You asked me if I would save you if you were going to prick your finger on a spinning wheel," I say. "Do you remember?"

Hettie nods.

"*This* is me saving you."

A quizzical look settles onto Hettie's face, replacing her sadness with confusion.

"The underground world is like the witch and the spinning wheel," I continue, hoping—praying—that this will click with her. "It's making you think it's good so you'll go back. And like the princess, you don't understand how bad it is. You're obsessed with this world, Hettie. You may not realize it, but you are. You fall into dazes and dream about it and talk about it all the time."

I watch Hettie's eyes as what I'm saying sinks in.

"Let me go and talk to Wayne," I say. "I'm going to find out as much as I can about this world. But I need you to be smarter than the princess. I need you to fight every urge you have to go back."

"I *am* fighting it."

"And," I say, forcing myself to sound stern despite my wavering confidence, "I need you to understand what this world is doing and that I'm trying to help you."

Hettie looks off to the side, but I move my face so it's back in front of hers. "Do you understand, Hettie?"

I can hear my heart beat in my ears. I hold my breath, waiting for her answer.

When she nods, I audibly exhale.

"I need you to say it."

"I understand," she says.

I feel the hot tears return to my eyes. I clench my jaw, willing them to go away.

"I'll be as quick as I can," I say. "Wayne doesn't like me. He doesn't want to give me answers. But I'm going to make him talk to me. We'll go from there."

"Okay," Hettie says weakly. I can tell she's still upset, but I don't linger. Instead, I slip on my shoes, leave Hettie with her crayons and paper—desperately hoping she'll find some peace in drawing—and go outside to mount my bike.

My determination exudes itself through my pedaling. I don't slow down or stop until I've reached downtown Larton, and even then, despite my aching lungs and the creeping hunger I feel after skipping breakfast, my resolve has increased tenfold.

CHAPTER 21
FIRE ESCAPE

The sight of the brownstone apartment complex, despite its unassuming appearance, makes my stomach churn and my heart race.

My uneasiness won't deter me, though, especially since it's nothing compared to the nerve-shattering terror that my nightmare provoked.

If the underground world has the power to get inside my head like that—to get inside of Hettie's—then I'd be an idiot to underestimate its power and even more of an idiot to give up on Wayne.

I dismount my bike and move it off the sidewalk, then return to the entrance of the complex and wait for someone to come out. I hope they won't question me when I enter without a key.

I sit outside the entryway gate and rest my elbows on my knees. Someone will have to come out eventually. Larton may be rural, but it isn't empty.

Ten minutes pass, then twenty, and I can feel the impatience start to set in.

I could wait for Ava to get off of work—or perhaps I could simply pop into the diner and ask to borrow her key—but I know that doing so will only elicit questions from her, and I'm not in the headspace to entertain her curiosity at the moment. Right now, my focus is on getting the answers I need.

When I hear the entry door of the complex open, I spin around. Two boys who look like they're in middle school stand near the gate. One holds a battered skateboard and the other walks with his arms crossed as if he hasn't a care in the world. I wish I felt like that.

When the boy holding the skateboard pushes open the gate, I jump up and reach out my hand to keep the gate open so it doesn't close and lock itself. Both boys look surprised at my eagerness.

I smile awkwardly at them. "Forgot my key."

The boy with the skateboard gives me a subtle smile in response, and his friend doesn't acknowledge me at all. I hold my breath as both go back to talking to each other and head down the sidewalk. When they turn the corner, I feel myself relax.

Once I'm inside the complex, I take the stairwell in bounds to the fourth floor. I don't hesitate or stop to catch my breath. Instead, I walk down the hall, which feels more daunting than it did when I was with Ava, and stand in front of apartment 427.

Now is not the time to overthink. I raise my fist and knock so loudly that it's more of a pound than a knock. To my surprise, Wayne opens the door immediately.

I hardly have time to read his expression because he grabs my shoulders and pushes me against the wall.

"What is wrong with you?" he hisses. "Do you not know when to stop? Are you that thick, girl? Do you seriously not remember what I *explicitly* told you last time I answered your questions?"

His breath reeks of alcohol and smoke. I push his hands off my shoulders, but I don't move.

"I don't care what you told me," I bite back with ten times his venom. "I don't care what you want. Do you really think *I* want to keep coming back here?"

Wayne glares at me, and if it weren't for how terrified I was of the underground world, I would be scared of him. His face is dead-white, his lips are shaking in anger, and his eyes that once held a haunted, forlorn look now emanate anger that is entirely directed at me.

"It's not getting better," I say through bared teeth. "My sister is not getting better. It's in both of our heads. I had a nightmare last night that was so real I nearly thought it was going to kill me. Then my sister tells me *she* had a dream, only hers made her want to go back to the well. So don't tell me again that I just need to 'give it time' and it will all get better because I think you're full of shit. I think you just want me out of your life. But that's too bad, Wayne, because I'm going to stay here until I get answers. You're the only one who knows a goddamn thing about this place and what it's doing to my sister...what it's doing to both of us. I want what you know."

Wayne blinks at me. The anger in his eyes fades in and out. I wish I could tell what he's thinking, but it's like trying to discern emotion out of a rock.

"Fine," he says. "But we don't talk here."

I stare back at him, blinking in shock. "Really?" I say. "You're...you're going to talk to me?"

He nods. "But we don't talk here," he repeats.

He motions for me to follow him. I do, completely stunned that he gave in.

"Where are we going?" I ask, keeping with his brisk pace and trying to glean any semblance of a reaction from him.

He doesn't answer me, but I don't push it. After all, he's going to give me answers. I'll finally know what's going on and perhaps be one step closer to helping Hettie get rid of her obsession with the well and what's beneath it. I'll know what my nightmare meant and what the world wants. I'll know what the trees are for, who the carvings are of, and why something as unfathomable as the underground moon exists. Perhaps Wayne knows how this world came to be, or maybe he even has ideas about how to get rid of it.

I follow him down the stairwell, glee coming to a crescendo in my chest.

I knew persistence would work. It always does, at least eventually. Though the viscous fear in my chest remains, hope alleviates a bit of it, making me all the more certain that knowledge will provide respite.

We exit the complex and Wayne pushes open the gate. He gestures for me to go in front of him, and I do, feeling lighter than I have in quite some time.

And then I hear the gate close behind me.

I whirl around and watch Wayne as he turns back to the complex.

"What are you doing?" The panic is evident in my voice.

"I told you to screw off," Wayne says without looking back at me.

I stand there, feeling more idiotic than I ever have in my life, as he enters the complex and slams the door behind him.

For five minutes—maybe ten—I remain, unmoving, unsure of what to do. How could I have been that stupid to truly think he was going to help? Finally, when I pull myself out of my state of shock and embarrassment, rage takes over. It fills my lungs and my throat, then my face and head, boiling over until I can no longer stay still. The rage morphs into aggression, and suddenly my limbs do not obey me. Using all my force, I slam my foot into the entryway gate— one time, two times, then twenty.

I want to scream. I want to break down the gate and his apartment door, and continue screaming and breaking things until he can't say no. Instead, I turn around and walk away.

I don't think I have the capacity to wait any longer for someone who can let me in—for Ava, for someone in the apartment, for anyone.

I feel the overpowering sense of failure creep in, then guilt, and I start to cry. Ashamed of myself for being so gullible and for breaking down in public, I turn into a dark and narrow alleyway at the side of the complex and try to compose myself, finding that the lack of light helps me feel a little less vulnerable and pathetic.

I try to blink away my tears, but the more I blink, the more come.

I may have been naive to trust Wayne, but at least I'm not selfish. At least I'm trying. How could someone who knows so much be so unwilling to help, especially if helping could save a little girl?

When I think of Hettie, I start to cry even harder. I told her that I would get answers, but my stupidity and gullibility robbed me of that chance.

I look up, following the wall of the complex to where it ends. I study the sky and the thin, wispy clouds above. In the distance, I see the moon—the real moon—faded by daylight but still present. It hovers in the sky, and its purity overtakes me. It isn't bad or good, it just *is*. It exists without wanting or needing; it doesn't pay mind to the people thousands of miles away. It is, in every way, different from the underground moon.

My eyes fall to my feet again but stop midway when I see a ladder. It's long, thin, and looks poorly put together, but it's a ladder nonetheless, and it's part of a fire escape that leads directly into the complex.

The hope that had so quickly deserted me only moments ago rushes back, and I approach the ladder on eager feet.

Overflowing trash cans, papers, and bottles force me to pick my way carefully. The ladder is a couple yards off the ground—much too high for me to reach on my own—but a desolate trash can a few paces away catches my eye.

I rush over to it and turn it upside down. A few bottles and wadded up napkins fall to the concrete, and once it's empty, I push my makeshift step stool beneath the ladder, feeling a soft breeze flit through my hair that beckons me to continue.

I can't believe I'm doing this, but the very little that is left of my motivation diminishes my doubt. I climb up on the trash can and reach for the ladder. The wind picks up, swirling the papers on the ground. The first rung is still too high up.

I groan aloud. Maybe this isn't worth it. Maybe I should just wait for Ava, or maybe I should go home and work through this with Hettie on my own. So far, Wayne has turned me away three times. What's stopping him from turning me away a fourth?

I lift my chin in disdain and jump down from the trash can, turning my back defiantly on the building. But as I step away and begin to move back toward the street, I think of Hettie. A surge of anger replaces my dejection and makes my face hot.

I jump on the trash can again, and this time, I lunge for the ladder. With one tremendous, hefty effort, I grab it and push my feet against the wall to pull myself up. I pause while

I breathe in trembling gulps of air. I lean against the brick wall for a moment and collect myself while I observe the ladder.

Bolts and rungs are missing, and the coating of rust on the metal railing chafes my hands. I'm determined now, though, and my hands grip tightly while I use my feet to feel around for a solid hold.

All of the sudden, like a shot, my face and chest hit the ladder. My arm jerks downward while a rung tumbles to the ground, making the whole structure shake. Tiny pieces of stone and brick sift down beside me. I clutch the railing in terror, desperately trying to regain balance.

I don't want to disturb the ladder any further, so I increase my tempo. Between the rungs, I can see the ground below.

As I struggle to keep my hold on the crumbling fire escape, I begin to feel a bit foolish for making such an effort to speak to Wayne. I shake the feeling off. That's the last thing that will stop me.

Instead, I shift my focus to the landing above. It's almost at the top of the building, but it gives way straight to the exit. Or, perhaps, in my case, an entrance.

On shaking hands and knees, I finally pull myself up to the platform. I stay for a moment, worshipping the grated metal beneath me. It isn't until I come to a stand that I put my hand to my face and realize my cheek is bleeding. I must have cut myself when I hit the ladder. I ignore the blood and reach out for the door, feeling the ingot push bar on my palms and hearing the satisfying click as the door opens.

I don't think about what I'm going to say or do. I don't bother to wipe the blood on my cheek away or compose myself. Instead, I follow the stairwell to the fourth floor, vowing that this will be the last time I come here uninvited.

I storm down the hallway, grateful that nobody is there to see me, and when I reach Wayne's door, I give it the hardest kick I can rather than knocking.

I don't just give it one kick. I continue kicking until the door opens and I'm face to face with Wayne.

Instead of blowing up at me, or yelling, or pushing me against the wall again, Wayne only utters a shocked laugh. Although this surprises me, I don't let my emotions show. I only glower at him until he speaks.

"Jesus Christ, kid," he says. "You're batshit crazy."

"Are you going to turn me away again?" I ask, struggling to regain my breath.

Wayne wavers for a moment. It's with pride that I realize he doesn't know what to say.

"I'm going to keep coming back," I say. "As long as my little sister is unsafe, I will *always* come back. You can turn me away again, but it won't be the last time you do."

When he still doesn't respond, I add, "This morning, my mom told me that we're staying here permanently, which means I'm more desperate than ever for information that may help me understand what's going on and how to protect my sister."

"And what makes you so sure I have information that will help you?"

"Honestly, I don't know if you do," I admit. "But you're the best chance I've got."

Wayne shakes his head. "I can't believe I chose to warn you that day at the well," he mutters. "So much for good karma."

I glare at him, inciting a defeated groan from Wayne.

But this time, he doesn't close his door. He doesn't tell me to leave or trick me into doing so. Instead, he opens his door even wider, staring at me with a mixture of disdain and awe that I'm too exhausted to mind. Then, with his eyes, he gestures for me to enter his apartment.

"Don't make me regret this," he says.

CHAPTER 22
AN ENERGY SOURCE

Wayne's apartment is dark—the type of dark that mutes every color but still allows for enough light to illuminate the shredded paper and empty bottles that scatter the floor.

I imagine if he opened the windows and cleaned up, his apartment would look almost exactly like Ava's. And yet, the chill that has cast its shadow over every inch of this place exerts a stubborn permanence—something that no amount of light can change.

Although Wayne sleeps and breathes and eats here, his apartment feels as though it were abandoned long ago, leaving behind an unsettling air that is just as desolate and miserable as its owner.

I look around for a moment, trying to make out the pictures on the walls. They aren't of Wayne, or his family, or anyone he really seems to know at all. They're of children. Each picture is of a separate kid. Some seem to have been cut from newspapers, while others are better quality. The one similar thing about them is that all the children look younger than twelve.

One particular picture catches my eye. It's one of the few that are actually in color, and it's of a little girl with long brown hair and bangs that fall in front of her eyes. When I notice her dimples, I gasp.

All of these pictures are of the children whose faces are carved into the trees.

"Who is that?" I ask, pointing to her picture, yearning for a name so that she may become more than just a carving.

Wayne shuts his apartment door, which makes the room even darker. He walks over to me, kicking the discarded pieces of paper and empty bottles on the floor out of his way.

"Cora Nittly," he says. "Nine years old. She disappeared on the tenth of December in 1983. Her body was never found. Her parents were quoted saying she was withdrawn and dazed in the weeks before she went missing."

He stares at me for a moment, then turns back around and makes his way over to his couch. Once he sits down, he pulls out a pack of cigarettes and a lighter from the coffee table in front of him. For a slow and drawn-out moment, we don't do or say anything. I watch Wayne as he puts the cigarette to his lips, trying my best not to look disgusted when he exhales. It doesn't work. It seems I'm never very good at concealing my emotions.

"Wipe the disapproval off your face," he says, taking a prolonged inhale and letting the lighter dangle from his free hand. "I didn't let you into my apartment so you can judge my lifestyle."

"I don't disapprove. My dad smoked." My voice comes out meeker than I'd hoped. I don't add that it isn't the cigarettes that disgust me—it's the memories they bring.

Wayne grunts in response and lets the cigarette dangle from his lips. "Bet your dad doesn't know how you've been spending your time, does he? Following someone more than twice your age around..."

I sit in a chair right across from Wayne and the coffee table. The chair is old and the leather on its arms has started to peel, cluttering the floor beneath it with shriveled flakes.

"My dad's dead," I say, crossing both my legs and arms. "So, yeah, I guess he doesn't know."

Wayne doesn't reply, but I can tell he hadn't expected my response.

I inhale the strong odor of the room around me. It's a mixture of hard alcohol, smoke, and bitterness. I wonder how long Wayne has lived like this, though I'm not sure that "living" is the right word.

"I'm not following you around because I enjoy it," I continue. "I'm worried about Hettie. I told you she's seven, didn't I?"

Wayne grunts again in response. "Ask your questions," he says, stubbing out his cigarette in the ashtray that rests on the coffee table.

I glance back at the wall with the pictures. "Are all of those children victims of the underground world?"

Wayne nods.

"How do you know?"

"Research," comes the short, uncouth reply.

I feel my temper rising again. I take a deep breath to subdue it. "Research? What does that mean?" I ask.

"It means I've done my research," he says curtly. "I've spent a good twenty-five years compiling every missing child case in Larton—those that didn't end with bodies being found—and tracing them back to the well."

I gape at him and lower my voice, once again worried that it hears me—that it knows what I'm doing. "You mean you've traced all of these children back to the well...to the underground world?"

"I suspect there are more out there than the ones I've found," Wayne says. "Missing cases that go back before 'missing cases' were ever recorded."

I glance back over at the pictures, just now letting the sheer number of them sink in. There must be a hundred, maybe more. Then I remember how many trees I saw in the underground world.

"The trees," I think out loud, pointing to the wall. "They're the children from the trees, aren't they?"

"That's them."

"I had a dream about the trees," I say. "Only I knew that they weren't trees...they were graves. I saw my face on one tree and my sister's on another." I inhale a sharp, shaky breath. Reliving the dream makes me more emotional than I would have thought.

Wayne looks both at me and beyond me. His emotions, which were once vacant, have come to life a bit.

"How many times did you go down there?" he asks me after a few moments.

I open my mouth and then close it. Despite my shame, I decide I need to be completely honest with him. "Three times before you confronted us and another time after that," I say, looking down at my shoes to avoid his reaction. Oddly enough, he remains calm. "Hettie went back a fifth and I went to get her with Ava, but we didn't stay there," I add.

"I don't understand how it got this bad...how Hettie has become so affected after only five times."

"It only takes once," Wayne says. "The first time you and your sister went below, it latched on. It began feeding right away. But you're older and it likes her better. That's why you see the change in Hettie."

My mouth suddenly feels very dry.

"What made you realize you shouldn't return?" Wayne asks.

I pinch my lips together before answering. "My name is Rosella Gill," I say. "Rosella, like the bird. The fourth time my sister and I visited, a Rosella landed on my arm." I study his face but still can't quite read his expression. "I knew then how much it understood...about me, about my sister...I knew that it knew who we were and what we wanted. And since you had confronted us the day before..." My voice falters and I struggle to regain it, "...everything just started to make sense."

When he doesn't say anything, I continue.

"Every time my sister and I returned to the world, it had something new for us. The first time it was glass animals, then a thousand colorful stingrays in the lake, and then jewelry hanging from the trees and music in the gazebo. Each time, the moon would grow brighter and fuller, but not like the moon above. This moon was aware of our presence. The entire underground world was. It knew Hettie and I were lonely and sad and we needed a sanctuary, and so it gave us one." I shake my head. "Honestly, after you confronted us, I didn't want to believe you. So, like an idiot, I returned with my sister. That was the time I realized you were right. Hettie didn't, though. She *still* hasn't. She's already gone back once when I wasn't home, and I'm worried she'll do it again. I've tried my best to explain to her what's going on, but she doesn't understand. I don't think she wants to."

My chest constricts and I lower my voice to a whisper. "Hettie has been withdrawn lately too. She started falling into dazes and lashed out at me when I told her she wasn't allowed to go back. Yesterday, she stared out our bedroom window for hours and didn't realize how much time had passed. When I came home and saw her, it took me a while to snap her out of the trance she was in. Her eyes..." I pause for a moment, feeling pins and needles run down my spine when I think of the way she looked when I found her. "Her eyes had changed color," I finally say. "They'd gone from blue to this dull, absent gray."

I sit up straight and uncross my arms, hoping that my feigned confidence will make me feel somewhat better. "And then, last night, I had a nightmare. Only, it wasn't a nightmare; it was *real*. I felt like I was dying this terrible death, and the moon was shining over me, completely full, taunting me. It hated me...I could feel it. This morning, Hettie told me she had a similar dream, only hers was good. She said the moon told her it loved her and wanted her to come back. She said it *missed* her. I know this sounds crazy, but I'm certain that the world—the moon—is angry with me for keeping Hettie away."

Although Wayne's face remains still, it's clear that he's listening. His eyes meet my own, and I notice incredible concentration in them.

Then, he stands up abruptly. I follow him with my eyes as he walks over to a bookshelf, positioned haphazardly next to his fridge. He snatches a massive binder from the top shelf, filled to the brim with loose pages. When he returns to the couch, he drops it onto the coffee table with a resounding thud.

First, I look at Wayne, then the binder, and then back at Wayne, waiting for him to talk.

"It may take the form of a moon, but it isn't one," he finally says. "Don't let it fool you."

I blink back my shock. "What?"

"It's not a moon," he repeats, opening the binder and pushing it toward me. "It's an energy source."

CHAPTER 23
LILA

I look down at the page in front of me, which is nothing more than a picture of the real moon and its phases. I remember when I asked Mother about the moon phases the night after Hettie and I had discovered the underground world.

"The underground moon doesn't have phases like the real moon does," Wayne says, "because it isn't a moon at all. The fuller and brighter it is, the more energy it has acquired and the closer it is to achieving its end goal: feeding off of the child, or children, it has enticed. Children like your sister."

My stomach does a nauseating flip.

"Once it's full, it has won. It feeds off its victim, then goes back to where it started and waits for another to refill its energy with youth and innocence. All the while, it accumulates trees. Call them what you will—graves, carvings—they're all the same to the underground world. They're all just trophies."

When I feel my hands start to shake, I dig my fingers into my palms to still them.

"There are *hundreds* of trees down there," I say.

"And there are hundreds of victims," Wayne replies. "Every tree you saw when you visited beneath the well was once a child who had a family, a life, and a future. But it took that from them, and now they're nothing but carvings. Nothing but memoirs for the world that swallowed them whole."

Wayne flips to the middle of the binder, where he has collected newspaper clippings from over the years.

"I've cataloged every article I could find detailing missing children in Larton," he says. "The first one I have is from the 1940s, but I'm sure that this has been going on long before that."

He points at a browned and faded article, laminated for preservation. The boy pictured looks only six or seven, smiling with gapped teeth and tousled dark hair. Above his head reads *'Mr. and Mrs. Lewis of Larton, Tennessee, offer*

$8,000.00 REWARD for any information leading to the whereabouts of their missing child, Danny Lewis."

My heart sinks as I read it. I try to remember if I saw his face carved into one of the trees, but the sheer number of carvings has left my mind muddled and my memories blurred.

I flip through more pages only to find that they're all the same. A laughing boy pictured with his brother from 1968, a beaming little girl with coiled hair and bright, intelligent eyes from 1979—all victims of a hidden fate, lost from their families and their futures.

Wayne sits back as I continue flipping through the binder.

"How do you know all of these children were victims of the underground world?" I finally ask, closing the binder so I don't have to look at any more missing faces. "How do you know they weren't kidnapped or went missing some other way?"

"Because I've seen most of their faces carved into the trees," Wayne responds, looking me straight in the eye.

I knew that would be his answer, but I wanted to hear it from him. If he's seen their faces, then I know he has been beneath the well, just like Hettie and me.

"A few of the parents who were interviewed about their missing children also mentioned their kids talking about a secret world with a moon in the weeks leading up to their disappearance," Wayne adds. "But what kid doesn't enjoy making up stories or playing imaginary games? I imagine for many of the children, those stories weren't uncommon."

He opens the binder again to a page with multiple articles stapled together. I suspect he has the whole thing memorized.

"For a while, police thought that maybe a kidnapper was in Larton who would entice children by telling them stories of a fantasy world with a moon. But that led nowhere. After all, no bodies were ever found, and the disappearances weren't close enough together to be traced back to a single suspect."

I scan the page. The articles questioning the existence of a single kidnapper range from the 1960s to the 1980s, and after that, just like Wayne said, they stop. Law enforcement seemed to have given up on the whole "serial kidnapper" idea.

"The rate of missing children in Larton is high," Wayne continues. "Higher than most places, at least. It makes sense that police would've thought some kind of child predator was at fault."

*The rate of missing children...*what Aunt Vivian mentioned when we first moved here—what Mother is always so worried about. A predator does indeed exist, but not the kind people would expect. How had I not drawn the connection sooner?

I continue scanning the page until Wayne impatiently closes it again.

"How many times have you visited?" I ask, looking up from the coffee table and back at Wayne. "And why can *you* see it? I thought you said it chooses who it wants to be seen by, and it only chooses children who need it. You're not a child."

"Maybe he used to need it," I remember Ava saying. Maybe he did—maybe once, he was like Hettie, Ava, and me: lonely, dejected, and in need of something better. But something went awry with his story, that much I know. He didn't become one of the trees in the underground forest. Had he realized something was wrong about the place, just as I had? Had he been warned?

Wayne shifts in his seat. His hands linger at his binder. After a moment, he turns it over and opens the last page, where a picture of two children has been placed neatly into a laminated pocket. A scribbled note in the corner of the picture dates it back to 1963.

When he places it in front of me, it's the boy who stands out the most. He's tall and thin, with dark hair, a pale face, and eyes that smile even more than his mouth. He looks eleven or twelve, maybe even younger.

Though the boy's eyes are innocent and lively, it doesn't take me long to realize that it's Wayne.

Next, I study the little girl beside him. It's his sister; that much is obvious. She has his eyes and hair, but she looks much younger. I study her dark, pin-straight hair and her delicate, upturned nose. Have I seen her before, carved into a tree?

"That's Lila," Wayne says, his voice cracking. He clears his throat, trying to cover up the despondency that has crawled onto his face. "She was five in that picture. I had just turned twelve."

I study her face, which is just as gentle and pure as Hettie's. I wonder if, in another world, they could have been friends.

"We moved to Larton when I was thirteen and she was six. A year later she was dead. I was too, in a different way."

I trace my finger around Lila. She has a delicate air about her, much like a fairy. Then, it clicks.

"I saw her," I say, my heart nearly stopping. "I...I saw her face. It was the third time we went there. Her tree had a necklace hanging from it. Hettie pulled it off and gave it to me."

For the first time, the emotion on Wayne's face is easy to discern. He looks as though he is about to shatter into a thousand pieces.

"I can't do this," he whispers. Then, he looks back up at me and says, louder, "I'm sorry, Rosella. I can't do this."

"What? No...Wayne, I'm sorry I said that..." I'm such an idiot. Why can't I just hold my tongue?

"I told you not to make me relive this."

"You're already reliving this," I argue, pointing at the binder and the pictures of the children on his walls. "You're reliving it every single day. Why is talking to me so much worse?"

"You're here because I let you in," Wayne snaps. "This is my place. You're a guest. That means when I'm done, we're both done."

I shake my head. I'm not leaving—not now. "If you don't relive this," I say slowly, making sure he hears every word, "if you refuse to talk to me and hide all of the information you have in your apartment for nobody but yourself, then hundreds of more children will die. All the research you've done will have served no purpose at all. This world will keep doing what you and I both know it does—taking children...feeding on them." Saying the last part sends a nauseating tremor throughout my body. "Hundreds of children will share Lila's fate. My little sister may share Lila's fate."

I don't know what to say or how to convince him. "Lila wouldn't want that," I whisper.

Wayne glowers at me. "Don't tell me what Lila would and wouldn't want."

"You can't possibly think she'd want other children to die," I say, offense be damned. "Nobody would want that. Please, Wayne. I don't know what to do to help my sister. I need your help. I don't know as much about this place as you do."

"I don't know what you expect me to do," he says, shutting the binder and pulling it toward him, along with the picture of himself and Lila. "I can give you the information I have...I can tell you about all the children who have lost their lives to this place...but you still wouldn't be able to do anything. You still wouldn't be able to stop it from taking and feeding and continuing to live off of children. It has been doing this for generations, and it will continue doing so until time comes to an end and there are no kids left to take."

"There has to be a way to stop it," I say. "But we will never figure out how if we don't start somewhere."

"We?" Wayne shakes his head. "No. I agreed to tell you what I know and answer your questions. I did not agree to go on a mission to destroy this thing. I don't even know if that's possible."

"There has to be a way," I repeat, if only out of blind hope. "There *needs* to be a way. Now that my sister and I are moving to Larton permanently, I can't spend the rest of my life just praying that Hettie won't decide to return one day. I can't live like that. *She* can't live like that."

"I get it," Wayne says staunchly. "But I didn't agree to that part."

"Fine," I say, crossing my arms. "You didn't agree to help me destroy it. But you did agree to tell me what you know. So, please, Wayne...for Hettie and all the other children who may be victims in the future, tell me what you know."

Wayne juts out his lower jaw and steadily inhales, then takes out another cigarette and lights it. "You're a real trip, you know that?" he says as he stuffs his lighter into his pocket.

"Thanks."

"Didn't mean it as a compliment."

I ignore him. "So what do you know?"

Wayne takes his time with his cigarette, inhaling and exhaling a few times before he speaks. "I know that the world lives off children. The younger, the better. You don't see any faces older than twelve down there for a reason. Older kids are harder to entice."

I swallow hard before I speak. "What do you mean?" I manage when my voice obeys me. "And...and if that's the case, why can I see it? Why can Ava see it?"

"Maybe it's hoping an older kid will come along who will fall prey to its tricks. Maybe it doesn't want to give up the chance for more food." Wayne curls his lip and shrugs. "Younger children are easier, though, that's for sure. They're more innocent; they believe the world is good from the get-go. Children like your little sister...like Lila...the world *loves* them. It loves their imagination, their trust, and their virtue. The outside world hasn't ruined them yet. Magic worlds don't warrant questions to young children. Once a child grows older, though, they become more skeptical. Everything that place prides itself on being is questioned and dissected." He studies my face for a moment, then asks, "How old are you?"

"Fifteen."

"And I'm guessing you were much more hesitant to enter the well than your sister?" Wayne asks. "And once below, you likely questioned where you were, who had made the trees, how it could possibly exist...you didn't accept it immediately. The very fact that you're so intent on figuring out more about the world is proof. You haven't accepted it yet."

"Well...yes," I say. "And no. I've always been the type of person to question things, but it wasn't until you warned Hettie and me that I started to think something was actually wrong. Even then, I *still* went back one more time willingly."

"And yet, your sister didn't question it even after I warned you two, did she? You told me she lashed out at you when you told her not to return. Of course she did. That's exactly what Lila did. *That* is why the world loves them. They're easier to convince and persuade. It likes easy prey."

I shudder. *Prey*—I hate that word. But what I hate even more than the word is picturing Hettie as it: something weak, slow, and easy to kill.

"I was only a year younger than you when Lila and I found the well," Wayne says. He's reluctant to continue, but he forces himself to. "Just like you and your sister, we needed it. My father was an alcoholic, and my mom was the person he took out his anger on. Lila and I wanted a sanctuary more than anything—a place to hide when he got too violent or yelled too much. And the world delivered. It gave us everything we wanted: music, warmth, and a place to escape to. I was enthralled at first, just as much as Lila was. We must have gone ten times. Every time we went, the underground moon would get fuller and brighter. I became very familiar with the world. I could remember almost every tree...every face."

Wayne looks beyond me as he speaks, as if looking at me directly would break him. He takes a shaky breath, then says, "I didn't realize something was wrong until the moon was almost full. Finally, I snapped out of my daze and back to reality. I realized how odd Lila was acting. Like your sister, she was withdrawn. All she could do was talk about the world—when we would go back next, how long we would stay—it was all she could think about. She didn't eat or sleep. My parents were too preoccupied to notice, of course, but I did. Suddenly, the world didn't seem so safe anymore. I told her we shouldn't go back, but she screamed at me. She told me that I was evil and the world was good. I didn't know what to do. Then, I started having nightmares. Nightmares like the one you had—terrible dreams about death and torture, and the underground moon was in every single one. It hated me for realizing its intentions. It wanted me gone so it could have Lila all to itself. I tried to tell her that something was wrong, but she wouldn't listen. And I ended up being too late."

Wayne puts his head in his hands for a moment, and I wonder if he's crying. When he looks back up at me, though, there are no tears in his eyes—only the same haunted, miserable look that stood out to me when I first saw him.

"One day, I came home from school and Lila was gone. I'd never seen my parents look so distraught—even my father. They'd called the police and had a whole search team looking for her. I immediately told them everything. I told them about the well and what was underneath it and that I was sure Lila had gone there. I even got everyone to accompany me to the forest. But when we got there, the well was completely gone. The grove was gone. Everything was gone, just like that. It had hidden itself so that no one else could see it. After that, my parents thought something was wrong with me. I guess I don't blame them." He pauses and draws a long breath.

"At first, they thought it was shock, then a thousand other things. They even had me hospitalized when I was your age because I had gotten so out of control. Just like Lila, I had become obsessed with the well, only for a different reason. I wanted to know where it came from, what it did, and why my little sister had become its victim. But it was a solo effort. Nobody believed me. It would've been a whole lot easier if I really *was* crazy."

Wayne's chin quivers. He clenches and unclenches his fists in a desperate attempt to steady himself, but when he speaks, his voice quavers.

"I didn't go back to the well until I was twenty," he says. "When I did, it was still there. Maybe it already knew I was aware of its presence, so it didn't need to hide. Or maybe it *couldn't* hide, since I'd already seen it. Regardless, it knew I wasn't a threat. It had stripped me of everything."

"Did you ever go back down?" I ask.

Wayne shakes his head. "No," he says. "Never. The farthest I could go was to the well itself. All the research I've done, all the hundreds of faces I've recalled, it's all from my memory." Then, in a weak and strangled voice, he adds, "I've never even seen Lila's tree."

I sit still, unsure about what to say. Perhaps I shouldn't say anything at all.

"I always knew she was down there," Wayne continues. "I had no doubts about that. But when you said you saw her face, it hit me harder than I thought it would."

I look down at my feet. "I'm sorry. I wasn't thinking."

Wayne doesn't respond. When I look back up, however, his eyes meet mine; he no longer gazes off into space as though he is talking to a ghost.

"You said your sister is seven," he says. "That's how old Lila was. It's the perfect age for the world to target because they're young enough to be innocent and naive, but old enough not to be watched as closely as they used to be. Teenagers are harder. Teenagers like you, like me when I found the well. Although it still doesn't hide from them, it understands that they're harder to grasp than children. They may be skeptical. Afraid, even. So it tries its best to pull you in quickly."

"How...how does it know all of this?" I ask. "How does it know who to hide from and who to lure in?"

"Every predator has a strategy to catch prey," Wayne says. "This thing is like any other organism. It needs to eat."

I bite down hard on my lip to keep it from trembling.

"Think about all the different ways animals get their food," Wayne continues. "Great white sharks attack from below. Rattlesnakes use their venom. Spiders weave webs. This place has its own method, and every few years, it manages to attract and feast upon new prey. But I imagine that like any other animal, when it finds its prey is being restricted—when it finds something is keeping its food from it—it lashes out. It gets desperate."

I swallow hard and find that even biting down on my lip doesn't work. Now, my whole body is trembling. *I'm* the thing restricting its food, and that's why it has been haunting me with nightmares and threats. Wayne doesn't need to say that part for me to understand.

"This thing *isn't* an animal, though." My voice is meek.

"Maybe not," Wayne replies. "But it lives and thinks and eats just like one."

The room falls eerily silent for a long and painful moment. I can hear the creaks in the walls and the sound of my own heartbeat, and just when I think those sounds may drive me insane, Wayne taps the binder in front of him. The sound is a welcome relief to the otherwise suffocating noises that fill the silence.

"This is twenty-five years' worth of research and guesses," he finally says. "It's the best I'll ever be able to do.

I can't tell you how this place came to be or how exactly it works, but I can tell you with enough confidence that it feeds off of children and their innocence. And the underground moon lies at the heart of it all. It's the thing that gains energy...that watches from above and consumes the prey that the world has enticed."

I wonder how full the underground moon is now. Hopefully, by keeping Hettie away, I've managed to stall its growth. Or perhaps it's working faster than ever, desperate to reel her in as quickly as it can. The latter thought sends a cold tremor throughout my body.

"This place is intelligent," Wayne says. "Not only does it know who to hide from and when to show itself, but it also knows what type of child is best to lure. I told you this when you demanded answers from me in the diner. It wants kids who need it. It likes it when they rely on it for comfort."

"That way, they continue returning," I think out loud.

"Sure, it definitely wants them to return," Wayne says. "But there's another reason why the world lures children who need it. What's something that sad and lonely children are usually missing in their life?"

I narrow my eyebrows.

"What are you and Hettie missing?" he asks. "What were Lila and I missing?"

"Family." My answer is immediate.

"Family," Wayne repeats. "And the children who are missing family—whose family may be neglectful, absent, or preoccupied—are children who may not always be looked after very well. How convenient, then, for the world to swallow them up while nobody is looking."

He reopens the binder, flipping to the pages with the newspaper articles and sorted pictures of previous missing children.

"I couldn't find information on all of these children," he says, "but the ones I did find followed the same pattern: they were lonely. Some only had one parent, others had two who worked all the time or had other issues...hell, some were even in the foster care system." Wayne flips back to the article from 1940. "Take Danny Lewis, for example. Pretty prominent family. They were able to offer eight thousand for information, which was a hell of a lot back in that day. The father was involved in government, and it was known at the time that his wife was struggling with cancer."

He points to a smaller article that he has attached to Danny's. The headline reads: *Mary Lewis, wife of Bill Lewis, passes away from illness a year after son's mysterious disappearance.*

"All of the children I could find information on were struggling with something," Wayne says. "And I'm sure the children who lost their lives to the underground world long before newspapers ever recorded 'missing cases' had their reasons too. That's what it loves: children who need it and who will be easy to feed on."

Wayne closes the binder again.

"It's a vicious cycle," he says. "It finds a child, or children, to lure down into the world, where it showers them with sparkling silver and music and warmth. Then, once it has successfully stolen everything from them and they are nothing more than a lifeless shell of a human, it devours them and adds their face to its collection of trees. Each time, the moon goes from crescent to full as it steals more and more of the child's purity, and then it starts over again. Like I said, it's an energy source. It grows as it acquires pure and uncorrupted energy from the children it entices."

A long, unsettling silence follows. I think about Hettie and how she has been acting recently. How close is she to becoming a lifeless shell?

"This world—the moon, the lake, and whatever it uses to captivate its victims—is poison in the guise of a blessing," Wayne says. "The children who have been affected don't realize it's poisoning them, so they continue going back for more. The poison changes them so that they're no longer who they were. Every waking moment of their life becomes dictated by an insatiable need to return, and when they're no longer really human, it has won. Then, it feasts."

I let loose a breath, waiting for the moment that this all sinks in. The moment never comes.

Wayne straightens in his chair and clasps his hands together. "That's all I know. Twenty-five years of obsession—of research and theories and guesses—and you've learned all of it in, what...an hour?"

"Thank you," I say. I can't settle on one emotion, so I decide not to settle on any at all. I'll leave the feelings for later. Right now, I need to process this.

Wayne nods. "Remember, since you're no longer a child like your sister but also not an adult, the world is hesitant about you," he says. "Now that it knows you're aware of its intentions and that you want to keep your sister away from it, it doesn't like you at all. Your nightmare should have made that pretty clear."

"If I threaten it so much, why doesn't it just hide itself from me?" I ask. "It hides itself from adults, so it clearly has the ability."

"I wouldn't go as far as to say it's threatened by you," Wayne says. I can't tell if he's being condescending or if this is how he always is. "What power would one fifteen-year-old have over something like that? It's not even threatened by me, and I have a good feeling it knows how much I hate it."

"Maybe it shouldn't underestimate us."

"Maybe *you* shouldn't underestimate *it*." He pauses and rubs his chin. Upon noticing that I'm unamused by his answer, he sighs loudly and with great irritation. "I don't understand every tiny way this place works, kid. I make my guesses, but I'm only human. I do the best I can with the little I have. My best guess is that once you've seen the well and what's underneath it, that's that—there's no reason for it to hide from you unless you bring someone along it doesn't know."

"Like when you brought the police to see it," I say, finishing his thought.

Wayne wrings his hands together. "All of this said, I can't help you protect your little sister." He says it sternly, as if I hadn't heard him the first time. "That's your battle. I don't know how long it will exercise its hold over her. Maybe another month, maybe longer...I can't say. All I have is this information, and all you can do is keep a close watch on her and make sure she doesn't try to go back."

I stand up. "Or," I say, watching Wayne's eyes, "it means I need to find a way to destroy this place."

Wayne laughs, but it isn't lighthearted. "How are you so sure that's even possible?"

"I'm *not* sure it's possible," I respond, walking back over to the wall with the pictures. I study the faces with the harrowing realization that even Wayne's research hasn't included all the children who have been taken. "But I have to try...for all of them. For my little sister." I turn to face Wayne and look him straight in the eye. "For Lila."

"I know what you're insinuating," Wayne says coolly. "And I'm still not going to help you. This is it. This is the extent of my involvement in your escapade."

"'Escapade? Are you serious?" I choke, struggling to keep my anger at bay. "You of all people should know how important this is."

"I know exactly how important this is," Wayne says. His forced calmness makes me even angrier. "But I also know how *dangerous* this is. I know that years of research have led me no closer to finding a way to get rid of it, and I know with even more certainty that some fifteen-year-old girl who just learned what took me twenty-five years to figure out is even less capable of doing so."

"You're right. You've done so much work," I say, gesturing to the pictures on the walls. "You've done way more than I've done...you know way more than I know. So why is the possibility of destroying this place so beyond you?"

"Because I'm a realist," Wayne responds curtly.

I bite my tongue. I don't know if I can argue with him anymore. He gave me what I came for, and I can tell that he is intent on doing nothing more.

Regardless of Wayne's decision, I've gotten this far, and there's no way in hell I'm stopping now. Not when Hettie's life is on the line. Not when the world that has taken all these lives continues to go unpunished.

"Fine," I say. "Thank you for speaking with me. Thank you for warning Hettie and me that day at the well, and thank you for not turning me away this time. I won't bother you again."

Wayne lifts himself from the couch and gives me a terse nod. "Do the reasonable thing," he says. "Don't go trying to destroy something that will destroy you."

I draw my lips into a thin, straight line. "You haven't tried to destroy it," I say. I look once more around his apartment, letting the overwhelming darkness, squalor, and obsession consume my every sense. "And yet, it has already destroyed you."

Wayne blinks at me. I'm not going to wait for a response. I return his curt nod and make my way to the door, realizing that it's harder for me to exit than it was to enter.

CHAPTER 24
DOWN BELOW

I take my time on my way home, despite how anxious I am to see Hettie. I need to think, and riding the empty road back up to Aunt Vivian's house allows me to do just that.

I never asked Wayne why he was at the well that day he ran into Hettie and me, but I decide it doesn't matter. After all, he already admitted that he is unable to bring himself to go back down.

As I continue coasting along the silent trail, listening to the pebbles beneath the wheels of my bike, I begin to pity Wayne. I understand why he hides from the world—why he doesn't let anyone into his apartment. Perhaps I would too if I lost Hettie the same way Wayne lost Lila.

I won't let that happen. I won't let this place take Hettie or any more children. I'm going to destroy it. The only problem is, I have no idea how.

There has to be a solution, though. I can't accept any other option, not with Hettie's life on the line.

I push my thoughts aside for the moment when I pull up into the front yard of the house. I don't bother to put my bike away.

I've been gone far longer than I had hoped to be, but I convince myself it was for a good reason.

Aunt Vivian must have left hours ago, and I don't see Mother in the kitchen, so I assume she's in her room. The kitchen isn't entirely empty, however. Hettie is sitting at the table, drawing.

I never thought I would be so happy to see her doing her favorite activity.

"You have blood on your face," she says when she sees me.

I put my hand to my cheek and feel the sticky, dried blood under my fingers. I forgot I had cut myself.

"I finally talked to Wayne," I say as I run my hand under the sink water and use it to clean my cheek. I haven't even looked at my cut yet. I hope it isn't too noticeable; I don't want any questions from Mother or Aunt Vivian.

"Hmm," Hettie mumbles in response.

I sit down across from her and glance at her drawings. The short-lived happiness I felt when I saw her at the kitchen table vanishes when I see her pictures.

The first drawing is of the forest with the carved faces, the second is of the lake next to the gazebo, and the third—the one she's working on right now—is of the underground moon.

"Is that all you've drawn?" I ask, bracing myself for her answer.

Hettie nods without looking up.

"Hettie," I whisper, "you're going to have to hide those."

"Why? It's not like Mommy or Aunt Vivian know where I got my ideas."

"Yes, but..." I purse my lips and lower my voice even more. "If they see these, they may get curious. I don't want them to ask you any questions."

"Ro," Hettie says, clearly annoyed. She looks up at me and puts her crayon down. "I told you I wouldn't tell them our secret."

Our secret. I'm not so sure this is a secret I enjoy keeping. Not like I did at first.

"It wouldn't matter if you did," I respond. "Mom and Aunt Vivian can't see the well, anyway. No adult can, except for Wayne."

I expect her to ask me why, but she just shrugs. "Good. They'd only ruin it." She looks straight at me when she says the last part.

I cross my arms. "Just like you think I ruined it."

When she doesn't respond, I exhale, hoping it will curb my returning irritation.

"Do you want to hear what I learned from Wayne? About the world?"

"I told you he's a liar."

I blink at Hettie as she resumes drawing.

"What happened to that agreement we came to earlier?" I ask. "Remember *Sleeping Beauty* and the spinning wheel?"

"This isn't the same," Hettie says.

"You're right, this isn't the same," I snap, uncrossing my arms and slamming the palms of my hands on the tabletop. "It's much worse. This world won't just make you fall into a deep sleep. It will kill you. You'll become one of those carved faces in the forest, but not before it has taken all of your innocence and everything that makes you *you*. And the underground moon? *That* is where all of your energy will go. It will keep getting fuller and brighter until it is full and you are empty. Even now it's taking parts of you, and you're not even in the underground world. Why can't you see that?"

Hettie lets out a muffled whimper, then grabs the three pictures she drew and violently starts to tear them apart. All

I do is sit there, unsure of how to react, watching her rip her drawings to shreds. She bunches up the shredded papers in her hand and stomps over to the trash can, where she throws them inside with uncharacteristic force.

I don't know whether to be worried about Hettie or relieved that I don't have to look at those pictures.

"Happy?" she snaps. "Now you don't have to worry about anyone asking questions."

I take a deep breath, trying to remember that this isn't Hettie. This is the world—the underground moon acting through her. It's changing her, so I do my best not to blow up.

"Hettie," I say as calmly as possible, "I learned a lot today from Wayne. A long time ago, when he was a kid, he went there with his little sister. Her name was Lila."

Hettie blinks back tears, but I can tell she's still listening to me, so I continue. "Do you remember the necklace you gave me that time we danced in the gazebo? The pretty one with the emerald pendant?"

Hettie nods.

"That was Lila's tree you took it from."

I watch her face very carefully.

"Wayne and Lila loved the underground world, and they returned again and again because it made them happy. But Wayne began to realize something was wrong, just like me, only he was too late. Lila died. The world took her, just like it's trying to take you, only that time it won. I'm not going to let it win this time, but I can't do it on my own. I need you to keep fighting."

"I know, I know," Hettie whispers meekly, refusing to look at me. "You already said—"

"I'm saying it again. I need you to fight every single urge, because if you don't, it may beat us. We really need to work together, Hettie. Do you understand?"

I don't add that I want to try to destroy it—to get rid of the underground world and the moon that has taken so many lives—because I don't know how Hettie will react to that. I can see it in her eyes; she's struggling to understand but wants to listen. She still loves the world and hates what I'm saying, but she's trying to grasp why I'm so desperate, and that alone gives me hope.

Hettie lowers her eyes to the floor. "I'm sorry I keep getting mad at you," she whispers.

"It's okay. I know it's hard. I know you don't understand why I feel the way I do and why I don't want to go back. But you're trying anyway, and that's what matters."

I stand up and walk over to Hettie so I can pull her into a hug.

When I feel her arms wrap around me, I forget about the well and the trees and the underground moon. Even though it's only for a moment, the warmth feels as though it could last a lifetime.

That night, as I lie in bed listening to Hettie's soft breathing from across the room, I think of ways to destroy the well and the world beneath it. I'm not even sure I know where to begin, but that doesn't stop me from trying.

If I learned anything from Wayne, it was that the underground moon acquires its energy through children—more specifically, through their innocence and purity. It waits until proper prey comes along, poisons its target with sweet lies and fantasy, then sucks the victim to a shell and leaves behind nothing but another face in its forest.

No amount of fairytale stories or books could have prepared me for this. I think about how Ava told me she had always entertained the idea of magic. And Hettie didn't even think twice about the underground world because magic wasn't something to be entertained at all—it simply existed, not requiring consideration. In her world, there were no questions.

I wonder if Wayne had believed in magic before he and Lila found the underground world. I wonder how shocked he'd felt when they discovered the spiral staircase within the well, and if, like me, he'd been hesitant and curious. After all, he had only been fourteen—stuck in the limbo between being too young and naive, and too old and tainted.

Suddenly, I feel hot anger rush to my face. Anger that this wicked place takes blameless children, anger that the innocence and purity that makes them so good is used against them.

It doesn't like adults, that much is clear. It's a cowardly thing that feeds upon the defenseless—that takes those who can't fight back. Perhaps that's important. I blink in the darkness, wishing I could expand on this idea with Wayne, but I don't think that will be an option. He made it clear that he's done helping me.

I turn to the side and rest facing the bedroom door, willing my eyes to shut. Silent shuffling alerts my senses, but I'm so exhausted that I don't pay any mind to it. Slowly, I fall deeper into darkness...

The shuffling has morphed into a soft, light pitter-patter. Somewhere deep in my subconscious, I wonder if it's a dream.

Someone is opening a door. Someone gentle and quiet.

Hettie.

Now I'm awake.

My head is heavy and my mind is bleary, but I quickly shake myself out of my sleep-induced stupor and realize that she's left the room.

Blood starts to pound in the back of my head. I tear off my sheets and jump up, then hurry down the hall to the kitchen.

Normally, if I woke up and realized that Hettie was out of bed, I wouldn't have cared. But everything has changed now. The very presence of that godforsaken well has me on edge, even as I sleep. I can't stay calm because there's always the possibility that the urge will get too strong and she'll go back.

I stumble into the darkness of the kitchen. I don't see Hettie's figure or hear her movements. I squint at the outline of furniture. I don't want to wake Mother or Aunt Vivian by turning on the lights, so I fumble my way through the dimly lit labyrinth of unpacked boxes and kitchen chairs on silent feet.

A sliver of light catches my eye, but it isn't coming from the window. It's coming from the door at the corner of the kitchen.

I lunge forward and pull it open, which Hettie has left both unlocked and slightly cracked. The sky is clear and covered with stars, and the moon—the real moon—casts a dim shadow over the grass.

When I see her only a few yards away, relief washes over me in waves.

"Hettie!" I whisper-shout as I rush toward her.

She hasn't gotten far. I don't want to think about what would have happened if I hadn't heard her get up.

I reach her quickly since she's walking slower than usual. When I grab her arm and spin her around to face me, I realize she's sleepwalking.

I've never seen anyone sleepwalk before. For a moment, I wonder if she's in a trance, but I dismiss the thought upon further observation of her face. Her eyes aren't the hazy gray they were when she fell into her daze, but they're just as emotionless. They close one moment then open the next; she's somewhere in the middle of being asleep and awake.

"Hettie, wake up."

"I'm going." Her voice is small and far away.

"Where?"

"Back down. I belong down below."

"No, you don't," I whisper fervently, feeling my heart beat in my ears. "You belong here...up above, with me."

"Rosella? Hettie?" I whirl around at the sound of Aunt Vivian's voice. I see her standing on the porch beneath the light. Her eyes are wide and her eyebrows are pulled together. I can't tell if she's scared or angry or both. "What's going on? Is everything okay?"

"She's sleepwalking," I say, taking Hettie's wrist and leading her back over to the porch. "I heard her get up and followed her out here."

Aunt Vivian exhales, surprised. "Has she ever done this before?"

I shake my head.

Mother must have heard us too. She appears behind Aunt Vivian and quickly rushes over to Hettie and me.

"She's sleepwalking?" Mother asks. "How did she get outside?"

"She unlocked the door in the kitchen." I look back at Aunt Vivian. "You should install an alarm system."

"I *have* an alarm system," Aunt Vivian says. "I don't know why it didn't go off."

I stiffen. "Did Hettie know where it was?"

"Not that I know of."

Mother and I lead Hettie, who is still not entirely awake, back inside. I follow Aunt Vivian over to the laundry room in the hallway. She flips open an alarm box hidden just above the dryer.

"It's been disabled," she breathes. "Hettie must have done it. I don't understand...it requires a code." She gestures at the little buttons inside the box, which glow green as she re-enables the system. "I don't think I told Hettie about the alarm system, so there's no way she could've known where it was even if she knew the code. I don't even think I told *you* where it was."

"You didn't," I say. "Did Mom know?"

Aunt Vivian nods. "Maybe Hettie heard me tell her what the code was."

I don't respond. I highly doubt it.

When we return to the kitchen, Hettie is awake. She sits at the table with Mother.

"I sleepwalked," she says timidly, trying to gauge my reaction. She looks down at her feet in an attempt to conceal her guilt. I can't tell if she thinks I'm angry with her, which makes my stomach sink.

"I know you did. It's not your fault." I sit down next to her, worried she may say something about the well or what's beneath it. If she does, I hope Aunt Vivian and Mother pass it off as a dream.

Aunt Vivian follows close behind me. "Hey sweetie," she says, patting Hettie's head when she notices she's awake. "Do you remember turning off the alarm system?"

Hettie shrugs. "I don't remember anything."

Mother furrows her brows. "Was Hettie in the room when you told me the alarm code?" she asks Aunt Vivian, who shakes her head in response.

"Maybe she overheard it," I say, despite fully knowing that's not the case.

Somehow, the world managed to know what even Hettie did not. If it exercises that much power over her, what else will it do to get her to come back? The thought frightens me, but I'm no longer surprised by the magnitude of its influence.

"I'm just shocked she went outside," Aunt Vivian said. "I hear of people sleepwalking inside of their houses, but this is rare."

"Do you remember where you wanted to go?" Mother asks Hettie.

Of all the questions she could have asked...

Hettie glances at me, then back at Mother. "No," she answers in a repressed whisper.

"I guess this means I need to change the code," Aunt Vivian says. "Especially if you're going to sleepwalk again, you silly goose." She ruffles Hettie's hair, evoking a tiny giggle from her.

"I'm so glad you heard her, Ro," Mother says. "That could be really dangerous."

I nod at her, but I don't say anything. My mouth has completely dried up.

If only she knew.

CHAPTER 25
PROTÉGÉE

I invite Ava over the following afternoon. Though I have a lot I want to tell her, it's her company I crave the most. I feel like every day is getting longer and harder to get through. For a little while, I just want to do something normal.

Most teenagers hang out with friends during the summer. They don't plot to destroy an underground world that wants to feed off their younger sibling. Maybe if I pretend to be normal for long enough, I'll start to feel that way.

Ava comes over an hour after her shift ends, carrying a paper grocery bag.

"I remember you said Hettie liked art," she beams as she puts it down on the kitchen table. "I have a whole bunch of paintbrushes and canvases I'm not going to use, so she can have them if she wants."

"She'll love that," I say. The unease of last night still pulls at me. I haven't spoken to Hettie about it yet, and I'm not sure I want to.

Both Mother and Aunt Vivian, though surprised at the incident, convinced themselves that Hettie overheard them speaking about the alarm system when we first moved here. Once Aunt Vivian changed the code, that seemed to be that. Children sleepwalk, after all, and they reassured themselves that as long as we take precautions to make sure she's safe, then all should be well.

I wonder what they'll think if she sleepwalks again and correctly guesses the new code. That won't be so easy to explain, which means I have to watch her even more closely than I've been doing. As if I need more reasons not to sleep.

When I go fetch Hettie from our bedroom, she seems present enough. I tell her that Ava brought art supplies over, which even brings a little glimmer of excitement to her eyes. The sight of it makes me want to cry out of relief. She's not all gone. Not yet.

"Ava likes art too," I say as I lead her back to the kitchen.

"You told me that," Hettie says, pulling at one of her curls.

"I'm sure she'd love to show you some tricks."

"What kind of tricks?"

I shrug as we both sit down across from Ava. "Hettie would like to know what type of art tricks you can show her," I say, gesturing to the paints in Ava's bag.

"Thousands and thousands," she quips, eliciting a small, crystalline giggle from Hettie.

It brings me comfort to watch the two of them together. Ava shows Hettie how she mixes colors and the best place to start when painting, and Hettie watches with those curious, cornflower-blue eyes.

I bring my knees to my chest as I observe them. It doesn't take long for their voices to fade away as I sink back into my thoughts.

The pictures of those children crowding Wayne's apartment wall flicker into my memory, followed by the articles in his binder, and then the carved faces on the trees. Danny Lewis, Cora Nittly, the girl with the coiled hair and radiant eyes, the two laughing brothers...all of them must have had futures that were unfolding brightly before them, and then, like that, their lives were gone.

I think of Lila and her delicate, porcelain face, and then my thoughts move to Wayne. I wonder if he is the sole survivor of the underground world—the only adult who can see it. Perhaps the word "survivor" isn't quite right, though; even Wayne admitted that he died after Lila did, only in a different way.

Wayne was unlucky. He hadn't had anyone warn him about the underground world. He figured it out himself, and by then it was too late.

I start to feel guilty about the way I treated him after he told me what he knew. After all, he likely saved both my and Hettie's life by warning us that day at the well. If he hadn't, would I have eventually realized something was wrong? Or like Wayne, would I have realized too late? Would I grow up only to become a miserable, tormented woman with a hidden past? Would the underground moon continue to haunt me, just as it haunts Wayne?

The guilt consumes me. I was so angry that he refused to help me destroy the well and the world beneath it that I hadn't thought about *why* he refused. I would apologize to him about the way I acted, but I have a feeling he doesn't want to see me again.

Despite my shame, I still haven't given up on my plan to stop the underground moon and the world it uses to lure children.

My resolve gets stronger every time I think of those children—of Lila and Hettie and the trees. Whether I have

Wayne's help or not, I'm going to try to destroy this place. And if it ends up being futile, at least I'll have tried.

"Ro," comes Ava's soft whisper from across the table.

I look up at her and wonder how many times she's said my name.

"Are you okay?"

I smile and nod. "Just lost in thought."

"Do you want to join us?" she asks. "We're going to paint a beach."

"I'm not an artist," I say, pursing my lips and then grinning. "It's more fun for me to watch you two."

Ava simply nods in response. She knows I'm not watching them, but she doesn't push it.

I try to focus on her and Hettie as they begin mixing blues and yellows, but no matter how hard I try, I can't.

It takes them a while to finish their painting, but I don't mind. Seeing how much fun Hettie has with Ava offers me slight liberation from my obsessive worrying.

When Hettie finally leaves the kitchen to hang up her new art in our bedroom, Ava turns to me and crosses her arms.

"Spill it, Ro," she demands. "You look like you caught the plague, and you were staring so hard at the floor that I thought it might melt. What's going on?"

"Do I really look that bad?"

"I'm kidding." She leans back into her chair. "But you do look stressed as hell. Did something happen with Hettie? With the well?"

"I finally got Wayne to speak with me," I say. "It took a lot of convincing, but he eventually gave in."

"When?"

"Yesterday. It took me a while, but I forced him to tell me everything he knows."

"Do I even *want* to know what you found out?"

I lean closer to her and lower my voice. Mother may be sleeping and Hettie may be at the other side of the house, but I'm still worried someone will overhear.

"This place has killed hundreds of kids," I whisper. "I guess I figured as much, but I didn't realize how bad it was before I spoke to Wayne."

"Oh," Ava says meekly. "Shit."

"All of those trees in the forest used to be children, just like Hettie...just like us...who were lured to the world and kept returning until it killed them. It feeds off of them. The underground moon acts as the world's energy source. Wayne said that it acquires children's innocence in the form of energy. That's why no adults can see it. I even tried to show my mom the other day, but the whole thing had disappeared."

Ava narrows her eyebrows. "What do you mean?"

"I mean it was completely gone," I say. "No trace of it whatsoever. There was no grove, no ring of trees, no well, no staircase...nothing. It was like it disappeared and used the forest to cover its tracks."

I bite my lip and look down at my feet. "It carefully chooses who it shows itself to," I continue. "It's wary of anyone older than teenagers, so it hides to make sure only a select few find it."

"I remember you saying that last bit," whispers Ava. "That's horrible. There were so many trees in that forest...so many carvings. How long has it been doing this?"

"I'm not sure," I admit. "Neither is Wayne. He isn't sure what created it or how long it's been around. The earliest case of a missing Larton child that he could find was from the 1940s, but he said he's sure it goes back further than that."

"So...it just continues acquiring and devouring children," Ava says slowly, "and the underground moon keeps gaining energy?"

"The younger the better, it seems," I say. "Children are less likely to question it. That's why it doesn't show itself to adults and why it's hesitant of teenagers."

"Teenagers? Why?"

I shrug. "Something about us being more likely to see through its lies and uncover its real intentions. We're not old enough to be corrupted, but we're not young enough to be wholly pure either."

"And Wayne told you this?"

I nod.

After a lengthy pause, Ava asks, "How did he figure all of this out?"

I remain quiet for a long moment, not knowing if I should tell anyone else about Lila. I have a feeling Wayne wouldn't like that, but when I see the concern on Ava's face, I tell her anyway.

When I finish, she sits very still and looks down at her feet, nervously running her fingers over the empty canvases on the table.

"I thought that might be the case," she whispers. "That's why he can see it as an adult. Because he saw it as a kid."

"That's why."

"Do you think he's the only one?"

"I have a feeling," I say, "but I can't be sure. This thing may have been around for hundreds of years...probably more."

Ava tugs anxiously on a strand of her hair.

"And now it wants Hettie," I continue. "It would've tried to take me too if Wayne hadn't warned us and I hadn't realized something was up. Now it's angry with me."

"Angry with you?" Ava asks. "It has *feelings*?"

"It seems to," I say. I tell her about my nightmare—about the way the full moon hung in my room as though it were threatening me. "When I told Hettie, she said that she had a dream too, only in hers, the moon was beckoning her. It told her it loved her and missed her."

"Oh," Ava says, holding her mouth in a circle for a moment as she thinks. "Holy shit."

"And it's unpredictable," I say. "Sometimes Hettie is fine, like she was when she was painting with you. Other times she's not. Last night she sleepwalked for the first time in her life. She disabled the alarm system, which I know she had no knowledge of before. It was the moon. I know it."

"You mean...you think the *moon* guided her?"

"She said it spoke to her in her previous dream." I shudder at the thought. "I wouldn't be surprised if it did again last night. It has more power than I originally thought, and I don't think it's going to give up anytime soon. That's why I need to destroy it."

"Are you sure that's possible?" Ava asks. Her face is paler than usual.

I shake my head and cast her a withering look. "No."

Ava folds her arms, deep in thought. "I've only seen it once," she says in a very calm voice, quite contrary to the distress on her face, "and I don't know entirely what it's capable of. But I guess knowing only a little bit is better than knowing nothing at all, especially if we're going to destroy this thing."

"Ava…"

"I'm going to help," she says, brooking no argument. "Hettie is your sister and you're my friend. Hettie is *also* my art protégée, and I'd be a horrible mentor if I didn't protect her."

I let out a surprised laugh and Ava responds with a grin.

"Are you sure?" I ask.

"Honestly, Ro," she says. "I want to help. In fact, I don't think I'm capable of *not* helping. I'd live the rest of my life with terrible guilt."

"Then you'd be the first," I say. "Wayne told me I was naive for thinking I could destroy it."

"Maybe," Ava says. "Or maybe you just have more to lose than he does if you don't."

"I'm not just doing this for Hettie, though." I pause and press my lips together. "Okay, I'm doing *most* of this for Hettie. But the other children who already lost their lives to this place deserve to be freed as well. Even if they're already dead, they shouldn't have to remain like *that* forever—stuck in those trees, stuck in the world that killed them." I shake my head, tears pricking at my eyes. "The underground moon doesn't deserve that. It shouldn't get to keep them. It shouldn't feel any semblance of victory whatsoever."

Ava nervously taps her fingers against the hollow side of a canvas. "Well," she says, "we may not be able to bring them back, but at least we can try to avenge their deaths."

I smile sadly at her, clinging on to the fleeting, yet ever so stubborn strand of hope that resides within me.

"Yes," I say. "We can try."

Ava sleeps over that night. At dinner, she cracks jokes and even makes Mother laugh. Aunt Vivian and her share the same sense of humor, and together they manage to distract me from my thoughts.

Hettie enjoys Ava's company as well. She even asks me if Ava can sleep on the floor next to her bed.

Ava and I make a silent agreement to take turns sleeping so we can keep an eye on Hettie and ensure she doesn't sleepwalk again. Ava takes the first shift when she realizes I can hardly keep my eyes open, and she wakes me up around three in the morning.

I let her sleep in my bed since the floor is hard and the thin blankets we laid out don't make a good mattress. She doesn't seem tired, though. I hear her toss for a while in my bed. The sheets rustle as she turns to face my direction.

"I can't sleep," she whispers after a while. "Do you want some company?"

I nod, but quickly realize she can't see me in the dark. "Yeah," I say. "I'd love some."

"Have you had any ideas about...the thing?"

"Not really." Using the blankets on the floor to push myself forward, I scoot closer to my bed so Hettie isn't disturbed by our voices. "Well, I had a thought a while ago, but it's not an idea."

"What is it?"

"I was thinking that if this world doesn't show itself to adults, it must be afraid of them, right? Wayne is the only adult who can see it, and that's only because he was introduced to the place as a kid." I lower my voice even further. "Maybe it's more than just the fact that it needs children for energy...maybe being *wary* of adults isn't the right description at all. Maybe..." my voice fades before I find it again. "Maybe adults *scare* it."

"You talk about it as if it's a person with feelings," Ava says.

"I think it's pretty obvious by now that it's closer to a person than a moon," I respond. "Or it's...a *thing*. A sentient thing—a thing that thinks and knows."

For a while Ava is silent. Then, she shifts and takes a breath. "Well, it makes sense," she says. She pauses, and I can feel her grin wryly despite not being able to see her. "We could just try to blow it up."

I snort. "I wish."

"I'm serious."

"With what? Dynamite? A grenade? This thing has been taking kids for a crazy long time. It's clearly magic...in some sense of the word. I don't think dynamite will work."

"It was only a thought."

Silence lingers in the room once again until Ava speaks. "If the underground moon *is* the energy source, then maybe it kind of acts as the heart of the world," she says.

"And...?"

"And nothing. That's the furthest I got."

"It's hard to imagine destroying something that I don't entirely understand," I say.

I hold my breath and clamp my lips together when I hear Hettie stir in her bed.

"She's just moving," Ava reassures me.

"I know." I exhale shakily. "It's hard for me not to think the worst."

"We'll know if she gets up," Ava says. "I promise."

When Ava finally falls asleep, I listen to the creaks of the house and Hettie's breathing. I try to use those sounds to calm myself. It works, if only for a little bit, and when the sun finally starts to come up, I feel oddly at peace.

Ava wakes up earlier than I would have expected, but since I have no mind to fall back asleep, we talk well into the morning. Around eight o'clock, after I hear Aunt Vivian leave, I ask Ava if she wants any breakfast before she heads to the diner for her shift.

"Do you have waffles?" she asks.

I look over at Hettie, who is still asleep, and grin. "Of course we do."

She takes a toasted waffle to go, and I see her to the door.

"Update me if anything happens," she says, smoothing her hair and taking a bite of her waffle.

"I will. Are you sure you don't want to ride my bike downtown? It'll get you there quicker."

Ava shrugs. "I like the walk."

After agreeing to call each other when she gets off, we hug each other goodbye and I return inside.

The house is quiet, as it always is in the morning. I hang around the kitchen for a while, wondering what it will be like to leave for school in the morning and do homework at the table in the afternoon.

The inevitable thought pops into my mind: what if I come home from school one day and find that Hettie is missing, just like Wayne did with Lila?

Hopefully, by the time school starts, this will all be a thing of the past. I simply need to focus on my goal: getting rid of the well and the wretched lie beneath it.

As if in response to my thoughts, the phone rings. I get to it quickly so it doesn't wake Mother or Hettie.

Something in my stomach flips before I speak.

It turns out I don't have to, though. The caller beats me to it.

"Is this Rosella...Rosella Gill?"

The voice is deep and familiar. And yet, it's not the same as I remember it.

"This is," I say tentatively.

"Oh...oh, thank God." It's Wayne. My heart nearly stops from the surprise. "I realized...I re...alized I screwed up."

He's drunk. Very drunk. Father used to come home every once in a while, in the years before he left us, smelling of liquor and speaking in slurs as though every thought required his utmost energy. Wayne sounds ten times worse.

"I didn't...I screwed up. I'm sorry. I..." He pauses for a very long moment, as though he has forgotten the word. "...screwed up," he finally finishes.

My throat and mouth suddenly feel dry. "How did you screw up?"

"You're right...about it destroying me," he manages. "I didn't think I realized...until you left. Well, I did...but I didn't admit it. I got all this...all this shit. And what's it done for me...for them? Nothing." He repeats it so loudly that I hold the phone away from my ear. "Nothing!"

"Wayne," I say, hoping that if I sound calm, he'll calm down too, "why did you call me?"

"Because I changed my mind," he says slowly. "I changed my mind...I want to help you destroy it."

It takes me a while to find my voice.

"You do?" I finally manage.

"Why the hell else would I've called you?"

"Okay," I say, forcing myself to sound composed. "Do you...do you want me to come over or something so we can talk about it?"

"Jesus...I don't know. I didn't...didn't think that far."

"How about we meet this evening at the complex?" I suggest. Ava should be off by then, and since she has agreed to help as well, I figure it would be best if we all spoke.

"Fine...fine." I hear Wayne cough on the other end of the line and for a moment, he's silent. Rustling echoes through the phone until he finally speaks. "Four o'clock?"

"Will you remember?" I don't want to offend him, but I don't think he has the mind to even recall this conversation.

"I'll remember," he snaps. The line goes dead.

I feel a trill rise in my chest. He's agreed to help—he's *actually* agreed to help. The persistent sliver of hope I've been trying so hard to hang onto grows in size, and I nearly skip down the hallway.

CHAPTER 26
INNOCENCE

Four o'clock does not come soon enough. I call Ava after she's off from work and we agree to meet outside the complex. In the few minutes before I leave, I watch cartoons with Hettie. As usual nowadays, she's present, but not entirely herself either. I crave the days when she would talk and ask questions every time we watched television. I used to get irritated with her—I'd tell her, "How am I supposed to know what's going on if you won't stay quiet?" —but now it seems I long for even the things which once annoyed me about Hettie.

Since we're alone together, I decide this would be as good a time as any to ask her about her sleepwalking.

"I've never seen you sleepwalk before," I say, trying to gauge her reaction.

Hettie takes her eyes off the television for a moment and looks down at her feet. "I didn't sleepwalk last night," she whispers.

"I'm talking about the night before. Were you dreaming when it happened?"

A look of distress rushes to her face.

"I won't be mad if you were," I say softly.

"I don't remember all of it," she says. "I just remember the moon."

"I belong down below," she'd told me when I'd asked her where she was going. I feel a cold shiver run up my arms and down my spine.

"Do you think the moon was making you sleepwalk?" I brace myself for her answer, but she ignores me.

"I didn't tell Mommy or Aunt Vivian because it's our secret," she says.

I cross my arms and sigh. "I don't want this to be our secret. I want this to be over."

"Not *you*," Hettie says, knitting her eyebrows. "It's my secret with the moon. *Our* secret."

I stare at her for a moment, feeling dizzy. "Since when?"

"Since you started telling me not to go back."

"And you said you'd fight the urge, remember?"

Hettie nods, crestfallen. "I remember."

Sudden, overpowering panic rushes through me. "Has the underground moon been asking you to keep any more secrets?"

"I told you I wouldn't go back," Hettie snaps. She looks near tears. "Stop asking me all the time."

I stand up and close my eyes, willing myself not to reply. I don't want to say something I'll regret.

"I'm going downtown," I say after a painful moment.

Hettie doesn't respond.

"Are you going to be okay while I'm gone?"

"I'll be fine."

I almost ask her if she's sure, but I decide against it.

Though I would have expected the tension between us to make it easier for me to leave, it doesn't.

Since I leave the house earlier than I had planned to, with only a quick word to Mother about when I think I'll be back, I decide to walk instead of ride my bike. I have the time.

It's still light outside, but not as hot as it is in the early afternoon. I like the weather; it reminds me more of Oregon and less of the South. Although I'm getting used to the humidity in Tennessee, I still pine for the cool, thin air that was once so familiar to me.

The sounds of crickets in the fields intertwine with the crunch of gravel under my feet. Birds chirp here and there, becoming scarcer and quieter the farther I get from Aunt Vivian's house.

I wonder if there will be a time when I think of Aunt Vivian's house as my own, but the thought evokes such discomfort that I refrain from thinking about it at all. It isn't that I don't enjoy Larton or Ava or even the summer weather here—it's simply the unfamiliarity, which I've always been so keen to avoid. That, and the insidious threat that lies within the forest in wait for us, only a few minutes away from Aunt Vivian's house.

Ava sits outside the complex when I finally arrive. She brightens and stands up when she sees me.

"Are you as shocked as I am?" she asks when I greet her.

"I still can't believe it," I say. "I didn't think he'd ever want to talk to me again."

A cynical grin spreads across Ava's face. "Well, nothing changes a person's mind better than time alone to be tormented by their thoughts."

"I didn't tell him you were coming," I admit. "It's pretty clear that Wayne isn't into surprises, so we'll have to be careful with how we go about it. Maybe I should do the talking. If I explain to him that you're here to help, I think he'll understand. I *hope* he'll understand."

Ava shrugs and nods. "Shall we go see him, then?" she muses, unlocking the entryway gate.

It's four o'clock on the dot when we arrive at his door, but my usual skepticism nags at me. What if he has changed his mind and turns us away?

Noticing my hesitancy to knock, Ava steps in front of me and raps her knuckles against the door. I wonder if she's really as confident as she's acting or if it's a façade. Either way, I'm glad she's here with me.

When Wayne opens the door, the smell of vodka and smoke shrouds my senses. As I expected, when he sees Ava, he turns to me and grimaces. "Brought your friend again, didn't you?"

Ava speaks before I can open my mouth. "I'm here to help," she asserts loudly. "Ro is my friend and Hettie is her sister, so I'm not going to leave even if you want me to."

So much for letting me do the talking. When Wayne glares at me, I only shrug.

Wayne shakes his head and motions for both of us to come inside.

Ava looks quite pleased with herself as she strides through the door, but her pride slowly turns to horror when she sees both the sorry state of Wayne's apartment and the pictures on his wall.

"Are these...?"

"I assume Rosella has told you everything," Wayne interrupts, shutting the door.

Ava nods, biting her lip. "Yeah, she has."

I straighten my posture despite wanting to disappear. "Ava is just as determined to destroy this place as you and me," I say.

"Mhmm," Wayne grumbles, staggering over to his fridge and taking a bottle of hard liquor off the top of it. "I wouldn't say 'determined' is the right word to describe my feelings about this. 'Convinced,' maybe, is better."

"What finally convinced you, then?" I ask.

Wayne takes his time opening the bottle, then trudges back over to his couch, where he falls back in exaggerated movements. He seems less drunk than he was when he called me but not sober by any means.

"I thought that would be clear to you," he drones, staring intently at the bottle he holds in his hand. I lower myself onto the same, crumbling leather chair I sat on when I spoke to Wayne earlier. Upon seeing that there's no other place to sit, I gesture for Ava to join me. It's a tight fit, but we manage. Wayne is sprawled on the couch and seems intent on keeping both of us at a distance.

"I...ah," I sigh through my nostrils and summon the tiny amount of confidence I can find. "I was too harsh when we last spoke. I was pushy...I'm sorry."

"Pushy is a bit of an understatement," Wayne says. I wince, bracing for a few insults, but he only shakes his head. "But you were right. This *has* destroyed me. Why let it destroy others?"

"That's the spirit," Ava says. I can tell she's trying to be optimistic, but when Wayne glares at her, she backtracks. "I mean...you're right."

"Can I ask you something?" I say after a few moments of silence.

Wayne raises an eyebrow and shrugs.

"Why were you so reluctant to help me destroy it in the first place?"

Wayne looks down and purses his lips, as though the answer pains him. "The nightmares," he finally says.

My heart does a triple beat. "The nightmares? Like the ones I had?"

"No. Well, yes, at first. Over the years that I accumulated evidence of those missing children, I had all the normal stuff. The moon was in all of my dreams, reminding me it was always with me...always a part of me. And then, there was a time—a brief time of my life, mind you—where I had done all the research I could and started moving on to figuring out how to destroy this place."

"You...you did?"

"A *brief* time," he emphasizes.

"Why brief?" Ava asks.

"Because it *knew* what I was doing. And then I had the nightmares...the ones that made me stop working toward trying to destroy it."

"What...what were they about?" I ask, not sure if I want to hear the answer.

Wayne puts his head in his hands and looks down at his feet, as though the answer is trapped in his throat, far too painful to come out. "They're not dead," he finally whispers, half to himself. He looks back up at Ava and me. Then again, directed more to us than himself, he says, "In my dreams, they're not dead."

Something in my stomach seizes and I exchange a terrified glance with Ava.

"The kids?" Ava asks.

"In my dreams...they're not dead."

My lips move, but no sound comes out. I try to grasp what he's saying, but I realize he's speaking more to himself than us as he repeats the same thing once again: "In my dreams, they're not dead."

"The kids aren't dead?" I finally manage.

Wayne swallows and nods. "They're alive, and yet they're not," he explains in a distant, exhausted voice. "They're trapped in the trees, not entirely dead. And the moon...it hurts them...it tortures them, and in my dreams, I listen to their screams." He doesn't make eye contact with Ava or me, as though admitting his fear makes him ashamed. "And I can't tell if my nightmares are true—if maybe the children aren't dead at all, and the moon will hurt them even more if I try anything. It will hurt Lila if I try anything." His eyes are teary, and suddenly the guilt I feel toward being so rude earlier grows tenfold.

"I'm...I'm so sorry," I say, my voice breaking. "I had no idea. God, if I'd known...I...I wouldn't have been such an asshole. I wouldn't have been so pushy."

My heart beats in my ears as I think about how angry I had been at Wayne for refusing to speak with me, then refusing to agree to help me destroy the world. I hadn't even considered the possibility that he was protecting those children—protecting Lila.

Wayne shakes his head. "How could you have known? How can *I* know if it's even true? It could be just a lie this thing makes up to stop me from figuring out how to destroy it...or not. It's the possibility of it being true that has kept me from doing anything. When I warned you that day at the well, they came back, and..." He tightens his lips and exhales through his nose. "It was like the moon was telling me that if I tried to stop you from going down there, it would hurt the others. I didn't know what to think or do."

"What made you change your mind?" I ask.

"You...your little sister...your friend," Wayne responds. "I don't know. All of it...all of you. And although I never wanted to admit it to myself, if it really is true that they're alive—that it continues to make them suffer—then maybe doing nothing isn't protecting them at all."

"So do you have any ideas?" Ava asks. "About how to get rid of it?"

Wayne frowns. "I wish I did. But since I gave up almost immediately..." He wavers for a moment, acknowledging his shame, then shakes his head and clasps his hands together. "I never got very far."

"There has to be something we can figure out," Ava says. The natural optimism in her voice, alongside my and Wayne's pessimistic natures, lights up the room, if only a little bit. It's as if a small flicker of sunshine made its way through the tightly shut blinds in Wayne's apartment. She clasps her hands and I see something light up in her eyes. "Ro and I were talking," she says, "about why this place hides from adults."

"Right," I interject, eagerness pricking at my fingertips. "Why does it do that?"

Wayne shrugs. "It doesn't need them. It doesn't *want* them."

"No...it has to be more than that," I say. "Is it scared of them? Scared of what they'd do to it?"

Wayne is quiet for a moment. I watch as he gathers his thoughts before he speaks.

"I've thought of that," he finally says. "You're hitting on something I've considered…I just never took the idea any further because of…" His voice trails off and I don't urge him to finish. He repositions himself and clears his throat. "Think about it: if it feeds on the uncorrupted and takes its energy from virtue and innocence, maybe the only thing that will destroy it is the exact opposite."

"Adults," Ava whispers.

Wayne takes a chug of his liquor, blinking rapidly as he swallows it. "Only it doesn't allow anything that isn't innocent underneath the well. That's why only children can see it." He takes a long pause, then adds, "Except for me."

"And us," Ava says.

"But one could consider both of you children. You may not be as young as most of the children it feeds on, but you're still young enough for it to prey on you. As for me, I saw it first as a child, and I have a feeling that I'm probably the only person it was ever unsuccessful with."

"It was unsuccessful with Ro." Ava looks over at me and smiles, but instead of feeling relieved, I feel even worse.

"Partially because Wayne warned me," I say. "I don't know how many times I would have returned with Hettie if it wasn't for him."

"Still," Ava says. "It was unsuccessful with you."

"Are you so sure it's done with her?" Wayne asks, setting the bottle of liquor down on the coffee table. "Or maybe Rosella was never even a target. Maybe the target was always her little sister."

"Whether or not I'm a target doesn't matter," I say. "I know for sure that Hettie is. And she isn't getting any better. She sleepwalked the other night...she disabled my aunt's alarm system and went outside. She wasn't planning on coming back."

"She told you this?" Wayne asks.

"No," I say. "Well...kind of. She wasn't awake. She couldn't control herself. When I caught her and asked where she was going, she said *'back down.'* She told me that she belonged down below."

The silence that follows is so cold it could crack ice.

"It does that," Wayne finally whispers. "It gets in your head."

"It won't after we destroy it."

Ava looks down at the scattered papers and bottles on the floor, then presses her lips together before she speaks. "And I assume that just starving it out won't do anything?"

"It will always get what it wants," Wayne says, his voice stiff. "One day, when I'm gone and you two are off living your lives, another child will come along and nobody will be there to save them. Starving it out won't work. It's been devouring children for generations. Best to kill it before it can kill anyone else."

Finally, I hear assuredness in his voice. He's made his decision and he's going to stick with it.

"The underground moon, then," Ava says. "That's the heart of the world, right? Maybe that's what we should target."

"How?" I ask.

Ava puts her head in her hands. "I don't know," she mumbles. "I like what Wayne said about impurity hurting the world."

"Me too," I say. "If the underground moon feeds on childhood innocence and youth, maybe corruption is exactly the thing that will poison it."

"The only problem is it's picky about who it lets in," Wayne says, "and it's more cognizant than it lets on. It isn't going to welcome in something that it doesn't know." He presses the back of his fingers against his lips before he speaks again. "But," he says, more slowly this time, "like I mentioned to you, Rosella, I can't help but wonder if after you've seen it once, it no longer has the ability to hide from you...not unless you bring along someone it doesn't know. I've returned to the grove hundreds of times, and it never disappeared. I used to wonder why; I wasn't a kid anymore, so why wouldn't it hide from me? But every time I went back, it was there, sitting in that grove as though it were waiting for me."

Sudden chills cascade throughout my body.

"But I can only guess," Wayne continues. "That's what I hate about all of this. I know nothing for certain, other than the lives it has taken. I want to believe I'm right…I truly do. But I can never be sure. None of us can. We have to do our best with the little we've got."

"Do you think it knows what we're planning?" I ask the question in less than a whisper, paranoid it may hear.

"Again, I'm not sure," Wayne says. "But what I do know is that all three of us have been down there before, whether ten times, five times, or only once. It's already in our heads. It already knows us." He grabs the bottle of liquor again and takes a swig. "Whether or not it completely understands our intentions is beyond me. I guess that just means the sooner we get rid of the hellhole, the better."

I wring my hands. "You've certainly done a one-eighty since the last time we spoke," I joke to lighten the mood. It doesn't work.

Wayne sits back and crosses his arms. "Maybe I needed someone as pushy as you to make me change my mind. How many more times would you have scaled the fire escape—or worse—to get the answers you wanted?"

"As many times as you would have turned me away," I say. A smile tugs at my lips.

"Wait...you scaled the *fire escape* to speak to Wayne?" Ava gapes at me. "You do know I have the key to the complex, right?"

"You were working," I say. "And honestly, I wasn't really myself."

Wayne stares at the liquor, as if he is contemplating taking another drink, but pushes it aside instead. He uses his hands to push himself up and walks over to a cabinet at the far side of the room. When he opens it, he takes out a gun.

Ava and I tense up as he returns to the couch and sets the gun on the coffee table. When he sees the unease on our faces, he puts his hands up.

"I'm not going to use it," he says.

"What's it for?" Ava asks quietly.

Wayne looks at the floor, then clears his throat. "A year after Lila..." His voice trails off and he doesn't finish his thought. "My father handled it terribly. And it just kept getting worse and worse...until he shot himself." He points to the gun. I can't tell if he's disgusted or despondent; as usual, it's hard for me to read him. "He did it with this. Four years later, my mother passed from a sudden illness, leaving me alone in the world with nothing but my memories of Lila to keep me company."

He coughs again to clear his throat, then leans back into the couch, looking as though he'd like to disappear.

"I nearly followed in my dad's footsteps more times than I'd like to admit," he says. "But it wasn't for the same reasons. I knew where Lila had gone, so there were no unanswered questions that haunted me. Instead, it was the moon. I've had nightmares for well over two and a half decades, which got worse when I first began thinking about destroying the underground world and which came back after I ran into you and your sister at the well."

I clamp my lips together. If Wayne's nightmares are anything like my lucid, visceral night terror, then I can't possibly imagine how terrible the past few decades have been for him. The worst part, however, is that I have a feeling his have been even worse than mine. The realization makes the blood drain from my face.

"I've lived in constant fear and obsession of it and all the lives it took," Wayne continues. "Even though I'm no longer a child, it still takes its toll on me." He laughs in a way that is void of humor. "Ironic, isn't it, that the place I escaped as a kid still tries to kill me years after I got away?"

He rubs his fingers on his chin. "My point is, whatever this place touches, it destroys," he says. "It destroyed me, it destroyed all of the children carved into the trees...I don't want it to destroy anyone else. Only, I've spent my life being too much of a coward to actually do anything about it. I hate to admit it, but you were right, Rosella."

"You had a good reason," I say. "A reason I was too stupid to even consider. And it's a valid one. If I thought Hettie would be tortured if I tried to destroy it, I don't think I would either." When Wayne doesn't respond, I add, "And you've done so much work. If it weren't for you, I wouldn't know half of what I know now."

"Regardless," Wayne says, "you asked me what made me decide to help you. It was regret. Regret that I hadn't done anything sooner. Regret that during the years I've been researching and making my guesses about this place, more and more children have been taken. Regret that my fear to destroy this place because of Lila and the others being hurt has kept them prisoners down there for longer than anyone deserves. I'm not going to let your little sister be one of them. I'm done regretting. I'm done being corrupted by my pain and guilt."

Something flickers in his eyes. Perhaps it's an idea, or maybe it's only a thought. He doesn't say anything, though, so I don't either.

CHAPTER 27
OUR SECRET

Although we don't come up with any answers about how to destroy the underground world, we agree to meet again in a day.

The lack of answers doesn't discourage me, though. If anything, the fact that both Wayne and Ava want to help put an end to this place gives me more hope than I've had in quite a while.

Ava accompanies me back to Aunt Vivian's house. When we pass by the fork in the road that leads into the tunnel-like forest, I clench my fists and quicken my pace.

"I hate knowing it's in there," I whisper to Ava as she catches up to me.

"It's not going to sprout legs and come after you," she says.

"It can come after me in other ways."

Ava runs her fingers nervously through her hair. "I haven't had any nightmares about it like you or Wayne have."

I notice the trepidation in her tone and try to respond accordingly. "You were only down there once," I reassure her. "I think you'll be okay. Honestly, I think the only reason it targets me is because it knows I'm trying to keep Hettie from it. As for Wayne..." I shrug. "I think it knows how much he knows, and it doesn't like that."

Ava is silent for a moment. "That isn't really what's bugging me," she whispers. "I've only lived in Larton for a year, and before I met you, I never left downtown. But what if I had come across it before you moved here?"

"What do you mean?"

"What if I'd come across the well and I hadn't been told by anyone that it was dangerous?"

"I'm sure you would have figured it out, Ava," I say. "You're smarter than you give yourself credit for. Besides, I don't think the underground world has ever taken anyone older than twelve. All of the faces I saw on the trees and on Wayne's wall are at least a few years younger than us. Most seem to be around Hettie's age."

"But it still shows itself to teenagers," she says. "Which means it must know there's some possibility a teenager could fall prey to its tricks. What if that teenager had been me?" She shakes her head. "I'd like to think I would have been smart enough—logical enough—to realize that something was wrong with that place. But to be honest, Ro, I don't know. If I hadn't met you and I was still in the same crappy mindset I was in last year, maybe I would have overlooked anything I thought was weird. Maybe it would've been the place I turned to...maybe I would have fallen in love with the underground moon and the world just like Hettie did."

"Or maybe you wouldn't have," I say. "Maybe you would have come to the same realization Wayne did years ago without me at all."

"Maybe. But there are hundreds of children who didn't realize what was going on. I can't fathom what it was like for them when it finally won." She looks down at the gravel as she walks and kicks a pebble ahead of her. "The worst part is that all of those children were probably feeling as lonely as I was—as you and Hettie were—when they found that place. But they were young and impressionable and sad, and that's what killed them."

A tear runs down her cheek. The sight of it surprises me. To see someone like Ava cry, especially when she wears confidence and good humor on her sleeve, makes my heart plummet.

"I know," I whisper, fighting hard to keep a steady voice. "What tears me apart is that the world didn't just kill children. It killed entire families. I'm sure that Wayne's dad wasn't the only parent who coped poorly with the loss of their child. I can't imagine knowing someone I love is gone, but at the same time having no idea where they went."

We approach Aunt Vivian's house and take the porch steps up to the door. They creak under our weight as the thuds of our shoes make the wood groan.

"That world...the underground moon...it's cruel and poisonous," I say before we go inside. "It's taken hundreds of lives, and I wish that weren't the case. But since it is, the only thing that would make me happy is knowing that it's gone for good and it can't take any more children—that all of the victims can finally rest."

"You and me both," Ava responds, drying her cheek with her sleeve.

The kitchen is empty when we enter.

"Where is your mom?" Ava asks.

"Sleeping, probably. We'll have to be quiet."

"How often does she sleep?"

I shake my head and draw my mouth into a thin line. "Too often."

We slip off our shoes in the kitchen and walk down the hallway on silent feet. The door to my bedroom is cracked slightly, and I can hear a voice—Hettie's voice—inside.

I put my hand out to stop Ava.

"Who is she talking to?" Ava whispers.

I look back down the hallway at Mother's closed door. "I don't know."

I strain to listen. Hettie's voice is low. I hold my breath so I can hear it better.

"No...no, I won't tell her," I hear her whisper. "I miss you too...I miss you a whole lot."

She giggles, as if someone said something funny.

"I already knew that," she continues. "I told you I wouldn't tell anyone. No, not even her. I remember. It's our secret."

Our secret. I push open the door. Hettie spins around in response. She's by the window next to her cot, but the rest of the room is eerily empty.

"Who are you talking to?" It sounds more like a demand for answers than a question, but I stand firm.

"Nobody."

"I heard you talking to someone."

"I was playing," she says coldly. "Since when am I not allowed to play? Are you going to start telling me I can't play now too?"

"I didn't say that," I respond, trying to sound calmer. "I heard you say 'it's our secret.' Who were you saying that to?"

"I'm *playing*," she repeats, crossing her arms. "Why do you care what I play? It's not like you even want to spend time with me anymore."

My lips part slightly and I stare at her for a moment. "Of course I want to spend time with you. What in the world would make you say that?"

Hettie doesn't respond, but I don't need her to. I know exactly what would make her say that—the same thing she shares secrets with and talks to when she's alone.

Wayne was right about the underground moon worming into people's heads. It's that sole fact which scares me the most. It isn't some hidden entity beneath a well; it's more powerful than that. It's everywhere—constantly stalking and manipulating its prey as it prepares to feast.

Ava and I exchange a knowing glance.

"Are you guys going to leave?" Hettie asks impatiently.

I frown at her. "That's rude to ask."

Hettie only shrugs in response. Realizing that she doesn't want to talk to me, I motion for Ava to follow me back down the hallway.

"She's not normally this bratty," I say when we sit down at the kitchen table. "She can be annoying, sure, but she's only been like *this* recently."

"She's only seven, Ro. And considering everything, it's understandable why she hasn't been acting like herself lately. We shouldn't be too hard on her."

"I miss her," I whisper, tracing the wood on the table with my finger. "I miss the way she used to be. She was a really good kid."

"She still is." Ava reaches across the table and gently touches my wrist in reassurance. "Somewhere deep down, she's still the Hettie you've always known. Once we destroy this place, she'll come back. I know it."

I nod and blink back pricking tears. "I hope."

CHAPTER 28
FREAK

After a lot of convincing, Ava gets me to agree to go back downtown to have dinner with her.

"It'll be good for you," she says. "You're going to run yourself into the ground obsessing over all of this."

I ask Hettie if she wants to come, but she turns me down—exactly as I expected. Mother is up and about when we leave, though, which makes me feel less uneasy. I tell her to keep an eye on Hettie while we're out, and her reply is the usual one: a sad, silent nod.

Ava and I choose a little pizza parlor a few blocks from the diner. The restaurant is small and warm, with only a couple booths and even fewer customers. As perfect as I think it is, we don't even sit down before Ava notices something and pales.

"Let's go somewhere else," she says, pulling at my arm.

"Why?" I follow Ava's gaze to a booth across the room with four girls.

"I'm not in the mood for pizza anymore."

One girl in particular, a brunette with long, wavy hair, stands out. She's the loudest of the four—the center of attention. Whatever she says elicits giggles from the three other girls sitting next to her.

Ava whimpers silently and sits down at our booth. She pushes herself back into the seat, looking very much like she wants to disappear.

"Who are they?" I ask, sitting across from her and trying not to look obvious as I stare at the brunette.

"That's the girl," Ava whispers. "Paige. She's the girl I liked...the one who turned all of her friends against me."

I watch the girl across the restaurant fling an ice cube from her drink at one of her friends, who shrieks in an obnoxiously high-pitched voice.

"We'll just ignore her, okay?" I say as Ava nervously fiddles with the napkin dispenser at our table.

Ava swallows and nods. "Yeah...okay."

Paige and her friends are loud—so loud that I wonder if they realize how annoying they're being—but I pretend like

I don't hear them. After ordering our pizza, I do my best to engage Ava in a conversation about all the fun things we'll do when school starts.

I realize, over the course of my attempt to distract her, that idle conversation actually helps me distract myself from my lingering worries about Hettie.

Just when Ava seems to forget about the presence of the girls across the room, all four get up.

"Shit," Ava says, cutting me off. "She sees me."

"I highly doubt—"

"Ava Lim?" one of the girls says. She's blond, like me, only she has a nasty aura about herself, much like a vulture cornering a dying animal.

When Paige's eyes meet Ava's, a look I can't quite read registers on both of their faces.

"Ava!" she calls, her voice sickly-sweet. She strides over to our table, her three friends at her heels, and smiles so venomously that I can't help but think I'd like to see her face carved into one of the trees in the underground forest. Although the thought makes a wave of guilt rush over me, I justify it to myself when I see how miserable Ava looks.

"How's your summer been?" Paige asks. "Fun?"

"It's been fine," Ava says. I can tell she's trying hard to put forth a confident demeanor, but she's failing. She's nothing like the bold, optimistic girl who had no issue raising her voice at Wayne earlier. Right now, Ava looks as though she might wither into nothing.

"Oh, I'm so glad." A mocking grin sweeps across Paige's face. "I thought maybe it would be as miserable as the school year was for you, seeing as how literally *nobody* wants to hang out with you."

I blink back my shock at her unabashed cruelty. When Paige turns to me, I feel hot anger rush to my face.

"Who's this?" she asks. Then, to me, she says, "I hope you know who you're hanging out with. She might try to come on to you."

"I know exactly who I'm hanging out with," I say. I glance at her friends, who are huddled behind her. "Do they know who *they're* hanging out with?"

Paige laughs. "I'd sure hope so. Better than hanging out with someone like her."

"Paige, just leave," Ava says in a voice that is little more than a whisper. "We're not bugging you."

"Oh, hon', I'm not trying to bug you," Paige croons. "I just wanted to see how you were doing. I know last year was tough for you."

Something in Ava snaps, but she stays composed. "It wouldn't have been tough if you weren't such a shitty person," she says coolly. "The only hard part of last year was realizing I liked someone who has no redeeming qualities whatsoever, other than her weak, copycat friends who worship the ground she walks on."

I bite my lip to keep myself from surprise-laughing.

Paige opens her mouth, but Ava interrupts her. "Don't worry about getting the last word in," she says, folding her arms and refusing to blink. "I'm sure it would have been something rude, and your friends would have had a nice laugh before they all went back to secretly hating you."

That catches Paige off guard. Even her friends blink back their shock. For a long moment, they stand there, staring at Ava. Paige shifts her gaze between me and Ava before whispering under her breath, "Freak."

Ava remains emotionless. "Better to be a freak than a miserable, lonely person."

Realizing she's gotten nowhere, Paige rolls her eyes and tramps out of the restaurant, her friends following behind her.

When the door closes behind them, I finally let myself laugh out loud.

"Ava, that was amazing," I say.

Ava giggles weakly and exhales. "I think I just about had a heart attack," she says. "But did you see her face? It was worth it."

"She needed to be shut up. I'm glad that you were the one to do it."

Ava grabs a slice of pizza and takes a bite. "I guess I realized there are a lot more things to be afraid of in this world than a couple of shitty high school girls."

I raise my glass of water to her as a salute. "If there's one thing I can say about this whole mess we're dealing with, it's that it sure puts a lot of things in perspective."

The rest of our dinner is lighthearted. By the time we walk home, it's clear that both of us have put our worries to rest, at least temporarily. Our laughter reverberates in the evening air, and the first glints of fireflies begin to dot the surrounding fields and roads.

"Did you see how fast I shut her up?" Ava says for the umpteenth time that evening. "She looked like someone had slapped her."

I grin in response and watch as the dust from the road gathers in the air.

"I can't believe I actually *liked* her," Ava continues. "But I guess the heart wants what the heart wants."

"I can't relate," I say, still grinning, "but watching you stand up to her gave me more satisfaction than I've had in quite a while."

Ava squeals and does a little jump. "I'm actually looking forward to school now," she says. "You and I are going to go on so many adventures." She pauses and looks straight at me. "After we fix this whole shitshow, of course."

The knot in my stomach, though slightly lessened by the spectacle at the pizza place, still lingers. "Once we fix this shitshow," I say, half-teasing, "I think I'll never stress about anything ever again."

Ava's giddy expression quickly turns serious, and she takes my arm before saying sternly, "We *will* fix it. I swear to God, Ro, we're going to kill this thing."

"We have to figure out how first," I remind her.

"We will," she repeats.

Our conversation comes to a halt as we continue on the remaining road to Aunt Vivian's house. I wonder what it would feel like to finally destroy the underground moon and everything else connected to it. I assume I'll feel the way Ava did after standing up to Paige, only a thousand times more relieved. That familiar glimmer of hope within me casts a reassuring warmth over my body. I revel in it and let it grow until we reach Aunt Vivian's house.

And then, just as quickly as it came to life, it dies. Parked outside of Aunt Vivian's house are police cars. Their sirens remind me of that night months ago, and the color of my and Hettie's still-wet manicures.

CHAPTER 29
THE CHILDREN

Mother.

The memory of her lying on the floor of the bathroom in April, still seared into my mind, comes back with resounding force.

I sprint to the porch, not bothering to check if Ava has followed me.

What if it happened again? What if she was successful this time? Perhaps she's already gone, or perhaps the ambulance has already come.

I fling open the door to the kitchen, my heart pounding in my ears and blurring all of my senses...

...and I see Mother sitting at the kitchen table.

I blink back my shock, then observe her tear-streaked face. Aunt Vivian sits next to her, paler than I've ever seen her before, and I realize that the police aren't here because of Mother at all.

Hettie is gone.

When Mother sees me, she begins to cry even harder.

"Where is she?" I gasp between breaths. "Where's Hettie?"

"Hon', we don't know," Aunt Vivian says, slowly getting up. Her limbs are shaking, but she manages to come over to me. "The police are here. They're going to help us look."

"She's gone?" I say, backing away from Aunt Vivian's outstretched hand. "Nobody saw her leave?"

I feel Ava's presence behind me, but I don't turn around.

A tall and gangly woman in uniform, also sitting at the table, turns to me and tries to smile. "We already have officers out looking," she says. "When's the last time you saw her?"

"How the hell did neither of you see her leave?" I shout at Mother and Aunt Vivian. The anger within me is so palpable that any last sliver of decency I might have had disappears. "How many times have I told you both to just watch her? It's not that hard! She's in the house all the time!" I turn to Mother, my eyes narrowed into slits. "She's your *child*, for heaven's sake!"

"Rosella," Aunt Vivian snaps. "Yelling at us isn't going to fix anything..."

"How dare you," I seethe, clenching my fists so hard that my nails break through a layer of skin on my palms. "How *dare* you tell me what is and isn't going to fix this? She's gone because both of you are so wrapped up in your own bullshit that being guardians has never occurred to you!"

I'm crying now too, so hard that there are no longer words to express my emotions.

"And she's gone because of *me*," I sob, burying my face in my hands. "Because I left her here and went out to get pizza like an idiot."

"Ro," comes Ava's soft voice. It's the one thing that brings me back. "I'm so sorry...I made you leave. I forced you to come downtown with me. God, I'm so sorry."

I shake my head. When I open my eyes and the blurriness subsides, Mother is the first thing I see. She's crying so silently that one could be forgiven for thinking she isn't crying at all, but I know her better. She's crying because everything I said was true, and yet hearing it from me— from her daughter who is supposed to support her throughout her illness—reminds her that I've grown hardened and resentful.

No. I'm not going to let this be me. I'm not going to stand here and let my resentment fester, because then I'd be little better than Wayne used to be. Mother and Aunt Vivian, as absent as they may have been, are not the culprits.

If my blame is to be directed anywhere, it's at the underground moon.

A glance at Ava tells me she's thinking the same thing.

I grab her hand and whirl around, slamming the door back open and jumping off the porch instead of taking the steps.

"Miss!" I hear the police officer call. "Miss Gill!"

Aunt Vivian says something too, but her voice is garbled in the distance.

I don't bother to look back. Ava and I run so quickly that the calm evening air feels more like a windstorm. The ringing in my ears increases tenfold as we reach the terribly familiar fork in the road. The tunnel into the forest looks more foreboding than it ever has.

"Get Wayne," I tell Ava.

She blinks at me, heaving to catch her breath. "What? No, Rosella, I need to come with you—"

"You need to get Wayne!" I grab her by her shoulders. "Bring him to the well...bring him *beneath* the well. Get him to help us. I don't know if we can do this alone, but I can't waste any more time here. I need to go beneath."

"And...and you're sure she's there?"

"There's nowhere else she would have gone. I can't let it take her...I can't let it win."

Ava doesn't protest any longer. She immediately turns down the main stretch of the road and runs, but I don't watch her go. I turn to the tunnel, taking no time at all to brave it, and sprint into its gaping mouth.

Though perhaps only a figment of my fear-infested imagination, the forest looks different than I remember it. The trees no longer sway in the summer breeze and boast their vibrant colors. Instead, their needle-like branches form spindles that clutter the sky above, and even the little aster flowers I remember admiring seem to have shriveled in the shadows.

I push on—harder, faster—momentarily worrying that perhaps I won't be able to see the grove at all. When I do, I feel conflicted between hating it and praising its presence. I remember Wayne saying that once you've seen the well, it can't hide from you. And yet, my instinctual pessimism wonders if perhaps the world *wants* me here—if it wants me to come looking for Hettie so it can kill me too.

It doesn't matter. I would rather it kill both me and Hettie than only her, and I'm certainly not going to go down without a fight, whatever that fight may entail.

The well sits in the middle of the grove, a speck of crumbling stones at the center of a carefully placed ring of trees. I realize now how much the trees look like they're guarding the well, especially now that I'm looking at it with a different perspective.

I don't stop to observe, though. Even if I wanted to, I don't think I could. My limbs have grown a mind of their own, and I sprint faster than I thought possible. The staircase within the well beckons me and I take its bait. I descend into the darkness so quickly that it isn't until I see the glint of silver that I register where I am: in the belly of a beast who detests me.

And then, I see what plagued my nightmares and Hettie's trances—what taunted Wayne for decades and continues to feast upon any sliver of innocence it can find.

The underground moon isn't full yet, but it's as close as I've ever seen it. The clouds that once hung in the sky are gone, and the moon hovers alone amongst a now entirely black atmosphere. Its magnitude is overpowering; the ashen glow of its barren face makes even the lake look silver, and if it had a mouth, I would suspect it to be smiling at me, taunting me and saying, "Look how far I've come. Look how close I've gotten to devouring your little sister whole."

Next, I see the trees. I try to match them to the pictures on Wayne's wall and the articles in his binder, but they look different than I remember. When it clicks, I catch myself from stumbling back in shock.

The eyes of the children carved into the trees are open. They no longer look as though they're sleeping peacefully; instead, they're staring at me with unmoving expressions as I maneuver about the forest. Perhaps it's a trick of the underground moon itself, or perhaps they truly are watching me.

I try to steady my shaking legs by remembering their names: Cora Nittly, Danny Lewis, Lila Reyes. They were all people once—not the lifeless carvings I see before me.

"You can't scare me," I whisper, more to myself than the moon. "You can't turn me away."

I continue through the forest, all the way to the gazebo where Hettie and I once watched a show of a thousand-colored stingrays, where we once danced to lulling music, and where I finally realized it was all a lie.

When I see her, everything around me fades into nothingness. She's not awake, or in a daze, or sleepwalking at all. She's asleep, only this sleep is so deep that I wonder if she'll ever wake up. She lies peacefully a few yards from the gazebo by the shore of the lake. Yellow fireflies fade in and out of color around her. It reminds me very much of the night we spent outside before we found the well— before any of this happened.

I'm not surprised that the moon knows about that night. Nothing that happens down here is a coincidence.

I run to Hettie's body and fling myself to the ground, brushing long tendrils of golden curls from her face and gasping when I expose the horror beneath.

Spider-like veins cover her face and neck. Her lips are a bluish-purple and her face has grown narrow, as though she's aged a hundred years in the span of an hour.

My muscles don't work. My voice doesn't work. I feel like I'm in one of those terrible nightmares where I'm trying to call for help, but nothing comes out. When I finally force my voice to obey, it manifests itself in suffocated rasps.

"Hettie...please..." is all I can manage. I shake her, much like I did when I tried to snap her out of her daze. But this is no daze; this is something much stronger and, if my worst fears are true, much more permanent.

As I desperately try to wake her from her comatose state, my vision grows blurry. I violently blink to get rid of my tears so I can see her better. Her skin...her face...what's happened to her? Has it already taken her? Am I too late?

I run my shaking hands down her body, realizing with even more horror that her arms and legs have been bound to the dirt with what looks like the roots of a tree.

I look back up at the underground moon to remind myself that it isn't full yet—that there's still time for me to figure something out before she becomes like Lila or any of the other children.

I grab the roots that encase her right hand and tear at them with all my might. I silently rejoice when they shatter under my fingers and her hand comes free.

Before I can get to her left hand, however, something snaps around my wrist and pulls me to the ground. Terror seizes me and I tug ferociously to free myself, but more keep coming. Whip-like roots, far larger than the ones that cover Hettie's arms and legs, entwine around my limbs. As I pull one hand up, another gets caught, and I'm left flopping like a fish as I jerk myself up and down to break the branches.

The air around me begins to feel stuffy and stagnant as the underground world closes in on me. It wants me dead. I'm more than just a nuisance keeping its prey away; now I'm a threat, and it wants me gone.

"I'm...not...letting you...take her," I snarl.

I try to push the branches off me, but my effort is of no avail. Still, I manage to pull myself up so I'm on my knees hovering over Hettie.

The roots I tore off her hand have already grown back, but I don't give up. I continue ripping them away, using all my strength to fight against the force of the vines that swathe around my body.

I cry out when one wraps around my neck, pulling my head down so quickly that it smacks against the ground and causes blotches of color to spot my vision. These are hardly branches at all—they're arms that mean to strangle the life out of me.

It can't end like this. And yet, it seems like it very well may. The force around my neck tightens. I'd claw at it if it weren't for the roots that pin my limbs to the ground. I try to look back at Hettie, but my vision is failing me. I release one last cry—as if that will do anything to help me—and then find that I can no longer make any sounds.

I'm suffocating. It's a terrible way to go. I'm gasping for breath and my head is foggy. I wonder how close I am to passing out. My lungs ache and I grasp at the air around me with what little movement my fingers can manage in the deluded sense that it will help. I'm not thinking clearly; my eyes are watering and probably bloodshot too. I've seen mice in traps with their necks snapped, and I assume that's very much what I'll look like when this is all over and done with...

And then, air pours into my lungs. I take a desperate, heaving breath. Someone has ripped the branches from my throat, and they continue pulling the rest off my body.

When I regain my vision, I realize that it's Wayne.

CHAPTER 30
POISON

The branches release their hold on me under Wayne's strength. I'm surprised he doesn't crush them entirely. When I'm finally free enough to move, I point at Hettie, who still lies motionless beside me.

As soon as Wayne gets to work on her, I feel another pair of smaller and gentler arms pull me up.

"Ava," I breathe, leaning against my friend and trying to muster as much energy as I can.

"Holy shit, Ro," she says between tears. "I thought you were dead."

"Not yet," I murmur, still struggling to breathe properly. "You convinced him to come down."

"It didn't take much convincing, surprisingly," Ava says. "Not after I told him you'd gone after Hettie."

I can't register any more shock at the moment, but I do feel a warm surge of gratitude. Wayne said that he refused to go back down after Lila died, and yet he put aside his crippling fear of this place when he learned that two kids he hardly knew were in trouble.

I look back over at Wayne, who has picked Hettie up, completely freeing her from the persistent roots that once attempted to devour her. She looks tiny in his arms, and for a brief moment, I wonder if Father would have cradled Hettie like that if he were still around.

Cool relief shrouds my senses until I see that Hettie's face hasn't changed; she still looks wilted and haggard. I choke out a strangled cry.

"We need to go," I say. "All of us, right now. It won't stop attacking us, not until we're dead."

"What about destroying it?" Ava asks. "Wasn't that our plan?"

"We don't know *how* to yet," I say. "We haven't had the time to figure it out."

"We may have," comes Wayne's raspy voice. Now that I can see clearly, I look into his eyes. They're still haunted and dark, just like the first time I met him, but something has changed.

"What do you mean?" I ask. "We never—"

"We need to get back to the archway first," Wayne says.

I don't question him. He leads the way, back through the forest and to the gleaming silver and gold of the archway…

…and he hands Hettie to me.

I take her in my arms, nearly buckling under her weight. Ava lifts Hettie's legs to help me support her.

"What are you doing?" I ask.

Wayne doesn't answer me. Instead, he walks a few yards away and into the forest, far enough so one or two trees conceal him, but close enough so I can see what he's doing. He looks around for a short, fleeting moment—perhaps re-orienting himself with the place he vowed he'd never return to—and stops at the carving of the fairy-like girl whose tree Hettie once pulled an emerald necklace from.

Lila's tree.

In that moment, I forget the roots that tried to strangle me and encase Hettie. I forget the gazebo and the lake and even the underground moon itself, which gleams above us and even now seems to be growing fuller. Instead, I see the place for what it truly is: a graveyard of children.

Wayne is very still and silent for a moment. He puts his hand up to his sister's face and runs his fingers down her cheeks. I wonder if he saw her when he first entered, or if he was so preoccupied with reaching me and Hettie that he put aside finding his little sister's tree until now. I'm inclined to think the latter.

When he turns around, I see the tears in his eyes.

"Wayne..." I say.

"All three of you need to leave," he says in nothing more than a whisper. "You need to take Hettie back up to where she belongs and let her grow up, far away from this terrible place."

My question comes out in a stammer. "What...what are you going to do?"

"I never thought I'd see her face again," Wayne says. "She would be thirty-seven right now if she were still alive. She'd have a job and a life...maybe she would even have kids of her own."

The stagnancy of the cold, dead air makes the following silence unbearable.

"But she isn't alive," he finally says, his voice quivering with hate. "Because this place killed her." He turns away from the tree. "You need to go."

"What about you?" Ava asks.

Wayne shakes his head and looks back at us. He doesn't move from Lila's tree. "The thing that will destroy this place for good is the thing that embodies the opposite of what this world lives on: something that is tainted with pain and loss of innocence."

When Ava and I don't respond, he straightens his lips into a thin line to keep them from shaking. He doesn't have to say what he means for me to get it.

"Oh, God...no. Wayne..." I groan. I'm interrupted by a shattering sound, as though the moon understands too.

"*Go,*" Wayne urges. He takes a very long breath and lifts up the side of his shirt, revealing his gun tucked into his belt—the gun that once belonged to his father.

"What did you...?" Ava chokes. "You took your *gun?*"

"Shut up and listen," Wayne says. "You both need to take Hettie and get up above. *Now.* Don't act like idiots and stand around. Let me do what needs to be done."

"What does that mean?" Ava stammers. She turns to me and raises her voice. "What does that mean?!"

Silence follows, and I can feel a change in the air as Ava finally understands it: Wayne needs to die down here.

I can't find the words. Perhaps there are none at all. And yet, as much as I scorn myself for thinking so, it makes sense. Even the underground moon acknowledges the truth; its light recoils, albeit ever so slightly, in Wayne's presence. Wayne is exactly the opposite of all these children; he's no longer pure like Hettie or Lila, or even Ava and me. Not after what this place has done to him.

I finally manage to speak, but all that comes out is a strangled plea. "Wayne...you can't."

He doesn't answer, so I raise my voice. "How do you know this will work?" I cry, my heart pounding in my ears. "This place has taken hundreds of children. How will a single death counteract it?"

"It only takes a little bit of poison to kill something," Wayne says.

"No...there has to be another way. You can't—"

"Just stop talking and listen. *You need to leave.*" I blink back my horror as he says, "Let me destroy this goddamn place."

As soon as Wayne says it—truly says it—with more conviction than I've ever heard him use before, a cracking explosion seizes the air. Thorny branches, twenty times larger than the ones that attacked me, shoot out of the ground and around the archway.

"Go," Wayne commands.

I don't know what to do. I could turn around and run— let Wayne die here and poison the world—but I'm not sure I would ever forgive myself.

"Ro," Ava says. "We should—"

More thorns and vines rip the ground as they shoot upward, leaving great black circles where they pierced the surface. Some cover the entrance of the archway, blocking us from reaching the stairs. The tinsel that once hung on the trees has transformed into sweeping black vines that sway in the non-existent wind. They thrash about like the arms of an angry kraken and begin to grow down the trunks of the trees until they hit the ground and spread outward. One swipes at Wayne's foot, but he staggers to the side to avoid it.

All the while, the underground moon lingers above us as bright as it has ever been, watching the spectacle beneath like a silver, hungry eye.

"Rosella," Ava pleads.

"Go!" Wayne shouts.

Hating myself, I turn around and head toward the archway with Ava. Hettie still dangles limply from our arms.

Ava and I try to both hold Hettie and move in tandem with one another, but our surroundings are so unpredictable that it becomes hard to keep the same pace. Vines continue bursting from the ground to create barriers. I look behind me and realize that the expressions of the children on the trees have changed from peaceful to almost menacing, reflecting the disdain that the underground moon feels for us. The stagnancy in the air grows into something even more musty and dead, the way an attic would smell long after being abandoned.

Although we manage to reach the archway quickly, a thousand emotions within me combine into ineffable guilt that makes it hard to leave. I turn around once more and glance at Wayne, who waits to ensure that Ava, Hettie, and I leave before he does anything.

Ava lets out a blood-curdling shriek as a thick, thorny vine wraps around her leg, digging into her jeans. I nearly drop Hettie in shock as it slithers up her leg, ripping her flesh with its barbed claws.

Panic floods into her eyes as she tries to pull her leg out from its hold, but it only digs deeper into her skin.

I shift Hettie to one arm and try to pull the vines from her, but they're so strong that I don't even think using two hands would work. Still, I try. I drop Hettie by my feet and use both of my hands to pull at the thorns around Ava's leg. I feel the barbs dig into my palms and do my best to ignore the dark blood that oozes out of them, but when the pain becomes too much, I pull back instinctively. Ava shrieks even louder as the vines tighten.

"Rosella!"

I try again; this time I wedge my foot under one of the vines and pull back with all the strength of my weight, but it does nothing.

Something moves in the corner of my eye, and I see the same vines wrap around Hettie, claiming her once more now that I've released my hold on her.

"Wayne!" I yell. The desperation in my voice twists itself into a cry so distraught that it hardly sounds like me at all.

And yet, it's all for naught. More vines covered in arrow-like barbs spring from the ground like rockets. They twist about each other to create a barrier between Wayne and the three of us.

It wants to kill us before Wayne can reach us. It's using all the energy it can muster. The underground moon flickers violently as it attempts to snuff out Ava and me before taking Hettie back for itself.

But what about Wayne? If he dies, the world dies…

An ear-piercing cracking sound sends a shockwave through my body before I can give the pressing question any more thought.

I see a small portion of the barrier vines wither and die. Another crack sounds, reverberating off the nonexistent walls of the underground world as even more vines shrivel in surrender.

Wayne manages to get through a small parting he's made, holding his gun defensively by his side as he brushes past the thorns. He reaches us in an instant, then puts the gun up to one of the vines around Ava's leg.

"No!" Ava wails. "Don't shoot!"

"It's not going to hit your leg," Wayne says firmly. "Stay still."

Another burst of angry vines breaks the ground close to us, and Wayne pulls the trigger.

Ava yelps as the vines ensnaring her leg atrophy and wilt, and with great effort on her part, she manages to pull her leg from the remaining bits of thorns.

She puts a shaking hand to her calf, now covered in blood, as Wayne attempts to pull the vines from Hettie. They're stronger this time; they've learned. Wayne puts the gun up to the vines and pulls the trigger once more.

I close my eyes as the sound echoes in my ears, then reopen them to Hettie's freed body.

"It can *feel*," I say, turning to Wayne as the realization hits me. The underground world can feel more than just hunger; it can feel pain as well. "How many more bullets do you have?"

Wayne shakes his head. "Three left."

"You...you didn't take more bullets with you?" Ava cries, wincing when Wayne glares at her.

"We were in a bit of a hurry to get down here, don't you think?" He swoops Hettie off the ground with ease and shoves her into my arms. I remain standing despite my legs, which are utterly intent on collapsing. "You three need to leave, *now*!"

"Wayne...this isn't right," I beseech him. I look back over at the archway. The vines have almost entirely covered the exit. "It isn't right for you to die...not here."

"Rosella, you..."

"Please, Wayne...I know that we can figure out another way...please come."

"For once in your goddamn life, Rosella, stop arguing and *listen*," Wayne snarls. "If you want so badly to remedy my death, then take this."

He violently reaches into his pocket, then grabs my hand and puts something cold into it. I blink as I stare at the key to his apartment.

"Get rid of the photos in my apartment when I'm gone," he says. "Make sure I don't look like the culprit behind all of the murders."

I swallow hard and nod, then shakily stuff the key into my pocket. "I...I will," I manage. It's all I can say—a promise I've never been more intent to keep.

"Good," Wayne says. My reassurance seems to have brought him some peace. "Now *leave*."

"The vines..." Ava says, shakily getting to her feet.

Wayne observes the barrier guarding the archway. He swiftly approaches it and presses the barrel of the gun directly to the twisting branches that cover the exit. A muffled, cracking screech of the gun sounds once more, and a small portion of the vines pull back like a hurt animal curling up in defense. The hole it makes is small, though— too small for us to get through. Wayne lowers his gun and pulls the trigger again, this time allowing for a marginally larger hole that Ava and I would be able to get ourselves and Hettie past.

He doesn't need to tell us to go again. The sound of the gun and the momentarily retracting vines is enough. Ava helps me hold Hettie, but her strength is considerably weakened. Our only luck is how close we are to the archway.

I see the underground moon flicker angrily in response as Ava slips through the hole in the vines. I push Hettie behind her before it fights back again.

This time, it targets me. It doesn't entwine about my body or attempt to choke me, though. Instead, the wilted vines barricading the archway grow back with the fervor of a last attempt. They grow too quickly for me to dive through, and I stumble back in shock.

Wayne slams his fist against the vines, but they don't budge.

"Ro!" I hear Ava yell from the other side.

Of course it blocked me. Hettie and Ava may be safe on the other side of the archway, but it can still punish me. It's painfully ironic that I saved my sister from this place, only to be trapped below and suffer the same fate. Although the underground moon is well aware that its time is up—that Wayne is intent on following through with his plan—my death down here would be a perfect final victory.

I would rather it be me than Hettie, though.

I still win, I think, mustering the weak triumph within me. *Hettie is safe. I still win.*

Though I don't say it out loud, I'm more certain than ever that the underground moon understands.

"Ro!" comes another one of Ava's distressed cries.

"Get Hettie up above *now*!" It's the only thing I can think to say.

"I can't leave you!"

"Ava, please!" I plead. "Please...get her back to where she's safe...if you don't, this whole thing will be for nothing. *Please.*"

I hear Ava utter a conflicted cry, but she concedes nonetheless. "I will," she says.

"And don't come back down," I say. "Stay above with Hettie. *Please*, Ava. She means the world to me."

"But..."

"I'll make it out," I reassure her, despite not being sure myself.

Ava hesitates, but only for a moment. "I'll see you up above," she says, her voice shaking.

I'm not sure how much either of us believe that, but I know one thing: I'm not submitting to this place just yet.

I hear Ava's footsteps as she takes the first few stairs back up above to safety. Despite carrying Hettie and walking with an injured leg, she moves quickly. I hear her steps grow softer and softer as she ascends. I listen until I can hear them no more, reveling in the unfamiliar calmness that has washed over me. Perhaps it's because I know that both Hettie and Ava are safe. Regardless of the reason, I welcome the tranquility with open arms, for this relief seems more permanent than anything I've felt in a long time.

"I have one left, Rosella," Wayne says, lowering his voice to utter a few curse words. "And I need the last one."

"Don't...don't worry about me," I say, choking on a sob. "If this world doesn't die, then neither of our deaths will matter."

Wayne shakes his head. "No. Not you. *Not you.* That wasn't the plan."

"We didn't *have* a plan—"

"You're not going to die down here," Wayne interrupts. "It has already taken too many...too many lives...yours is *not* going to be one of them."

I grit my teeth and press my tongue against the roof of my mouth, willing myself not to cry. And yet, as hard as I try, I can't help it.

Another shattering explosion rocks the world in an angry scream. The stagnancy of the air turns into a howling wind that moves the tinsel-turned-vine leaves of the trees along with it. I curl my hands into fists, feeling my clammy palms against my fingers.

Suddenly, the world begins closing in on me. It's as though the night sky has formed walls that intend to crush me. That pulling, converging black hole from my nightmare surrounds my body, and I can't tell if it's all in my head or if it's truly happening.

Perhaps it's best to come to an end right here, right now, before I think any more about all the things I'll be missing—about Hettie and Ava and the home my family could have made in Tennessee.

"Listen," Wayne says. His voice reverberates as though we're in a cave, bouncing off the walls that the sky has formed. "This world will not kill me on its own because if I die down here, then *it* dies."

"I...I figured as much..."

"But it will still try to kill *you*," Wayne says, speaking faster than ever, "because you're still young...your death will still give it purity and innocence...all the things it needs to survive. Mine won't...mine will kill it. I need to kill it before it gets to you, okay? I can't...can't let it win with you...can't let it win ever again."

"How do you know?"

"I know...I just know. When I die, you need to do everything you can to get out. Understand?"

I nod rapidly in response, even though the idea of leaving him here makes me sick.

"I...I understand."

The sky continues lowering in on us, and I can't help but think that perhaps it was never a sky at all. Perhaps it only looks like a sky, the way the underground moon only looks like a moon.

It's an energy source.

Standing here, in this very moment, I can sense fear, and it isn't coming from Wayne or me. Although it may seem like this place exercises inconceivable power over us, a profound sense of desperation lingers in the atmosphere. The underground moon lives and feels much like a beast does. Powerful, maybe, but certainly not invincible.

"Wayne," I say, my voice breaking. "Thank you."

"Don't watch," he responds. This time, it's his voice that breaks, and he steps away from me. "And when it happens, do everything you can to get out."

"I will."

"Whatever it takes."

I nod and squeeze my eyes shut as the world continues closing in on me, more and more until I feel as though I will not be able to move again. I still can't tell if this is all in my head or if the world truly intends to crush my bones and suffocate me.

For a long moment, the only sounds I hear are Wayne's muffled footsteps. I wonder how far he is from me; the remaining barrier the vines made encloses us into a confined space near the archway.

Still, when his gun sounds, it seems as though he is a thousand miles away.

CHAPTER 31
A DYING LIGHTBULB

When I open my eyes, the night sky no longer moves inward. Instead, I feel as though I am suspended in a gaping, black hole.

No more ice-cracking explosions shake the ground, no more gnashing vines grow from the trees, and no more snake-like branches claw at my body in an attempt to strangle me.

First, I see the trees. The eyes of the children have closed; they look the way they did when I first discovered this place with Hettie. Slowly and with great hesitation, my eyes wander back over to Wayne's body. I don't want to see him, but I feel I must.

The gun dangles limply from his hand and a pool of dark crimson oozes from his head. I don't observe the portion of his face that is no longer there; it's too much for me to take in.

I suddenly start to feel a very heavy weight on my chest. I stand still, and for a moment, I'm not sure if I can move at all. There seems to be both an abundance of space around me and no space at all. Time moves forward, and yet I am utterly confined to this very moment.

Wayne is gone. Slowly—very slowly, the world follows suit.

A low, rumbling sound reverberates under my feet. I step back, closer to the barred archway, as the rumbling grows louder until it isn't rumbling at all—it's shrieking. Then I hear voices. They're high-pitched, as though children are screaming.

The underground moon grows brighter. I shield my eyes from its overpowering light as the white rays touch the lake, then the trees, and then Wayne. In horror, I watch as the gun in Wayne's hand disintegrates, followed by his hand, and then his entire arm. The wind, if there is even wind at all, blows the dusty remains away. I expect it to blow Wayne's body away with it, but it does not. Instead, spindly branches of a nonexistent tree entwine about his feet. Then, with violent vigor, he is propelled upward and off the ground as hooked branches pierce through his stomach and neck. There are no cracking sounds as the branches break through his bones, and no blood follows either. Any last bit of humanity inside of Wayne has been entirely drained from his being.

I feel as though my soul has stepped away from my body. Perhaps it's the only way I can cope. Still, I utter an agonized cry as the needle-like branches spiral upward, suspending Wayne's body in the middle of them. Although I feel my voice inside my throat, the world around me no longer permits sound.

I look back at the trees and the faces of the children. Their closed eyes flutter slightly, despite being only wood, as though something disturbs their sleep. The barrier of the vines withers away, revealing even more of the forest that lingers behind Wayne's body. The last tree I look at is Lila's. The memory of Hettie grabbing that emerald pendant from the branches flits into my head before the light of the underground moon becomes so overwhelming that I can't see the trees or the carvings at all.

And then, everything stops.

The night sky, which looks far more blue than black under the piercing beams of moonlight, begins to curl and peel like old wallpaper, shriveling as it dies. Suddenly, the world seems much smaller than it ever has, as though this whole time it has only been as large as a single room. As the sky flakes away, the lake dries out as well, and somewhere in the distance I hear sound again. It's that of crumbling wood and a crashing chandelier. I strain to listen as the gazebo caves inward and buckles underneath its own weight, falling into what is left of the lake.

The next things to go are the trees themselves. Though I still can't see them clearly in the blinding light, it's impossible to miss the way they sway as they fall to pieces and become nothing but dust. The faces on the trunks cave in and wither, leaving behind nothing at all, as though each tree—each child—never existed to begin with.

It all happens so quickly that I hardly have time to orient my thoughts. It isn't until the light dies down that I realize the vines that once barred me from the archway have disintegrated completely.

Wayne's body and the branches that suspended him no longer exist. There's nothing for me to mourn or glance at one more time, for he has become nothing but dust, just like the forest around him.

I don't take any longer to observe the dying world before me. I can't afford to. I need to get back up to Hettie and Ava. I need to burn the pictures in Wayne's apartment so he isn't wrongfully accused of the children's deaths. I owe him that.

I lunge toward the archway, which has turned from glimmering gold and silver to an ugly tarnished gray. Before I step over the threshold, I notice it: the last part of the world to die.

The underground moon, which once looked so beautiful despite everything it was, flickers like a dying light bulb. It no longer emits its ethereal ashen beams, and although it is almost full, it's weaker than it has ever been.

It is the moon in my nightmare—the moon that lies and takes and devours—but it no longer scares me. Wayne's sacrifice has taken all of its power. With a sliver of pride, I watch as the flickering grows faster, then stops entirely.

Just like that, in less than an instant, the underground moon dies. Its light—and its legacy—snuffs out for eternity, and as soon as it does, the already withered world around me begins to erode even faster.

I need to leave *now*. I spin around, thinking of nothing more than getting through the archway and up the stairs.

Faster, faster, faster.

I push on up the stairs through blurred vision and a light head until I feel the warm Tennessee air on my face.

CHAPTER 32
THE STORY

The first thing I see is moonlight—real moonlight.

I inhale the smell of grass and fresh air, and I slowly still my dizzy head as I make out the figures of Ava and Hettie.

Ava sits in the grass, cradling Hettie's head in her lap. Her long, dark hair falls over her face as she gently smooths Hettie's curls with a shaking hand.

When she sees me, she starts to cry.

I stumble over to her and let myself collapse to the ground, revering the feeling of grass against my skin and the beauty of the star-covered sky above. Ava's shaking voice reminds me that I can still hear.

"Is it gone?"

I nod. The tips of the grass gently prick my neck. "It's gone."

"And Wayne?"

I pinch my lips together and nod. Ava doesn't ask any more questions; she can tell I don't want to answer them.

I'm too exhausted to cry, and despite my shaking body, I don't feel scared. It's as though any emotions I was once capable of having are now dust like the world below—like the trees and the faces and Wayne himself.

I flip over onto my stomach and touch Hettie's head.

"She hasn't woken up yet," Ava says, "but look."

She points to Hettie's face. Even with only the faraway moonlight to use as a light, I can see that the spindly veins that once covered her skin have disappeared. Her youth has returned and her eyes flutter softly, much like the way the children's eyes did—only Hettie is very much alive.

I pull myself to a sitting position, then lean over to her and gently kiss her forehead, feeling her golden curls tickle my cheek. Although I still can't quite grasp my emotions, a single tear falls from my lashes and touches her hairline.

The picture of the sleeping princess in the book of fairytales flashes at the back of my mind. Her golden hair and porcelain face undeniably mirror Hettie's; both lie unmoving in their peaceful sleep, unaware of the world around them.

As if in response to my thoughts, Hettie opens her eyes. When I see that deep cornflower blue, all of my emotions flood back to me. Now I can cry.

When I start, I can't stop. I cry for Hettie and the children, for the families that never got to see their sons or daughters again. I cry for Ava and how much undue danger this whole thing has put her through, and I cry for Lila. Most of all, I cry for Wayne, who is gone now—who *wanted* to go—and who nobody will ever mourn for or remember, except me and Ava, despite the fact that he died a hero.

I cry until I can't breathe, and I bury my face into my hands.

"Ro." Hettie's whisper is louder to me than my own sobs. I want to see her face, but I don't lower my head from my hands because I don't want her to see mine.

Her cold fingers curl around my wrist; it's what finally gets me to move my hands. Her head still rests in Ava's lap, and I can't tell if she's too weak to move or if she simply doesn't want to.

"Remember the story?" she asks.

I nod, sniffling. "I remember."

Hettie's face twists a little bit and she starts to cry too. Not only does that make me cry harder, but it also causes Ava to start crying again. We sit there in the grass, under the light of the real moon, huddled together and sobbing.

"I'm really sorry, Ro," Hettie says. "I'm really, really sorry."

I shake my head. "It isn't your fault. It's the underground moon's."

"It told me you hated me," she says. When she blinks, tears fall from her cheeks onto Ava's knees. "It told me I was alone and...and I wouldn't be alone if I went down below. And I didn't listen to you because it was so loud...in my head, in my dreams...it wouldn't leave."

"I know," I whisper. "It's not your fault."

"You're not mad at me?"

"Oh God, Hettie, no," I say. "Remember the spinning wheel? The princess was in a trance. She didn't know she touched it until it was too late."

"But it's not too late for us, right?" The hope in her voice makes my heart tremble. I think of Wayne and wonder if I'll ever be able to tell Hettie what happened to him. If I do, will she live the rest of her life blaming herself for his death?

Still, I nod. "It's not too late."

"I thought it was too late when I was down below," Hettie says. "I realized...and it started making me feel very sleepy. I couldn't even call for you because I couldn't speak anymore..."

"It's gone," I say. "You're safe. I'm here...I'm here and Ava's here."

And the thought crosses my mind that maybe, in some way or another, Wayne is too.

When we leave, I don't succumb to my curiosity to look back down the well. I know I'll see nothing.

⬤

More police have shown up at Aunt Vivian's house by the time we return. I don't mind them, though, because when I see Mother lingering by the porchlight, all I can think about is how much I want to run to her and embrace her—to hold on to both her and Hettie and never let go. When she sees Ava and me with Hettie, she starts to cry and nearly leaps off the porch as she sprints toward us.

I ready myself for some kind of scolding about leaving during a serious situation, or perhaps a lecture to Hettie about the danger of running away. When she reaches us, however, all she says is, "I'm sorry."

She says it five, six, and then ten more times, and she pulls both Hettie and me into the tightest hug, squeezing us so hard that I think I may suffocate. But this time, I don't mind.

"I'm so sorry. God, I am so, so sorry." She can't stop saying it, and then we're all crying again for what seems the ten-thousandth time that night—perhaps for different reasons, perhaps for the same.

Mother finally releases us, and even then, the questions about where I found Hettie don't come. I suppose they'll come later, when all of this madness ends. It relieves me, actually, because it means Hettie, Ava, and I will have more time to come up with answers.

Aunt Vivian exits the house shortly after Mother finally stops crying. The tall policewoman who was in our kitchen follows her, raising what I suspect is a walkie-talkie—I can't see her well from where I am—to her mouth. As she alerts the other officers, Aunt Vivian rushes over to us, crying, which is a rarity for her. Although we had all managed to stall our tears for the time being, seeing her cry breaks us all over again.

I wonder if Hettie will spill everything in this moment. Now that the underground moon is finally dead, perhaps everything she was holding in to appease it will come flooding out. But when she glances at me, I realize we're on the same page. For now, perhaps forever, we will remain silent.

As my reality slowly sets back in, I feel the weight of Wayne's key in my pocket.

CHAPTER 33
DEATH AND JUSTICE

In the days following, Ava and I set to work cleaning out Wayne's apartment. Ava hauls her father's paper shredder up to the fourth floor so we can get rid of the pictures and the articles. Luckily, nobody notices us.

It becomes cathartic, considering everything, to get rid of Wayne's things. Though at times I feel averse to destroying over two decades of research, I remedy my hesitance by reminding myself that we're doing this to protect him from false accusations. There would be nothing worse than seeing Wayne blamed for the death of these children, when in reality he saved them—he set them all free.

Whether out of respect or mourning, Ava and I don't speak as we go through his things. For hours, we simply pick up trash and empty bottles, shred photos, and set his apartment to a proper state.

I imagine that someday, people in the apartment complex will realize he's gone. Perhaps it will happen after his rent doesn't get paid, or perhaps someone will come by and knock on his door, then out of worry alert others that he isn't there. People will talk; some will say he simply got up and left, others will comment on his aloof and mysterious nature. And then, slowly, he'll be forgotten. But not by Ava. Not by me.

It takes four days to completely clean his apartment and shred the contents of both his wall and his binder. It's the binder I leave for last, mostly because I know what's inside of it—the only thing that will ever remind me of the sacrifice Wayne has made.

I'm not sure if I'll be able to shred that picture of him and Lila. Not yet, at least. The thought of destroying it makes me feel like I'm snuffing out any last happy memory of Wayne. I leave it until the last day when the apartment is almost completely clean and all that's left to shred are the articles in the binder. Neither Ava nor I have opened it yet, and when I finally work up the courage, I'm surprised by what's taped to the front page.

It's a crinkled piece of binder paper with spidery, almost illegible handwriting. Although I know it's Wayne's, what surprises me most is who it's addressed to.

I peel the paper away from the page and sit gingerly on the couch, holding it in both hands.

"Ava, come here," I whisper, inhaling shakily.

She sits down next to me. I can feel her eyes scan the page. "Is this from...?"

I nod. "Wayne."

She clamps her lips shut as we read.

Rosella and Ava,

We agreed to meet one day after our conversation, but by the time that comes around, all you're going to be met with is an unlocked door and this letter, which I hope you'll find. Luckily, we won't need to be meeting anymore, so don't go looking for me (that means you, Rosella).

The answer about how to destroy this place has always been at the back of my mind, but the nightmares and the possible threat of those children suffering kept me from contemplating any further. I had clues—bits and pieces of ideas that didn't really come together until we spoke earlier. What I said about the world requiring corruption to destroy it is true, that much I'm sure of. We know it hides from adults, and everything I've learned about this place tells me that it's because adults are like poison to it. You only need a little bit of poison to kill something, and I'm hoping that poison will be me. I'm the only one here who both has access to the well and is exactly what this world hates. I've been stripped of all my innocence because of this godforsaken place. My father killed himself and my mother died shortly thereafter. I've been plagued all my life with nightmares, fallen into alcoholism, and hidden away from the world while I accumulated research and mourned the deaths of hundreds of children, my sister most of all. This world has destroyed me, Rosella. You were right.

Suddenly, my eyes are so teary that I can hardly see the page. I push on, determined to finish the letter.

If something dies beneath the well that counteracts everything else that has died down here, then the world itself will perish. And so, I've come to the conclusion that I need to die down there. I hope to God that by the time you're reading this, the world and the underground moon residing over it will be gone forever—that if you go back to the forest, you'll find no grove, no well, and no staircase leading down into that terrible place. I'm fairly certain that will be the case.

When you came to me demanding answers, Rosella, all I could think of is the harm I might be bringing to those children if I helped you—if the underground moon knew I helped you. And then you kept demanding answers, and when I realized how dire the situation was, another realization came to me: I'm doing more harm than good by refusing to help out of fear, rather than biting the bullet and finally figuring out how to destroy this place. Now I've figured it out, and I'm not going to wait around any longer.

But I need you two to do something for me: I need you to move on. That means no obsessing over this, no guilt, no going back again and again to check if it has reappeared. Live your lives, because you're young and you deserve that much.

Death isn't just. The children trapped in that place know that better than anyone. But my death will mean something if it happens down there.

-Wayne

By the time I finish the letter, I'm crying. Ava is too. For a while, we sit there—hugging and weeping and mourning all together, because that's all we're able to do.

"I don't know if I'll ever be able to tell Hettie what he did for her...for us...for all the children that would have been victims in the future," I say when I finally find my voice.

"Then don't," Ava responds softly. She wipes her eyes. "I don't think Wayne is the type of person who would mind."

I look down at my feet and feel Ava's hand on my shoulder. "Even so," she says. "*We* know."

I swallow. Even after crying, the lump in my throat remains. "He must've...must've been planning to do it before this all happened," I say. "Hettie just got there first."

"He did it, though," Ava whispers. "He realized—*really realized*—what had to happen, and he did it." She shifts to face me. "You know what will always stick with me? How *scared* he looked when I got to his apartment and told him what had happened...that you'd gone after Hettie."

She shakes her head to herself. "I've never seen anyone look so frightened. It was like..." Ava's voice trails off.

"Like what?"

"Like he was experiencing Lila's disappearance all over again. He ran so quickly to that well, I couldn't keep up."

I feel my face shrivel and I begin to cry again.

It takes us a while to fully gather ourselves. Once we do, we get rid of the rest of the binder, though I'm unable to part with both the picture of Wayne and Lila and the letter.

And so, rather than subject them to the shredder, I fold them up and put them in my pocket. Ava doesn't mention it. Instead, she hands me Wayne's lighter and smiles.

"For when you're ready," she says, and I place that in my pocket too.

When we finish, we stand in silence in the middle of the apartment. I run my finger over the shriveled leather of the chair by the coffee table.

Ava places the lid gently back on the shredder and walks over to me.

"When are you guys leaving?" she asks.

"In about a week," I respond. "We should only be gone for a few days."

My stomach lurches a little bit when I think about returning to Oregon. Aunt Vivian and Mother decided that summer would be a good time to solidify our plans to stay in Tennessee, so we decided to fly to our old house, collect our things, and bring everything back here.

Oddly enough, the thought doesn't upset me as much as it once did. A small part of me, which grows a little each day, actually *wants* to make Larton my permanent home. Perhaps it's because I met Ava, or perhaps it's because I now know the threat of the underground moon is gone.

On our way home after the first day cleaning Wayne's apartment, Ava and I had checked, briefly and out of sheer curiosity, if the grove and the well still hid within the forest. We found nothing at all—nothing but trees and leaves and little aster flowers. Whatever force or entity made the grove and the well died with the underground moon, snuffing it out altogether and leaving only the forest behind.

Even so, I don't think I'll ever be able to enter the forest again without thinking of what was once there, but I believe my nerves will subside with time. For now, there are more important things to focus on.

"I don't think we have anything else to do here," I say as Ava hauls the shredder over to the door.

I leave the key Wayne gave me on the coffee table. The incoming sunlight makes it shine a dusty gold, and when we finally leave, I don't bother to lock the door.

CHAPTER 34
HOPE

On the plane ride to Oregon, all Hettie can talk about is how we're going to rearrange our room back at Aunt Vivian's. She makes plans for where she'll keep her art and where I'll stash my clothes, and she asks if we can paint the walls blue, which I agree to.

I actually enjoy the conversation and become invested in the future layout of our bedroom. By the time we step foot inside our old house, Hettie has drawn out six separate ideas.

There's a musty smell about the hallways, and I'm torn between heart-wrenching nostalgia and discomfort over the memory of what happened in April.

Mother and Aunt Vivian bring in boxes, and Hettie immediately gets to work putting her belongings inside of them. She even helps me bring some of my things out. Watching her bound around the house with excitement about the change to come evokes warmth in my heart. Even though it's uncharacteristic of me, I'm optimistic.

Mother seems comforted by the idea of change as well. She comes to me around midday, though we're far from done packing everything up, and sits next to me.

I look up from rearranging my suitcase and smile at her. When she smiles back, I notice that her expression, though still slightly sad, is not as empty as it once was.

"Are you excited to move in with Aunt Vivian?" she asks. Her voice is hesitant, as though I'm going to say no and resent her for making the decision.

"Of course I am." There's relief in her eyes after I say it.

"Good," she responds. "I know it's not optimal, but—"

"It's perfectly optimal."

Mother blinks. "Really?"

I smile again and nod. "I think we'll be happier there—safer—with Aunt Vivian."

Mother looks down. "You were right, you know," she whispers. "About medication. About trying something. When we get home, I'm going to look into it."

I let out a surprised exhale. "You will?"

"I really thought I could handle it all myself, to be honest," she says. "After April, I told myself I was going to get it under control." She swallows and folds her hands together. "But that was stupid of me. I would tell myself all these things when I was in bad places. First it was that you and Hettie were better off with Vivian, then it was that if I just waited, it would pass..." She shakes her head and cuts herself off. "But then Hettie went missing, and I realized how wrong I was—that there's no time to just wait around for it to go away, because it won't, and it has affected even the safety of my daughters. And you don't deserve that."

I reach out and give her shoulder a gentle squeeze. "You know I'll be there for you, Mom. The whole way. Forever."

"I don't expect anything less from Rosella Gill," she says. "But I want you to try something for me—something more important than being there for me, or Aunt Vivian, or even Hettie. Something I don't think you've done in a long time."

I raise an eyebrow. "What?"

"I want you to be there for *you*," Mother says. "After everything...after how much you watched over Hettie, after how you kept her happy when I wasn't there...you deserve it, Ro. You deserve to just be fifteen."

The comment shocks me. I can't tell if I want to smile or cry in response, so I don't do either. Instead, I wrap my arms around Mother in silence and listen to the sound of her breathing while she strokes my hair.

The morning before we return to Larton, Hettie and I take one more walk through the Oregon forest as Aunt Vivian and Mother help the movers haul everything into their trucks.

The deep summer greens, which change color ever so slightly as we walk farther into the folds of brambles and coast redwoods, hum with the gentle songs of birds and crickets. Ever since we left Oregon, all I could think about was the day I'd come home and see the forest again. And yet, in this very moment, despite all its beauty, my heart doesn't ache when I think about leaving.

I wonder the extent to which I've changed since moving to Larton. Certainly more than I thought I would, and in ways I never could have imagined.

Hettie's soft voice mirrors the rustling of the leaves in the coppice above.

"Ro," she whispers, "do you think we'll ever go back to the forest in Larton?"

"I think so," I respond, keeping my eyes on the trail before us. "We can't refuse to go back because of what used to be there. That would mean it still has power over us."

"I still think about it," Hettie says. "I don't want to. I don't want it to have power over me. But there are times when I think about it...about what it used to say to me. And I feel like it's still there."

I'm silent for a moment. "It will take time, I think. For me too. But we'll work together to get through it."

"Sometimes," Hettie says, "it would tell me that you hated me. Especially near the end, it would tell me you wanted nothing to do with me, but that was okay because *it* was there for me. The underground moon was there."

"I know," I whisper. "It does that. It got into my head too, in a very different way."

I pause and observe Hettie's curls bounce as she walks, wondering what I should say—how much I should say.

"That man, Wayne," I venture slowly, "he found the underground moon and the world beneath the well as a kid too. It took his little sister, and for years after her death, it still got in his head. But he didn't have his sister there to help him. He was alone. That won't be you and me. We'll have each other, and any time the memories get too hard or too scary, all we'll have to do is ask each other for help."

I want to add more—about how it's *because* of Wayne that we'll have each other. But I decide I'll save that conversation for another day, when the time is right.

"Do you think we'll ever tell Mommy or Aunt Vivian?"

"I don't know," I reply. "I'm not sure they'd really be able to understand even if we did. But one day, if we decide to…"

"If *you* decide to," Hettie says, smiling gently. "It should be your decision."

"Why?"

Hettie shrugs. "Because you know better than me," she says. "And even if I wanted to tell them, I don't think I could if you weren't with me."

This time, I don't respond, because there's nothing to say.

We continue walking for a bit longer until Hettie gets tired and we turn around. Even once she's gone back into the house and gathered her belongings, I stay outside for a while longer, looking out at the trees that are the color of my eyes and the sky that is the color of Hettie's.

While I watch the world around me, I think about going back home to Larton and spending time with Ava and Hettie. I think about all the art lessons Hettie will ask Ava to give her, and all the days we'll go downtown to the diner. Most of all, I think about how safe we'll be, and when the real moon comes out at night, we'll love it more than we've ever loved it before.

There will be days, I'm sure, where the memories of what happened below the well will become crippling—

where I'll drown in my silent mourning for Wayne and Lila and the children and their families. But I'll have to be strong, for Ava, for Hettie, and for myself as well. As I inhale the sweet summer air, I think that I am much more equipped to do so than I've ever been.

My pocket feels heavy, and when I know I'm alone, I reach into it. I've kept the picture, letter, and lighter with me for a while, and for some reason—here in Oregon—I finally feel ready.

I sit on the porch steps that face the forest and hold the picture and letter together. Then, slowly, I put Wayne's lighter to them, and when they begin to char from the flames, the sadness within me lessens just a little. I watch the fire gnaw away at the last memories of Wayne and think he would be happy to know I parted with them—happy that Ava, Hettie, and I are going to do our best to make things normal again. Before the fire reaches my hand, I toss it into the dirt and cover it up, still hearing those little crackles as they grow softer and softer.

Afternoon birds circle the trees, and the tattoo of the Rosella on my wrist feels as present as ever. For once in a very long while, the hope within me is permanent.